Get a Clue

AMULET BOOKS
NEW YORK

TIFFANY SCHMIDT

BOOKISH BOYFRIENDS

Get a Clue

PUBLISHER'S NOTE: This is a work of fiction. Names, characters, places, and incidents are either the product of the author's imagination or used fictitiously, and any resemblance to actual persons, living or dead, business establishments, events, or locales is entirely coincidental.

Cataloging-in-Publication Data has been applied for and may be obtained from the Library of Congress.

ISBN 978-1-4197-3968-2

Book design by Brenda E. Angelilli

Published in 2021 by Amulet Books, an imprint of ABRAMS.

Printed and bound in U.S.A.
10 9 8 7 6 5 4 3 2 1

ABRAMS The Art of Books
195 Broadway, New York, NY 10007
abramsbooks.com

FOR ST. MATT.
OF ALL THE LOVE STORIES
THAT EXIST IN THIS WORLD,
OURS IS MY FAVORITE.

Detection is, or ought to be, an exact science, and should be treated in the same cold and unemotional manner. You have attempted to tinge it with romanticism, which produces much the same effect as if you worked a love story or an elopement into the fifth proposition of Euclid.

—Sir Arthur Conan Doyle, *The Sign of the Four*

1

Boredom is a sign of a lazy mind.

This was my dad's catchphrase during rainy weekends, snow days, and the long afternoons I'd spent rinkside while my older brother, Miles, played hockey. He said it whenever I complained that there was nothing to do, adding, *There's always something to do if you use your imagination.*

But Dad had never been in Mr. Milverton's Earth Science class. Imagination can take you only so far in a room with drawn shades and bare walls, where the closest thing I had to entertainment was timing how long it took my teacher to monotone "Four legs on the floor" if I tipped my chair back.

I yawned without bothering to hide it. Mr. Milverton was never going to like me—and not because of chair tipping. I'd ensured his loathing in October when I causally mentioned an upcoming pop quiz to a few classmates.

When we'd shown up prepared and anticipating it, he'd marched me to the headmaster's office and accused me of looking in his planbook.

I hadn't. And my suggestion that planning online would be more secure *and* eco-friendly hadn't been well received. Neither had my explanation of his tell: the day before pop quizzes, he chewed his mustache and said, "*Looking forward to class tomorrow.*"

So, yeah. I was not in contention for teacher's pet.

That would be Bancroft. He was a solid B student. The sort who tried, but not too hard. What he lacked in studiousness, he made up for in toothy grins and answers like, "I'm not sure. What do you think, Mr. M?" He'd fist-bump on the way out of class and say, "Cool lecture today, Milvernator," and our teacher would flush flattered pink from the top of his sweater vest to the roots of his gray hair.

In all fairness, the role of favorite should've gone to Clara Highbury. In other classes she was a people pleaser. Here, she veered into *try-hard*. She volunteered to distribute materials, was the first to jump up and shut off the lights when Mr. Milverton used the projector—despite her seat being dead center of the classroom. One row over and one seat back from mine. My best friend, Rory Campbell—well, really one of my *only* friends, but regardless, she was The Best—sat in front of her. And every time Clara's eager hand shot up, Rory's brown hair swished from the momentum. Like I said: Clara should've been the favorite.

But Mr. Milverton didn't call on her. Her persistent attempts to participate made him purse his lips and look away. I'd been keeping track in my notebook for a week. In that time he'd asked fifty-seven students for answers. Only fourteen had been girls. Only once had it been Clara. Those statistics were grimmer once I factored in our class size of twelve. And it was a fifty-fifty split between those identifying as guy or girl.

See, Dad, I wasn't lazy. Since nothing in this class had been stimulating, I was keeping my mind busy with my own projects. Or...trying to. I yawned into my collar and looked around.

Gemma sat behind me. Her nails were bitten down again, which meant she'd broken up with her sometimes-girlfriend from Aspen Crest Academy. Dante was totally checked out. He had his phone under the desk and based on the airline app he had open was leaving a day early for spring break. His flight to Vail left at ten thirty. First class.

I wasn't going anywhere. My parents were college professors. Their spring break didn't match mine. Even if it had, our vacations were road trips and bargain-hunted hotels. They didn't involve boarding passes, or first class, or jet lag.

Dante clicked to a map of ski slopes. In front of him, Bancroft was stealthily scrolling his iLive page on his phone. No, wait. It was Elinor's iLive page he was scoping. She, sitting in front of Rory, was oblivious to his interest. When she wasn't typing notes, she was using her stylus to doodle hearts on her screen—while staring at Umberto on her left.

Mr. Milverton cleared his throat. "Who can tell me"—Clara's hand shot into the air—"which scale measures the intensity of an earthquake from one, microseismic, to ten, extremely high intensity tremor?"

He ignored her and pointed at me. "Mr. Baker?"

The answer came from a sidebar in last night's reading. I'm sure most of my classmates had skipped it. Besides Clara, obviously. And me. I lifted my chin. "The Rossi-Forel scale."

He nodded and pointed at Umberto. "What's the difference between P and S waves?"

I was off the hook until next class, so I pulled my phone out of my pocket. I had the data in my notebook. Now I wanted proof.

Unfortunately, these desks were not designed for anyone taller than five six. After last spring's growth spurts, I was five inches past fitting and could barely wedge the phone underneath. I shifted my knee so the camera wasn't filming the pen marks on the bottom of my desk. The back of Elinor's head came into view, along with Mr. Milverton's profile.

"Who can tell me what an L wave is?"

I panned the classroom, catching the swish of Rory's hair as Clara's hand rocketed up. After a two-second delay, Dante raised his and was called on immediately.

Mr. Milverton had Atticus answer next—he hadn't even raised his hand. He never did. It never stopped Milverton from calling on him. Even when Atti was sleeping, Mr. Milverton would have someone poke him awake and repeat the question.

Clara added a soft "Oh!" the next time she raised her hand, but it was Gemma's bitten nails he pointed to.

By the end of class I'd added another nine tallies to the "Questions Asked" column. Another seven to "Boys." Neither of the remaining two were Clara, but she'd made Rory's hair swing all nine times.

Mr. Milverton dismissed us, saying, "Some of you might want to review that reading."

It was his new tell—and not even a subtle one. We'd be having a pop quiz tomorrow.

"Highbury," I called.

Clara stepped to the side of the hall. "Hey, Huck. Are you coming to the meeting today? Gemma will be there. Hannah and Sera and Shi—"

I shook my head, but flashed some dimples to soften the no. I'd get to a Hero High Pride meeting one of these weeks, but as much as I appreciated Clara being a good ally, this time I wanted to help *her*, not the other way around. "Aren't you mad Mr. Milverton doesn't call on you?"

Clara was fair. Her blond hair was lighter than mine, and hers rotated from curly to straight on an alternating-day schedule. She was the type of girl who color-coordinated her notebooks to the covers she put on her textbooks and her glittery nails to her sparkly shoes. The type who greeted everyone with a smile, even if she hated them.

She didn't hate me—we got along pretty well—but she'd hated that question. "I'm not the only one in class." Her smiled dropped. "Why do you want to know? I didn't ask for your help."

Right. That was my biggest problem with Hero High: It was the last day of February, and I'd been attending since the first day in September, but no one here asked for my help. Back at my old school I'd been that person—the one everyone turned to. Want to take him to prom? I'll come up with a promposal. Need to get on a teacher's good side? I knew the specialty coffee in their travel mug. After-school job? The hardware store was hiring or the Bensens needed a babysitter. I knew everyone's pronouns, their crushes, their best and weakest classes—I was a matchmaker for romance, tutoring, and more. Mr. Gershwin had me help pick the school musical. Coach Mortimer came to me when she needed a team manager. Principal Bellinger consulted me about school morale and rumors.

Here, I had no purpose. Clara was already the Hero High fixer. I was the new kid.

"What are you two up to?" Rory must've noticed we weren't following her and doubled back to find us.

"Nothing," Clara said. "Huck was offering his help with something, but I'm fine. I don't need it."

I didn't miss how her gaze and voice hardened, but they were like waving red before a bull. She might not think she needed my help, but she was wrong. What was happening was *wrong*.

I blurted, "There's going to be a pop quiz tomorrow."

Rory groaned. "Another one?"

Clara looked over her shoulder at the classroom door and dropped her voice. "You're going to get us all in trouble. If you want to cheat, keep me out of it."

"It's not cheating. It's observation."

But before I could clarify, a booming "Huckleberry!" resounded down the hall.

Hero High had all sorts of private school traditions, from the basic—uniforms, small classes, people with posh backpacks and fancy vacation homes—to the things that made the school unique, like mosaic tiles embedded all over campus as tribute to the school's founding donor, Reginald R. Hero, a famous artisan tile maker. But my favorite tradition was the Knight Lights program.

When I moved from Ohio to Pennsylvania in August, I'd known starting a new school would be awkward—but I'd assumed *all* freshman would be new. I didn't realize that ninety percent of them had attended the same private middle school. Rory and I made up forty percent of the non-Mayfield Middle Academy students: She came from a local all-girls charter. I came from a tiny public school five hundred miles away. Knight Lights was the Hero High mentor program that paired each incoming student with a sophomore. Curtis Cavendish—the only person who called me "Huckleberry," which, incidentally, was not my name—was mine.

"Just the mentee I was looking for." Curtis slung an arm around my shoulder, and my gut gave a guilty hitch. Because here's the thing I'd learned recently about Curtis: his younger brother was hot.

The hottest person I'd seen since packing up my bedroom in Rio Grande, Ohio. And now I spent every conversation with Curtis searching for smooth ways to interrogate him about Winston. They looked related, but not alike. Both of them had the golden skin and dark eyes of their Egyptian mom. I'd met her; she was petite, so I assumed they got their height from their white dad. Ditto their detached earlobes. But Curtis was all careless cheerfulness. Win's smiles were rare. At least that was the conclusion I'd drawn, based on how everyone on Rory's driveway had reacted when he'd aimed one at me.

Win and I had met only once, spent a total of ten minutes talking, and Curtis had been my friend all year—my lacrosse teammate and my mentor who constantly left home-baked treats in my locker. Guess which brother I dreamed about. Spoiler: it wasn't my straight, platonic friend.

Still, I didn't want Curtis to think I was using him to get to Win.

Not that it mattered. Winston Cavendish didn't go to Hero High. And while I was a master at matchmaking *other* people, I had zero firsthand experience with dating.

It's just...Win had looked at me in a way no one had since the move—like he saw me. Like I had answers. Even if the questions were "What book are you reading?" and "Can I render you speechless with a smile?" *Sherlock Holmes* and *heck, yes*.

While I'd been daydreaming, Clara had escaped and Rory had said she'd meet me in the art room for lunch. I turned to Curtis. "What's up?"

"How do you feel about baseball? Playing, not watching." Curtis mimed a slow pitch. "The team's short on players; I'm recruiting."

If my parents heard his offer, they'd be speeding to a sports store for balls and gloves, building a batting cage in their garden, and inviting the team over for cookouts. They'd also been way overinvested in my lacrosse team all fall—actively disappointed when Toby May's season-ending injury bumped me up to varsity, where I'd been the only freshman.

But since Dad's burgers were the most appealing part of any baseball scenario, I hesitated. "I haven't played since T-ball."

"We'll train you up," he promised. "Even if you're awful, you'll fit right in. C'mon, everyone loves baseball."

This felt like an opening. Cool. I could play it cool. I cleared my throat. "So does your whole family share your baseball fervor?" Fervor? *Fervor?* Yeah. Not cool.

Curtis snorted. "Wink only plays sports via remote control."

I nodded. I'm sure his sister was great, and someday I'd ask what "Wink" was short for, but I was leaning forward for news about her twin.

"And Win . . ." Curtis laughed.

And Win what? How was that an answer? There were so many ways I'd finish that statement: *And Win could take* me *out to the ballgame anytime he wanted. I'd buy him all the peanuts and Cracker Jacks*. I gestured for Curtis to finish his thought.

"Win actively avoids *anything* I like."

Yikes. Since theoretically Curtis liked *me*, that didn't bode well for my chances. "Why?"

His omnipresent smile flickered. "You know how some people are motivated by sibling rivalry or thrive with competition? Win's pretty much the opposite."

I was still puzzling out what the heck that meant when he added, "Anyway, just think about it."

"Oh, I *am*." He blinked at my thick-throated answer and I shook my head. "I mean, I will. Baseball. Yup."

"Practice starts after spring break. We'll talk." He held out a fist for me to bump, then headed down the hall. I stayed where I was, a mortified roadblock for the next group of students filing into Milverton's room. Was he any less misogynistic to this class? The analytical part of my brain wanted to stay and observe, but lunch beckoned. As did the promise of Rory's teasing sympathy when I confessed my latest crush-tastrophe.

Food first. Then figuring out how to convince Clara she wanted my help. Then, if there was still time before math, I'd mentally replay my awkwardness until I died of humiliation.

2

The video I'd recorded in science class looped on my computer screen. Mom and Dad were at some reception on campus and wouldn't be home until late. I'd made coffee and a bowl of Frosted Flakes. Breakfast for dinner and them not hassling me about my lack of plans: tonight was a win.

But this video: solid fail. It was all there on the screen. Clara's pinched eagerness. Rory's flying hair. Milverton ignoring the girls in a way that was blatant and deliberate—at least to me. Rory wasn't big on volunteering, but she didn't bother in science. Gemma's hand never made it past the halfway point, like it wasn't worth the effort to fully extend it. While Elinor, Kat, and Mira were completely checked out, Clara looked like a desperate contestant on a game show.

Clara said she didn't want my help, but which was worse: being a lazy white dude who stood by while Milverton got his patriarchy on, or trying to play hero when Clara told me to butt out?

I needed to send it to Phil and Susie for their takes. They were my best friends back in Ohio and had always been good sources of advice when I wanted to vent about social injustices or my celebrity crushes. Not that *any* actor or actress had ever inspired the levels of ridiculous fixation I felt about the guy whose iLive profile I had open in another tab.

I couldn't see much—just the few profile pics Win had made public. I'd sent him a friend request the night we'd met on Rory's driveway. She'd called it a "meet-cute"—I called it a "meet-dead-end." Because I hadn't seen him again and he hadn't accepted me as a friend. So really, me scrolling his page was pathetic and creepy. I should stop.

And I would. Tomorrow. Maybe the day after. Okay, endpoint TBD.

But first, the science video. Photography and videography were *not* my mediums. There were classmates in my Advanced Art studio who could've made this look polished and fancy, but I knew only basic editing. I couldn't fix the weird angles or crop out the bottom of the desk, but I could at least mute the sound of Milverton's nasal questions and add a voiceover. I could probably add a filter that gave everyone cat ears . . . but that seemed unnecessary.

I cleared my throat and tapped the microphone icon: "Hey guys. Welcome to Hero High freshman Earth Science. Where the material is dumb as rocks and the professor's attitude toward women is more dated than fossils. See exhibit one . . ." I rattled off the data from my notebook, but the video didn't need much narration—Milverton's actions spoke for themselves. As did the lingering shot of Clara's crushed expression when she lowered her hand.

I typed up a message to go with the video: `If this was your teacher, what would you do?` I'd send it via iLive's private messenger, but first I'd earned a break to admire Win Cavendish.

The fact that my friend request was still pending after nine days was probably a signal that Win wouldn't want me doing a deep scroll and pausing on a picture of him from last summer. It was taken in profile, him on a beach. Shirtless. But not like, *Hey, check out the gun show*. This was a photo he hadn't known was being taken. He was midlaugh, looking at someone to the left of the photographer. The sunset behind him was stunning or whatever, but I couldn't look away from his smile. And, fine, his bare stomach too.

Luckily my phone interrupted before I actually started drooling. "What's up, Campbear?"

"Hey, you left a book at my house," Rory said. "You know, the day you fell in *love.*"

"Hmm." I tapped my lip. "I seem to remember another person who was recently deeply invested in a one-sided romance." It'd taken months of matchmaking prowess to get Rory and her boyfriend, Toby, together. But they've been bonded like epoxy since New Year's Eve.

"Good point." She laughed. "Plus, Win was digging you. This was not one-sided."

"I've got an unaccepted friend request that says otherwise." I clicked back to his feed.

"Weird. Anyway. Want me to drop off the book? I need an excuse to get out of my house before Merri ropes me into redecorating Lilly's room for Eliza. Can you even imagine how mad Eliza will be that Merri's gone through all her stuff?"

"Sure. Come on over." I swiveled in my chair. Eliza Gordon-Fergus had recently moved in with the Campbells while her scientist parents were stationed at the South Pole, where she was currently visiting them. It was during the move-in that I'd met Win. And while Rory was always welcome here, she was wrong. Eliza might bluster about Merri's redecorating, but she'd be deeply touched and wasn't half as bristly as she wanted people to think.

"You leaving now?" I should send the video to Phil and Susie before she arrived. All I had to do was click—"Shoot! No. *No*. How fast can you get here?"

"You okay?" Rory's voice went high. "I'll be there in ten, but what happened?"

I cringed and swiveled away from my computer. I'd clicked—but not on sending the video to my friends. Instead I'd made a rookie stalker mistake: I'd clicked *Like* on a six-month-old photo of Win. Panic sat in my lungs like the weight bar that time during lacrosse practice when Curtis had spaced out while spotting me for bench presses. I reached out with a jittery hand to send the stupid science video, then slammed the laptop lid, unplugged it, and shoved it in a drawer.

I had my head down on my desk when Rory let herself in. I mumbled an explanation without moving. "On a scale of never-leaving-the-house to witness-protection, where does this land?"

"It's not that bad," she said. "Just click *Unlike*."

"He was online," I said against my arms, the words making my face flush hot again.

"Oh. Then he's already gotten the notification. How old did you say the photo was?" I groaned and she patted my back. "Maybe it'll be a reminder to accept your friend request."

"Or a big red flag that says *Stay away from the guy who's obsessed with you.*"

"First: I was there when you met. Merri agrees; he was vibing with you. I thought you guys were going to exchange saliva before names." She patted my back again. "Second: Hello? What happened to the guy who wouldn't let me give up on Toby? Where's my hopeless-romantic Huck?"

"He died, Campbear," I said. "Of embarrassment." This was why I focused on *other* people's crushes and kept my own safely on celebrities. As for exchanging saliva? Yeah, no. My first kiss wasn't going to be some impulsive, public thing. And it was probably safe to assume it wouldn't be with Win either.

"What can I do?" Her phone beeped in her bag, but she ignored it.

"Distract me." If I had to slip-click, why couldn't it be on a picture of him and his siblings? But, no. It had to be shirtless.

"Okay." She pulled a massive book out of her tote and dropped it on the desk. "Let's talk about Arthur Conan Doyle's *Complete Adventures of Sherlock Holmes*. Why did Ms. Gregoire assign it and where are you in it?"

"I haven't started." It was my parents' latest attempt to force me to "put myself out there at Hero High." They'd said if I didn't do a spring sport, then I needed more than just orchestra. "Some extra assignments to keep busy—perhaps a book club!" I'd called their bluff; they'd called Ms. Gregoire. And while it wasn't a book club per se, it was a book she'd picked for me. But if I let Curtis talk me into baseball, Mom and Dad would back off. Frankly, they'd throw a parade and hopefully, finally stop worrying that the move had ruined my social life. "I'm thinking I'll return it."

"No!" Rory hopped off the bed, upsetting my cup of pens. She swept up a handful and pointed them at me. "You can't."

"Or you'll ink me to death?" I laughed and shoved her hand away.

"Huck." Rory bent so our eyes were level. Only I hoped mine weren't open that wide, because she looked ridiculous. "You need to tell me *everything* Ms. Gregoire said when she gave you the book. Exact words if you remember."

Of course I did. "'It's only fitting my most perspicacious student should study literature's most perspicacious hero.'" I'd had to look that word up to make sure it wasn't an insult—it meant "perceptive and discerning," which, true. "And, 'You'll learn a lot from Sherlock.'"

The whole thing had been weirdly intense. I mean, Ms. Gregoire was my favorite teacher and she was always enthusiastic, but that day she'd been eerily earnest.

"Hmm." Rory chewed her bottom lip. Her phone beeped again, but her eyes stayed fixed on mine. "That doesn't sound very romantic. But you need to trust the process."

"Campbell, you're making zero sense. What are you talking about?"

She held up a hand. "Hit pause on the eye-rolling and hear me out. Ms. Gregoire does this thing with books. She picks one, you fall in love. She set up Merri and Fielding. Me and Toby. Eliza and Curtis. Apparently even Trent and Lilly, though he won't give us any details."

I scratched the back of my neck. Rory was a born cynic about everything but Toby. And art. She was the antithesis of her effervescent sister. So who was this quixotic imposter, or what was the punch line? My phone rang, but I hit the Ignore button. Probably my parents on their way home.

"Do you remember when I asked you to start making sense? Can we skip to that part?" I squinted at her. "Are you doing some weird impression of Merri? If so, I don't get it. Also, *I* set up you and Toby."

She shrugged. "Well, you, and Ms. Gregoire, and *Little Women*."

I remembered her whining about reading that book for extra credit, but... "I still don't understand."

"Just... read your book." Rory picked up my hand and placed it on the cover. "If Ms. Gregoire gave it to you, it's important."

I shivered. The tingles I was feeling weren't coming from *her* touch—platonic, thank you very much—but from the cloth-covered cardboard beneath my fingers. It was a low-key buzz, like when you touched a radiator as it kicked on, or the hum of fluorescent lights. If Rory'd noticed, she didn't react, but I snatched my hand away. I didn't like things I couldn't explain. And I couldn't explain this. I wiped my hand on my pants.

The book was going back.

"Who's blowing up your phone?" I pointed to her bag, the illuminated screen glowing through its canvas sides. Mine was ringing too, but that was likely part two of Mom's voicemail—where she reminded me that cereal wasn't dinner and coffee wasn't a nighttime beverage.

"Probably Merri asking my opinion on twinkle lights or feng shui." Rory dug through her bag. "Toby's at piano and Clara's—" She paused as she read the top text on her screen, then scrolled through others with stiff, frantic fingers.

"What's up?"

"Um, Huck..." She looked from her phone to the power cord dangling off my desk. "Did you post a video takedown of Mr. Milverton?"

"What? No." My stomach was already knotted, but it clenched. "I sent it to two friends in Ohio."

She clicked on the iLive app then thrust her phone at me. "You sent it to *everyone*. According to the latest comment, they're currently playing it on the local news."

3

My navy-and-red school tie was choking me. It had been all day. I dug a finger between it and my collar, but it didn't relieve the pressure in my throat.

I dried my hands on my pants and wished I could as easily fix the sweat sticking my shirt to my back. There was something about waiting, something about this room—an antechamber to the headmaster's office—that made me feel small. Since I wasn't actually shrinking, I'd distract myself by deducing the *why* of it. I stood and made a slow study of my surroundings: maroon area rug on marble floors, my parents seated in adjacent wingback chairs, the dark wooden side tables stacked with brochures.

I turned to face the wall and the answer practically leapt off it: the portraits.

They were overly oversized—unless the former headmasters had been giants, these were larger-than-life depictions. Framed with more gilt than necessary and hung higher than any designer on Dad's favorite HGTV shows would recommend. The overall impression was of mammoth people staring down their noses from lofty perches.

I sat back in my chair with a satisfied thump, no

longer choked by my clothing or having a crisis about my hard-won growth spurt having been revoked. I was still sweating though.

"Please stop fidgeting," Mom begged as she sat furiously knitting—but wasn't that just glorified fidgeting? "I know you're nervous, but we'll figure this out."

Easy for her to say. She and Dad had arrived on campus at dismissal. I'd had to be here all day. Through the people staring and talking about me, unsure if they should be hostile, impressed, or amused. Though, if my parents knew this, they'd probably be pleased that everyone on campus finally knew who I was. All it'd taken was a viral scandal and ruining Clara's life...

I knew this thought wasn't fair or accurate, but then again, neither was the World Wide Web. The thing about the internet was, it's like toothpaste. Once something was out, you couldn't squeeze it back in. I knew because I'd tried. I'd deleted the original post—the one that in my cyber-stalk-fail flail I'd accidentally sent to *all* instead of Phil and Susie—but it had already gone viral, which I would've realized if I'd checked my phone. Those calls had been the local news station asking for my comment.

And that was before the meme. I swallowed. Whatever happened in the headmaster's office, it wasn't going to be the low point of my day. *That* had already happened.

I felt ambivalent about the video—foolish for misclicking—but it was the truth and it was problematic. But the spliced-down version that some jerk had created? I got queasy just thinking of it and the apology I owed Clara.

I hadn't had a chance to give it though—she wasn't in school today. But her face was *everywhere*, on every tablet and laptop and cell phone screen. A desperately eager expression and a hand that zoomed into the air over and over on a loop. The "clever" captions were legion: `Tryouts for a deodorant commercial. Every woman on The Bachelor. If Hermione went blond. Me, when my gym class picks teams.`

Every time I'd glanced at Clara's empty desk in science class, I'd legit wanted to cry.

The school admin, Mrs. York, appeared in the doorway. "The headmaster asked me to pass along that he'll be a few more minutes. He's finishing up an interview."

She smiled tightly in response to my parents' "Don't worry about it. Tell him to take his time," then disappeared to her desk.

I stared at my tapping thumbs. If the low point of my day was the Clara gif, the high point had been Mr. Milverton's absence. Except—I tugged at my tie again—I hadn't meant to get anyone fired. Or humiliated.

Or for anyone besides two people to see the clip.

And for bonus humiliation funsies? I'd checked: Win still hadn't accepted my friend request.

I leaned my head back against the wall—there was plenty of room beneath the closest picture frame—shut my eyes, and groaned.

"Do you have a headache? I've got Tylenol. Let me just find it." Mom handed her needles to Dad, who had his nose buried in some book he'd plucked off a shelf. He moved the yarn out of the way and turned the page. *Thanks for your concern, Dad.* All that was missing was his glass of merlot and Sondheim CD, and he might as well be sitting on our deck. Mom looked up from her cavernous purse. "Do you have a drink? Ask that nice Mrs. York to direct you to a water fountain."

"I'm fine, Ma-ahhmm." Her name became something between a stutter and a moan, because Headmaster Williams's door opened and the person who appeared wasn't the stodgy administrator—well, he was there too. But my eyes were fixed on the guy at the receiving end of a perfunctory handshake who looked as uncomfortable in his tie as I was in mine.

"I'll be right with you," Headmaster Williams said before shutting the door and leaving me face-to-face with the student he'd been interviewing. Because did I mention I'd stood up? Not out of any show of respect for the headmaster, but from some weird jack-in-the-box instinctual need to get closer to Winston Cavendish.

"Win? Hi?" Neither of those should be questions.

"Hey, Huck." He grinned down at the feet he was shuffling. "I didn't think I'd see you. I know you go here, but it's the office and why would you be—Why *are* you here?" He glanced up with raised eyebrows, and the angles of his arch and chin and cheekbones made me momentarily hate Rory, because I wanted to capture his expression and save it forever. Her artistic specialty was portraits, and mine was pottery. Which was zero percent helpful. Rory gave Toby adorable sketches; what could I do, offer Win a super-duper romantic homemade mug? I tilted my head; actually, if it came prefilled with coffee, that might be a gift worth trading my first kiss for. Even if it was lopsided or lumpy.

The mug. Not Win—who was neither of those things.

As my scattered-focus silence stretched, his jaw tightened. "Not that it's any of my business. I'm well acquainted with principals' offices. No judgment." Except he was clearly judging himself, and I didn't deserve absolution.

"I accidentally made a viral video about the school."

"That was you?" His eyes sparked. With amusement? Approval? I'd need to spend more time with him to be sure, but whatever it was, he glanced at my blatantly eavesdropping parents and tamped it down. "That teacher was... How's Clara?"

I blinked in surprise—then realized he *knew* Clara, would've gone to school with her at Mayfield. But it wasn't only their association that caught me off guard; it was that his concern was for *her*. All day everyone had been so caught up in the hype and scandal.

"Absent." I could barely say the word without gagging, and vomit was not a good look on anyone. I reached to cup the back of my neck and my sleeve grazed his. Had I stepped closer, or had he? Because we were pretty much breaking every rule of personal space. In front of my parents. "How was your interview? You're transferring?"

"Trying to." His eyes shuttered and he stepped back. "I should go."

"Oh. Right. And I'm—" I gestured to the headmaster's door.

He grimaced. "Good luck. See ya."

"I hope so." My earnest words came first—then the realization that Win's had been a closing, not a question.

But before my embarrassment and panic could battle for emotional control, Win grinned. "Me too."

I was staring at the doorway and jumped when Dad's hand landed on my shoulder. "So Pucky, who was that?"

The name printed on my birth certificate was four letters long: *H U C K*. This didn't stop Curtis from adding "-leberry" or my parents from substituting a *P* for the *H*.

"Puck," or if they were feeling extra sentimental, "Pucky." Not after the trickster fairy I've been told my dimpled grin resembles, but the sports equipment for dad's favorite game. And like my ridiculous nickname, there was no point in *me* playing it cool. My parents and I had been close for every one of my fifteen years, despite their annoying post-move obsession with making sure I was "well adjusted"—aka *popular*— and no way was I convincing them Win was "just a guy I know" or anything acquaintance-like.

So, I was zero percent surprised Dad put down his book and Mom abandoned her yarn. Each of Miles's dates and girlfriends had been analyzed and scrutinized like future grandbabies depended on corsage color preferences. I swore Miles went to college out of state to prevent them from showing up at his dorm on Sunday mornings with cinnamon rolls and surveys for him to complete about his plans from the previous night.

And while they'd spent the whole school year trying to expand my friend group beyond Rory and Curtis, I'd never given them any fodder for their romantic machinations. Mom and Dad exchanged looks of anticipation.

Since there was no chance of escaping, I sighed and answered. "You know Curtis? That's his younger brother. He's a freshman at the public school, Chester High. Not here."

"But, *an interview!* Maybe he will be." Dad waggled his eyebrows. "Maybe he'll need someone to show him around campus."

I bit back a grin. I'd volunteer to tour-guide the heck out of Win, except... "He wouldn't start until September." And I couldn't endure half a year of crush-limbo.

"Good point. We'll need something sooner." Dad steepled his fingers and began to pace. Maybe I should've been embarrassed, but I liked that Dad saw *us* as possible. I liked a plan. And I was primed for Baker Brainstorming Sessions from years of watching Dad and Miles fill whiteboards with potential date ideas. "What do you know about him? Sports? Hobbies? Does he play any instruments? Oh, does he like salsa music?"

Mom shook the Tylenol bottle to get our attention. It rattled like the egg-shaped maracas she'd used when she taught toddler music classes. "Can you two focus, please? We're not here for *The Dating Game*." She held out two pills and when I rejected them, offered me a butterscotch candy instead. "Though he was very handsome, and I'd be happy to hear about him later."

Which meant I could likely persuade them to stop at Cool Beans for coffee if I made them think I was a reluctant participant in this conversation. The reality was far more humiliating: I *wanted* to talk about Win, and they were the best option. For one thing, they won gold medals in the supportive parents category. For another, there were only so many times I could rave or whine about him to Rory, Curtis was clearly no-go for all conversations about his brother, and it wasn't like I could say, "Hey, random classmates, want to hear about my crush's earlobes?"

Let the bargaining begin. "You know what goes well with interrogations?" I asked. "Biscotti and extra-dry cappuccino."

"Well played and we'll see." But Mom's smile slipped

when the office door opened and Headmaster Williams said, "Please join me."

Despite there being three chairs on our side of the desk versus the one on his, the power balance wasn't tipped in our favor. Part of this was structural: the chairs we sat in were shorter. The other part was decorative: the row of awards facing us, all proclaiming his greatness and authority.

Headmaster Williams set his elbows on his leather blotter and leveled me with a look. "Why don't you start? Tell us what you were thinking when you posted that video."

"I wasn't thinking anything—it was an accident," I said slowly. "But I can tell you what I was thinking when I recorded it: that everyone deserves an equal opportunity to participate."

He nodded stiffly. "While we can agree on that sentiment, it's your actions I can't condone."

"Sir, I'd been planning to send that video to two people for advice. It was never meant to be public."

"It should never have been recorded!" Headmaster Williams reached into a drawer and pulled out a slim black volume. "This is the school handbook. I have a form with your signature indicating you have read and understood its contents."

I'd read a digital copy during our drive from Ohio and knew exactly which section he was going to flip to.

"There are a number of policies in here that you've violated, but namely the ones from the section on electronics and privacy." He read aloud: "*Students are not to use the image of any students or faculty without their permission.* Do you understand this?"

I nodded, appreciative that he didn't do that gotcha

game of naming everyone in the video and asking one by one if I'd had their permission.

He flipped to another section. This one was titled "*Grievance Procedures*." Dad scooted closer and Mom muttered a quiet "Oh, dear" as Headmaster Williams's fingers lingered beside the word "infractions."

"No one is condoning what was taking place in that classroom. I was appalled and disheartened by what I saw, but we have established protocol you should have followed. And nowhere does it suggest making this hallowed institution the subject of mockery for social media and morning talk shows."

"Yes, sir." I clutched the armrests so I wouldn't tug on my tie.

"I've spent the day on calls with concerned parents and disgruntled alumni. People are threatening to pull donations, students, and applications. Reginald R. Hero Preparatory School has had a sterling reputation for a hundred years. You undermined that with forty seconds of video. And have you seen the gifs?"

"Of Clara?" I swallowed.

"Well, she's certainly in them—but these ones demean the school."

My "I'm sorry, sir" sounded like a croak. Mom patted my leg.

"Mr. Baker, you are new to Hero High this year, yet this is not your first time in my office."

Crashing the after-hours Rogue Romeo party in the school theater in September hadn't been my brightest decision, but I couldn't regret it. My parents had been desperate for *any* sign of a social life, and while I may not have made friends at the party, Rory and I had bonded in the resulting Saturday detentions. Nothing creates camaraderie like scrubbing paint off a stage.

Still, I put on a penitent face. "Yes, sir."

"This is your second strike. And if—"

"Might I make a suggestion?" Dad interrupted. Mom whispered a second, more emphatic "Oh, dear!" and I braced myself.

Headmaster Williams blinked in surprise that someone had dared to talk over him, but gestured for Dad to continue. "Before we get ahead of ourselves, let's take a breath. I had a chance to peruse your handbook while we were waiting out there."

I'm not sure whose eyes went wider, the headmaster's or mine. *That* was what he'd been reading? I rubbed the back of my neck, unsure if Dad was about to be brilliant or a liability. From the look on Mom's face, she wasn't sure either.

"Now, it seems to me that other parts of the handbook are relevant too—specifically the 'core values' of mutual respect, equality, and responsibility to a greater community. Or the section of your mission statement about 'ensuring a safe, supportive learning environment to provide *all* students with the opportunity to flourish academically and personally.'" Dad tapped the tips of his fingers together. "Is it safe to assume you agree Mr. Milverton wasn't representative of those beliefs?"

Headmaster Williams's mouth puckered as he nodded.

"Great, then we're on the same page." Dad sat back in his chair, and I fought the urge to clap. "As someone who is also well versed with the pressures of academia and the peculiar trials of raising teenagers, I've come up with what I believe is a logical consequence for Huck."

Clapping urge gone. Dad making Headmaster Williams eat his handbook's words? Great. Dad brainstorming ways for me to meet up with Win? Yay! Dad in fixer mode suggesting punishments? Much less cool.

"The way I see it, Huck needs to demonstrate knowledge of the stated boundaries for video and privacy, and he should help mitigate the damage he's done to the school's reputation."

"In an ideal world, but I—"

Dad was not to be stopped. "Assign him to make a video that showcases Hero High's best qualities. Filming within the parameters of the school rules, of course. It'd be a great opportunity for him to engage with his classmates while creating something that promotes the school."

I wished I'd taken Mom up on that Tylenol, because I had a sudden, massive headache. Of *course* Dad would turn this into a social project as well as a punishment.

Headmaster Williams's expression was strained. "While I appreciate your insight and I hope Huck spends his break contemplating his actions, I'll be spending mine putting out PR fires and organizing sensitivity trainings for the staff." He glanced at a framed picture of his kids, sophomore Sera and junior Fielding. Had I wrecked their breaks too? "And hiring a new science teacher, because Mr. Milverton has retired, effective immediately."

"Good." Mom's voice was firm. "Those poor girls."

Headmaster Williams blinked out of his to-do list, looking chagrined as he said, "Indeed. But a project like the one you've suggested would require significant supervision, and with these additional duties, I don't have time to devote to it."

"I wouldn't dream of expecting *you* to advise him, but surely there's another faculty member who could." Dad turned to me. "You're always raving about Ms. Gregoire. Think she would?"

When Headmaster Williams leaned forward and clasped his hands on the desk, I knew my spring break was also forfeited. "I like this idea. But make no mistake, Huck's on probation. One more misstep and he'll be asked to leave the school."

My parents and I overlapped in our "Yes, sir" and "Thank you, sir."

"I want this done quickly." He scanned the calendar on his blotter, then pointed to a square. "Friday, March twenty-ninth. The last meeting of the admissions committee is that afternoon. It's always the most contentious. I want the video to play there, to remind everyone *why* we work so hard to select our incoming students. Letters of acceptance and denial are mailed the next morning, and I'll share your video on social media as the future students are receiving their acceptances. We need to put out a positive narrative—convince those students that Hero High is where they want to spend the next four years of their schooling. Understood?"

It was March first. That gave me twenty-eight days. "I'll get right on it—as soon as I talk to Ms. Gregoire."

Which is how I ended up trudging across campus and knocking on the classroom door of my favorite teacher while my peers were already an hour into their spring break.

I hoped Ms. Gregoire would come up with some clever reason this project was unnecessary. Instead she opened the door with a smile. "Headmaster Williams just called and filled me in. I love this idea, don't you? It pairs perfectly with your Sir Arthur Conan Doyle reading."

"About that..." I reached into my backpack and pulled out the book, ignoring the echoes of Rory's proclamations about this story being my destiny or whatever. "I might sign up for baseball. And with this project...I don't need this anymore. I won't have time."

"Oh, Huck." Ms. Gregoire was an emoter. Her feelings were big and they were obvious. Usually variations of excitement or anticipation or enthusiasm, but right then I was blanketed in sympathy. It made goose bumps spread up my arms. "You need Sherlock more than ever. In fact, priority number one over your break isn't the video. It's reading that book. It'll fortify you for what's to come."

4

I loved everything about coffee. The caffeine, the smell, the sound it made when it was being poured. The warmth of a mug between my hands. The taste—so sharp and bitter, alive on my tongue. But especially the caffeine.

And when the world frustrated me, regular coffee wasn't enough. I dug out the French press.

I measured grinds with exactitude. Filled the canister with water, stopping precisely at the line etched in the glass. Set a timer and waited for it to steep. And when I thrust the plunger down, compressing the grinds while siphoning off the strong, rich brew—well, it was the most satisfying thing that had happened all week.

Which said a lot about the state of my spring break.

My room was sending pretty strong crisis-bunker vibes. Besides the French press hidden below my desk, there were coffee mugs on every flat surface. Empty, half-full, cardboard, ceramic. I'd had to banish Mom's cat, because Luna kept knocking them over.

And Mom—if *she* had peeked in and seen how flagrantly I was violating the "no more than two cups a day" rule... well, grounding would be counterproductive, but I could see them grabbing the Hero High directory and trying to schedule play dates with random classmates.

I thanked the gods of door locks and doing my own laundry that she and Dad had no reason to wander in as long as I ventured out when they got home from work.

But while they were gone, it was just me, coffee, and, on two different laptops, a tablet, and my phone, Clara's face.

I hadn't yet apologized. I'd tried, repeatedly, but her phone went to voicemail and the mailbox was full. Rory had stopped by her house, only to learn that Clara had decided last minute to spend the week in New York with her dad.

If I couldn't apologize with words, I'd do so with actions. I hadn't read any *Sherlock* or done anything for the video project. I'd been too busy teaching myself search-engine optimization, so I could do the opposite and try to eliminate or reduce the spread of Clara's gif. I'd lost track of the number of image-removal requests I'd completed. There were no legal grounds for it to be deindexed in searches, but the more copies I got taken down, the less there were populating results. In the first four days of break, I'd gotten it from number twelve to number seventy-two when you searched for `eager+gif`.

That felt like progress, so I set down my coffee when my phone rang. And after checking that it wasn't yet another reporter looking for an interview, I picked up. "Hey, Campbell."

"You answered!" Rory said. "But, do you know Larken?"

"Sometimes I think you think I don't listen." I moved three empty mugs so I could lean a knee against my desk. "I was there when Merri spent twenty minutes telling us 'Larken is the new feminist pop-rock icon.'"

"Yeah, well, sometimes you *don't* listen." Rory laughed. "Like any of the times you've been looking right at me, but totally lost in your head."

"Fair point." I picked up a mug and took a sip—then spat it out. Wrong mug. And it had clearly not been the right mug for several days.

"Back to Larken." Rory's voice grew serious and I sat up, still wiping my tongue on my sleeve. "She just posted the meme on iLive."

"Please be joking." I was already opening the app: `@IAmLarken: Me, trying to get a designer to dress me for awards ceremonies. Can a fat girl get some fashion love? #BodyPositivity #BigisBeautiful`

I slammed the laptop lid. In two seconds a wannabe singer—fine, she was actually very talented—had undone sixty hours of burial work.

"I guess it's game over for hoping it goes away?" Rory said.

"I'm not giving up."

"You never do." Rory paused. "But maybe take a break? Step away from your desk. Have you been outside?"

"Yes, Campbell, I've been outside." Dad had made me shovel the driveway yesterday. Because nothing says "spring break" like a fun March snowstorm.

"Good. It's not just Clara I'm worried about. Any gray hairs are both your faults."

After we hung up, I rooted around my desk until I came up with the correct mug. I'd just taken a sip when my bedroom door swung open. Luckily the coffee was now lukewarm, because I spilled the rest down the front of my shirt. "What the heck, Curtis? Ever hear of knocking? Or doorbells? How did you get in?"

"I knocked. You didn't answer. Your front door's unlocked." He shrugged. "My Knight Light mentor sensors detected trouble in the force—I decided to come check on you."

"I'm fine." Except for the fact that there was a literal puddle of coffee on my collarbones and my shirt looked like a Rorschach test.

Curtis raised an eyebrow and gave a slow scan of my room. "Yeah, I can tell."

So my bed was unmade and there was laundry and a towel on the floor from the last time I'd showered, which had been . . . sometime this weekend? What day was today? Tuesday?

"It smells like a barista died in here," Curtis said as he stacked empty cups. "Get changed. You're coming over to play catch."

My first instinct was to protest that I was busy—but stupid, freaking Larken. I scrubbed a hand across my eyes. Maybe throwing something would be cathartic.

"Will your brother be there? Win?" Like he didn't already know his brother's name. I gritted my teeth and tried to dim my lightbulb eagerness.

"That'd be him." Curtis grinned. "But he's at school."

"Oh. Right." I tugged my wet shirt off and added it to the laundry pile. I really needed to empty the clean clothes from my hamper so I could refill it. I flipped open the lid and grabbed a fresh T-shirt from the top. There—that was a start.

"Huckleberry, you said you like guys, right?" Curtis asked, and I froze with my head and one arm inside the T-shirt.

"Well, yeah. Some guys, some of the time." I hadn't settled on a label yet. Bi? Pan? Gay? Queer? Did I *need* to know mine already? Sometimes it seemed like everyone else did. They'd had kisses and dates and figured things out. And I...

I was glad my expression was hidden behind the Buckeyes logo on my shirt, because there was zero chill on my face. There was also probably zero chill in standing here tangled in fabric like a toddler who couldn't dress himself. I twitched everything into place and turned toward Curtis, whose eyes glowed with amusement and mischief.

"Think you could like my brother?"

My attempt at a nonchalant "Maybe?" earned me some skeptical eyebrows, so I begrudgingly added, "Win's hot."

Curtis puffed out his chest. "He takes after me."

"No, he doesn't." Curtis was all easy smiles. Sometimes they were *too* easy. Sometimes they were performative. Win was sandpaper; he was grit and unpolished edges that I had no desire to ever polish... but wouldn't mind rubbing up against.

"I was there when you two met." Curtis looked me over. "I don't know why I didn't say something sooner."

I shrugged, but *seriously*, with all my failures to be subtle, I was starting to doubt Curtis was as smart as his recent science fair win suggested. "I don't know if he's into me. I tried friending him—"

He waved away that comment. "He's never on social media."

I blew out a breath. "Yeah, but he's... I'm..." There was a huge difference between smitten daydreams and reality. In the former I was suave. In real life, not so much.

Curtis smirked. "I've never seen you insecure before, Huckleberry. It's cute. I get it; you're a fragile, post-meme creature right now. And Win's all prickly cactus, no agave nectar."

Eh, that was one interpretation. But maybe if I drank *all* the dregs in this room, I'd be caffeinated enough to fake confidence. Or maybe I should do the much more productive thing and continue to obsess over my ignored friend request from afar.

"But no worries, as your mentor I'm here for all your needs. I can totally see you and Win together—he just can't have any idea that I approve of you two."

"What?" I blinked at the plot twist. "Is this because he's 'antisibling rivalry' or whatever that means?"

"He's not anti it in that he doesn't experience it—more that if Win thinks he and I are going to compete or be compared, he nopes out or gets defensive. Win's... complicated." Curtis resumed stacking cups and avoided my gaze.

Complicated, out of my league, and unwilling to friend me? "Let's just forget the whole thing."

"No." Curtis unearthed my sneakers and tossed them to me. "This *is* happening. Just know I'm going to pretend to disapprove."

I threw a shoe back at him in exasperation. "This is officially the worst pep talk ever."

He laughed and unhooked a sweatshirt from my closet door. "Like you really needed one."

I blinked. I *did*. And I couldn't understand why Curtis and Rory didn't get that. How did everyone else make the transition from impossible crushes to possible kisses?

"But I'm putting this out there: if you and Win hit it

off, I want all the credit. And if you go Chernobyl, then I'm Switzerland and you don't blame me. I'm not down for hostile Knight Lights meetings or lacrosse games. Sound good?"

I shrugged. It sounded... overwhelming.

"Now, come on, mole person. Let's go play catch."

Curtis marched me around the back of his brick ranch, pausing only to collect a ball and two gloves from the garage. I shuffled my sneakers in the snow and looked around the small, fenced-in yard.

"You know the saying 'keep your eyes on the ball'?" Curtis threw as he said this, and I let the ball plop in the snow so I could keep my eyes on him. Because, yes, I'd heard that, but my parents had always emphasized "Look at someone when they're talking to you."

I tossed the ball back and he added, "That's the whole secret. 'Eye on the ball' and you're golden."

"It's hard to see the ball when it's the same color as the snow." I made an attempt to reach his next throw, but between sun glare and slush shoes, it sailed past me.

"Also hard when you have absolutely no desire to play catch," Curtis said with a grin.

"Am I that obvious?" I kicked at the snow until I found the ball. "It's not my sport. Too much standing around. I need the constant movement of lacrosse or skiing."

"How do you feel about swimming?"

"Most public pools are virus-ridden cesspools." It was an evasion, not an answer. "If you can smell chlorine—run. A clean pool is odorless. The chemical smell comes from the chlorine reacting with human waste and—"

"Now that's a fun topic," said Curtis. "Please make that your pickup line for Win. And let me watch—I want to see how it goes over."

My stomach tightened. *Should* I be planning pickup lines? Not that one, obviously.

"How about running?" Curtis pulled off his glove and I gladly copied. "I'm doing a half-marathon, and my training partner abandoned me for the South Pole."

That'd be Eliza. Curtis's girlfriend looked like a cover model and studied like she planned to follow in her parents' Nobel Prize footsteps. She and Curtis had covertly flirted with each other for weeks before they'd owned up to dating. I didn't understand how everyone else *hadn't* noticed, but there'd been no misreading Eliza's discomfort the one time I'd brought it up. Thankfully they'd made everything public and official before she'd headed to Antarctica for an extended spring break measuring ice caps or something.

"I don't hate running," I said.

"Good. I'll let you off the hook for baseball if you do my long run with me this weekend. Now let's go in the house, my feet are freezing."

An hour of video games later I had my jacket on and was tying my sneakers when the front door opened. The twins entered in a jumble of conversation and coats.

Win froze when our eyes met. I did too. Was it possible to take my coat back off in any suave manner? To find an excuse to stay? To ever say "Hey" to him without sounding like I was holding in a sneeze?

"Hey," he echoed, still holding my gaze.

Curtis leaned over the couch. "How was school? Did you play nicely with others?"

Win raised an eyebrow. Man, he had good eyebrows—eyelashes too, the kind that announced all his emotions in bold font. But it was his eyebrows that killed me. They excelled at two modes: confident and vulnerable. Right now those arches were set to stun. "Play nice? Never."

"You don't know how good you have it with your fancy spring break." Wink collapsed dramatically on the love seat in a ball of pink down and faux fur.

Curtis stretched out across the couch, tucking his hands behind his head. "My classes are just that much harder than yours—we private-school folk need a week to recover from our arduous studies."

Wink laughed, but Win's jaw tightened. "Remind me of that part where your media teacher lets you watch manga and your French teacher has 'pastry Fridays'?"

Curtis grinned. "Don't forget Knight Lights' sledding day, mentor-mentee baked goods, and the time Dr. Badawi let us re-create melting videos from iLive." Win yanked the throw pillow from beneath Curtis, but he laughed as his head landed on the couch cushion. "All this could be yours too, if you aced that interview last week."

It was like all the good humor and oxygen evaporated from the room. Wink stood, Win stiffened, and Curtis looked chagrined.

It had gone so quiet that the *tzzzzh* of my jacket zipper sounded obscene. "I'm, uh, going to go."

"We're not going to fight; you don't have to leave." I thought Win was talking to me, but he'd turned to his sister, who'd been slinking toward the hallway. "In fact, I'm leaving."

Now he faced me, his eyes still blazing with a heavy emotion I couldn't name yet. "You headed home? I need to go that way; I'll walk with you."

I shoved my hands into my pockets, squeezing them into *yes* fists. "Sure. That'd be cool." I breathed a silent prayer to the gods of attention spans and self-absorbedness that I was the only one who noticed Win hadn't said *where* he was going, and I hadn't told him where I lived.

"Ugh, make your own friends, Win." Curtis's faux-disapproval voice was passable, but I couldn't look at him, because I doubted his poker face was. "Are we on for a run this weekend, Huckleberry?"

"Sure." But before the brothers could get contentious again, I bolted out the door.

"Is Curtis recruiting you for the race too?" Win asked once we'd reached the sidewalk and I'd turned left toward my house. I'd tried to do it smoothly, pretending not to notice he had paused to let me navigate.

"Nah, I'm a training stand-in while Eliza's gone."

"Maybe he'll get some actual training done then. I swear he and Eliza just make out in the woods."

"Oh." My cheeks heated and I had all the mental pictures—but not of Eliza and Curtis. Of *me* and the other Cavendish boy. "Yeah, we won't be doing that."

"Eliza's cool though," said Win. "I don't know what she's doing with my brother."

Curtis's rivalry insights helped, but I hadn't fully decoded the animosity between them. It was constant, and if you took it at face value, brutal. And yet, it rang hollow.

Like a rote script they were both stuck delivering. Back when my brother lived at home, Miles and I had argued. But when we were mad, we were *mad*. The interactions I'd witnessed between the Cavendish brothers were like cayenne on a cupcake: they looked spicy, but underneath, they were sweet. Win and Curtis truly liked and loved each other—so why did they constantly pretend they didn't?

Win coughed and I realized I'd been quiet too long.

"What's Wink's full name?" I blurted. "I've been trying to figure it out and I keep forgetting to ask. Wilhelmina? Or something Egyptian I'm never going to guess?"

He laughed. I wanted to do a victory dance for having caused it. Instead I looked away so he couldn't see my expression go heart-eyed emoji. "Lincoln. Wink's a Curtis-ism."

"Ah. That makes sense." Curtis's nicknames were infamous. But I was finally alone with Win, so we needed to stop talking about his brother. I took a deep breath. "So there's a thing I do. I call it 'The Question Game'—but there's no points or winners or anything. Basically it's that I'm awful at get-to-know-you small talk, and..."

I scrunched my hands in my pockets and wondered if I was failing at pickup lines or simply doing them my own way. I glanced sideways to see how he'd reacted. Win was giving me an expectant look, one I knew too well and that Miles accompanied with a flick to my forehead while saying, "*Pay attention*."

"Sorry, could you repeat that?" I asked.

Win shrugged. "I said, 'Small talk is the worst.' How do you play?"

I unclenched my hands and exhaled. I couldn't have done another block of unstructured stress-walking, trying to flirt while making sure I didn't get lost in my thoughts or get *us* lost. "We take turns asking questions and answering. You can ask anything. Like, 'favorite drink?'"

"Cranberry juice."

Tart and sweet, like him. "Black coffee." Eh, did that mean I was bitter? "Now it's your turn."

A tiny crinkle appeared over his left eyebrow as he mused. "Favorite reality show?"

"Okay, I watch this with my parents—and before you laugh, it's fascinating as a way of analyzing body language and motives." Dad and I always competed with predictions; Mom watched it for the dresses. "*The Bachelor*."

He recoiled. "That's my least favorite." This didn't shock me. I'd already deduced he'd hate televised rejection. I knew his answer wouldn't involve competition even before he said, "I'm digging *Tidying Up with Marie Kondo*. But fair warning, I'm a slob."

I would not picture his bedroom. I would *not* picture him *in* his bedroom. While I was focused on not doing these things, I skidded on an icy patch and Win's arm shot out to grasp mine.

Technically his touch steadied me, but I felt even more off-kilter. My voice cracked when I said, "Okay, my question..."

Sometime between "favorite animal?" (his guinea pig, Hudson, and for me, otters) and "favorite season?" (summer for both of us), our footsteps had changed. They were slower, looser. Closer.

"If I could travel anywhere I'd—" I looked over my shoulder to where Win had lagged. He was bent over a snowbank, fishing something out. A fuzzy purple mitten. So small the whole thing would've fit one of his thumbs. He shook it off, then carefully arranged it on a black spire of the closest yard's fence.

And I couldn't help but grin.

He looked up and caught me, caught up to me. "What?"

I shook my head, but my grin had only grown.

"No, seriously," he said. "What?" But he was grinning too as he nudged my shoulder with his.

I didn't know what that meant; I only knew what I wanted it to. I wished I was brave enough to reach out and take his hand, the one that could've fit that mitten in its palm. The one that wanted to make sure someone's tiny fingers weren't cold.

My hand wasn't. Was his?

I searched for words—a way to combine them that was clever, but not a "dad joke" like Rory teased me about. Less corny, more flirty. *I'll be your mitten.* Or *I got your hand-warmer right here*. "Smitten" rhymed with "mitten"—was there anything there?

I winced. Yeah. No. I was so grateful telepathy wasn't real and that this humiliation was only happening *inside* my head. And maybe—just maybe—that meant I should stop sniffing him. I doubted I was as subtle as I was trying to be. He smelled like spicy dude deodorant, but there was something else too, something sharp and chemical. And layered over both of those were whatever pheromones made me want to keep leaning in and taking lungfuls.

"Do you have a cold?" he asked. "I might have a tissue."

So, yeah, that was a no on subtlety. I cringed and mumbled, "I live on this next street." Though I was tempted to find some longer way home so we could keep walking.

He nodded. "Finish your answer. Where's your dream vacation?"

"Iceland. Or maybe Australia, but I don't know about the whole spider thing."

Win laughed. "I'll come and squash them for you."

"Would you? At least the poisonous ones." We were almost at my driveway. Should I attempt a front-door maneuver? What would that even look like? Why hadn't I drawn a schematic of my front porch and ever diagrammed out this possibility? Though if the free fall panic in my stomach was any indication, I was in no way ready. I could invite him—

"Huck!" I turned toward the voice. Merri, the adorable and effervescent middle Campbell sister, was standing next to Rory on my front porch.

"Hey," I said. "What are you doing here?"

"We came to do a welfare check. Rory said you were hermitting."

"But clearly you're fine and we'll go now." Rory flashed me apologetic eyes as she tugged Merri's sleeve.

Her sister ignored her and beamed at the guy beside me. "You're Curtis's brother, right? I hear you might be transferring to Hero High. Fingers crossed!"

Win looked like a deer in headlights.

Merri could be . . . a lot. As demonstrated by the fact that she bounced through the snow to offer him a hug before he'd even answered. He stepped back and thrust out a hand instead. "I'm Win."

"Win? That's so cute. And you're with Huck—who should really be named *Hunk*, am I right?"

I prayed to the gods of civil engineering and city planning

that some undiscovered sinkhole would open beneath my front walk and swallow me whole.

Rory yanked her sister backward by the hood of her coat. "I swear we're not related. And I'm forever sorry for bringing her along."

"No, it's okay." Win's serious expression cracked into a smirk. "Normally I reject anyone that enthusiastic out of principle, but this time I have to make an exception and agree."

Merri opened her mouth, but I threw up both hands like a highly stressed crossing guard. "Everyone freeze." Shocking me, they did. "Campbells, I'm fine. Win, thanks for walking me home—I mean, keeping me company on your way to . . ."

He grinned. "I was walking you home."

"Good. I was hoping." My hands were still up, but now the corners of my mouth were too. "I'm going to leave right now, before anyone says anything else. Because that's the perfect ending. So everyone shut your mouths until I'm through the door." I pointed to it with one hand while making a shush sign with the other.

Once on the other side, I slid to the floor and grinned against my knees while raining celebratory fists against the foyer rug.

Win thought I was a hunk.

5

Rory showed up the next day with a Cool Beans latte and an apology for Merri's behavior. I waved it off—"Did you miss the part where Win agreed I'm a hunk?"—but downed half the latte before we'd made it to my room.

She looked around and whistled. "I'm getting serial-killer vibes. Or college student before finals. Maybe I should take that cup—clearly you don't need more caffeine."

"Don't you dare." I held it out of reach. "Things got messy. Want to help me clean up?"

"I'll supervise. I haven't had all the shots required to handle this without a hazmat suit." She sat on the end of my bed as I loaded my arms with old coffees. I would've needed to do this today anyway. Mom had been making suspicious comments about our missing mugs. It took three trips to the kitchen. Then I washed my hands, because Rory was right, there was something funky growing in some cups.

"Done."

She looked up from her phone and gave a pointed look at my laundry pile but didn't say anything.

"What's up?" Because if she'd wanted to apologize, she could've texted; if this was a hangout visit, she wouldn't be so quiet.

"So, Huck." She was sitting on the bed like a kid waiting for the flu shot. I braced myself. "Remember when we had that conversation about me and Toby—how people aren't projects?"

I nodded. Of course that was *before* I got her and Toby together, so...

"Clara said she didn't want your help with Milverton."

"But—"

"You should've respected that."

I scratched at coffee stains on my desk. "It was an accident. And I didn't do it just for her. She's not the only girl in his classes."

"But she *is* the only one in the gif." Rory sighed. "And the one who's gone into spring-break hiding."

"I'm going to fix it," I said. "This Larken thing is a setback, but—"

"Maybe you should let it go. Accept that you can't."

I lowered my head. "I don't know how to do that."

"Then you need to start your reading assignment from Ms. Gregoire." While I'd been making trips downstairs, Rory had unearthed the massive book with the black cover. She hefted it toward me, and even though I hadn't caught a single pass from Curtis yesterday, and even though I wasn't expecting her to *throw a book at me*, it settled gently in my hands. "We never finished our conversation about her, and I'm still trying to figure out why she assigned you *this* book, but I trust the process. You need to read it. You get that, right?"

I looked down at the silhouette of a detective in his famous hat holding a magnifying glass. Ms. Gregoire's agreement seemed to ring off the pages: she'd called this book "priority number one over break." And while I wasn't sure I bought into the whole woo-woo, supernatural reputation our teacher had, if it was this important to Rory, I'd play along.

"Fine," I said. "If it will make you happy, I'll read it."

"Good!" Rory stood and patted my arm. "Start now."

I was supposed to meet Curtis for a nine o'clock run on Saturday, but it wasn't until I tried sipping from an empty mug that I looked up from my book and saw that it was nine thirty-four. I shoved my feet into sneakers and figured the sprint from my house to his would count as a warm-up.

It was Ms. Gregoire's fault. And Sir Arthur Conan Doyle's. Since I'd opened *The Complete Adventures of Sherlock Holmes* three days and nineteen short stories ago, I'd dreamed of poison and bodies and treasure and Scotland Yard. It killed me to be putting distance between my eyes and the pages where orange "pips"—which I'd looked up; they were just seeds—were being used as a harbinger of death.

For thirty seconds after I knocked on the Cavendishes' door, it was silent, then footsteps and a lock and knob turning. The door opened to reveal Win with a glorious case of bed head and sleepy eyes. If I hadn't already been bewitched by him, I would've lost the battle in that moment.

"Oh. Hey." He scrubbed a hand over his mouth to hide a yawn. Then stretched and revealed a sliver of stomach between his flannel pajama pants and rumpled T-shirt.

Happy birthday to me!

"It's your birthday?" He yawned again, and now I was the

one covering my mouth—because apparently I'd said that aloud.

"Um, I have plans with Curtis."

"For your birthday?"

"No. No birthday. I mean, I have one, obviously. But today isn't it."

"Come in." He blinked sleepily, and I prayed to the gods of brain fog that he wasn't awake enough to process what had just happened. "I'm not sure where Curtis is, but you can wait."

"Sorry I woke you." Did I want to come in? *Heck, yeah*. But he had the look of someone who could be back asleep in three minutes. "You don't have to entertain me. I'll text Curtis and—"

"It's no problem." His eyes widened in quick blinks, like he was trying to wake himself up. When I still hesitated, he asked, "What's your favorite breakfast? I'm not offering to make it, I'm question gaming."

I grinned and stepped inside. "Coffee and cereal."

"Man, if I'd known it was that easy, I *would've* offered." He padded barefoot into the kitchen and opened a cabinet of mugs for me. As always, I went for the biggest, but first I pointed to the one with a paint handprint that had been cracked and repaired.

"Yours?"

"The handprint or the handiwork?" he asked. "The print is Curtis's. Wink's the one who dropped it, but I got caught gluing it. So if you ask my parents, I'm responsible for breaking it too." I had follow-up questions, but he shut the cabinet and pointed to a press-button coffee machine. "My favorite breakfast is juice and pancakes."

"Cranberry?"

He paused with his hand on the fridge door. "You remembered."

I shrugged. "That's kinda the point. To get to know you." But my cheeks were hot. I'd always been the kid who remembered too much. It was never clear when that was cool as opposed to creepy. Win looked flattered I knew his juice preference, but how would he feel if he knew all the other personal facts I'd consciously and subconsciously collected and cataloged? In *Sherlock Holmes* people didn't react well. At best, they treated it like a parlor trick. At worst, they were offended. Either situation made Sherlock out to be something *other*, an oddity because of how his mind worked. I knew what that was like. To be queer—or whatever label I picked—*and* have a brain that never turned off... sometimes it felt like a double serving of *not-like-everyone-else*.

I turned to the coffee maker and pressed the Brew button, addressing my question over my shoulder. "Where is everyone?"

"No clue about Curtis. Wink slept over at her friend Reese's. My parents are at work."

Right. They were physical therapists who owned a small practice. Opening on Saturday made sense for patients who couldn't come during the week. Again, too much information, so I just held my mug and nodded. "My parents are planning their garden. My brother, Miles, lives in Manhattan. He's probably sleeping off his night."

"Did you have big Friday night plans?" Win asked his question while shoulders-deep in the refrigerator. I was usually the avoidant one; he was direct, so his lack of eye contact did the opposite of what he'd intended: it added emphasis to a question he was trying to make casual.

I wondered when we'd get back to conversation without subtext.

Where is everyone? = How long are we alone?

Friday night plans? = Do I have competition?

At least that's how I was reading his question, because it was how I wanted him to be asking.

Win poured his juice then leaned against the kitchen island, a full glass in his hand. The jewel color sparkled in the pendant lights as I watched him bring it to his lips. My body language was mirroring his—lower back against the counter, legs stretched into the space between us. I matched him sip-for-sip. It was a visual signal of my interest, but would he know to read it?

Win's forehead furrowed. "You don't have to tell me."

"Oh." I'd been leaping forward in my mind and forgotten to answer. Right. I did that. And he didn't know me well enough to call me on it. "Um, it was a weird night." I explained I'd been catching up on homework when I got a message on iLive.

My tongue tangled on the site's name and I shot him a flush-cheeked look. If he noticed, he ignored it as completely as he had my friend request. "Who was it from? I hate that site."

"Larken. You know, the singer?"

"For real? You know her?" He wasn't starstruck, just amused.

"No. But I reached out after she used the Clara meme and asked her to delete her post. Some damage is done; it's been screencapped and included in a dozen articles on body positivity and inclusive fashion, which I'm all for—just not at Clara's expense. Luckily, she got it. She took down the post and wrote a new one about being more careful with images from the internet."

"Wow." Win's feet were closer to mine. He'd slumped slightly. If I did the same, my running socks would brush his bare toes. "How's Clara? We were at Mayfield together but haven't been in the same classes since they started sorting us into smart kids and not. Guess which of us was honors?"

It seemed unlikely that he wanted me to respond to his self-deprecation with a pep talk, but I also wasn't going to encourage it. I decided to ignore it. For now. "I've called and emailed. She hasn't responded."

He crossed the three feet of floor to stand next to me. "At least you're trying to fix things. That's not nothing." I could smell the juice on his breath, the pine of his deodorant. I hoped my own was doing its job, because I was testing it. Win opened a cabinet. "Do you want Cheerios, granola, or raisin bran?"

"Cheerios." I was positive that in the entire history of the world, that word had never sounded so breathless.

His arm brushed mine as he set the box on the counter. "They're plain, not Honey Nut. My parents have this strange rule about keeping foods in the house that'll kill my brother."

I cleared my throat. "Fun fact: Honey Nut Cheerios probably don't contain nuts." He stepped away to grab bowls. "Curtis is only allergic to peanuts, right? The 'nut' part of the cereal comes from 'natural almond flavors.'" Win pointed to the drawer behind me, so I moved and he got spoons. "'Natural almond flavors,' however, mostly come from ground-up peach and apricot pits."

"Yeah, that's probably not going to convince my parents." Win shrugged. "Especially after I almost accidentally killed him recently. But good to know."

Was it? Or was it one of those facts I found interesting and other people humored? I couldn't read him well enough to tell the difference. As for Curtis—the story I'd heard was that he'd eaten an unmarked peanut dessert at the science fair banquet.

Win was testing me. The realization solidified as I made mental connections between our conversations. The thing about honors classes: Did I judge him for not being in them? No. The comment about "killing" Curtis: Did I condemn him for the mistake? Not even slightly. He was putting his perceived flaws on display to see if I reacted. But if these were tests, had I passed? Diagnosing the situation didn't mean I knew how to handle it.

I followed him to the table, but instead of tipping my chair back, I leaned forward, studying him. He scooped his spoon outward, stirred between bites, chewed on the left side of his mouth, and pressed his lips together when he swallowed. None of those things should've been hot. And yet they were.

"Normally I work Friday nights, but... I don't have that job anymore," Win said. There was more to that story; I made a mental note to follow up. "And Curtis was moping about missing Eliza, so I let him pick a movie. Mistake. I don't know why he thought a rom-com about a blond scientist would help, but he spent the whole time whining. 'If Eliza were here, she'd be objecting to the lack of safety goggles in this lab.' And, 'I can't wait to tell Eliza they were handling hydro-something acid with bare hands.'" Win shook his head. "He's pathetic. When she dumps him, I'm moving in with my grandparents."

My cereal turned mushy as I tried to figure out the Cavendish brothers' strange blend of affection, mockery, and cynicism. Curtis described Win with words like "detonate," "implode," and "cactus," and Win used "pathetic" and was anticipating the breakup of a happy couple. Yet Curtis was low-key matchmaking us and Win endured what sounded like a terrible movie to keep his brother company. I would've let Miles mope solo—or at least demanded control of the remote.

Win was looking at me. Right. My turn to contribute something to the conversation. "So I was supposed to come up with an idea for a reputation-fixing video for Hero High over break. I got nothing. Thoughts?"

"First, film steadier. I got motion sick watching that video clip on the news."

"Hey, I was filming under my desk. You try doing that steadily."

Win laughed. "Based on your fallout? I'll pass."

My own laughter sputtered to a stop. Was it okay to joke about this? I doubted Clara was. That I was flirting instead of holed up in my room—was that progress or selfishness?

"Well, I'm your guy," Win said, and I jerked my head up. "To help with this project. Video and photography—those are my things. I used to work at Frame Me. You know, the photo studio with the cheesy mug-shot theming on its sign? I can help with any camera questions or editing."

"Used to work?" It wasn't quite a direct pry—he could answer with a simple "Yup" and I'd let the subject drop, but I'd found that if you gave people an ambiguous opening, they'd fill in as much as they were comfortable.

"Yeah." He rubbed his lip between two fingers. "I think Mr. Rivera might be slipping—you know, mentally? He kept saying I wasn't showing up when I was supposed to. But I was? And while I didn't love the photo shoots with stressed parents and crying babies, I liked everything else about the job." He shrugged, forcing a smile. "*Many* people in this town have decent passport photos because of me. That's not nothing."

"No, it's not." I laughed because he wanted me to, but I had so many questions for a time when this firing was less raw.

"At least now I've got my weekends back. Wink and Morris are happy about that."

"Morris?"

"Friend. But he and Wink's best friend, Reese, can't be left unattended with Wink. Unless I'm there too, they fight nonstop."

"Eliza and Toby get like that over Merri. For a minute I couldn't tell if Eliza loathed or secretly liked him."

Win grinned. "For my brother's sake, I hope loathed? I don't know Morris and Reese's deal, but Wink hates when they go at it."

The last part was unsurprising. I'd already noticed she was conflict avoidant, practically fleeing whenever her brothers started to bicker. As for Reese and Morris—I'd have to see them together to deduce, so I let the subject drop and followed Win to the couch.

We sat on opposite ends and somehow didn't need the question game to keep the conversation going. "Tell me more about your project."

One of my favorite things about Win was how he gave

me his attention. I didn't feel like I had to earn it by being charming or witty. He made me feel worthy of it.

My attention tended to wander. Or at least it splintered. If attention was a river, mine had tributaries. It flowed all over the place, gathering observations. It never asked my permission and didn't discern between what I *should* be paying attention to and what I *was*.

The problem was, I didn't know how to separate what I *wanted* to see from what I actually did. If I wanted proof Win was into me, sure, I could collate that: the way his body was angled toward mine, the fact that he was here instead of sleeping. He'd walked me home, agreed I was a hunk.

But I had evidence for the opposite too: the way Curtis talked about his brother's love life, and how Win was so cynical of Curtis's relationship. If he was interested in me, would he be telling me they were "pathetic" or joking about their breakup? Wouldn't he have at least answered my friend request?

Also, what was the *why* of his attention? Back in Ohio, people liked me, but they didn't like-like me. Maybe it was being a not-straight kid in a small town, but more likely it was *me*. I exhausted people. I exhausted myself. Despite my efforts to tone it down, Win couldn't be more than a few encounters from moving me into the friendzone.

Maybe that would be for the best? I was so uncomfortable in this place of uncertainty. So distracted by it. And Win made me want to pay attention, to be present and process what was going on in front of me. To stop cataloging his expressions—the way he tilted his head and leaned in—and enjoy the effect of it.

He played with the fringe on a throw pillow. "So, what do you like, Huck Baker?"

I mentally applauded myself for not answering "*You*," and offered a random truth: "Puzzles."

"Like, the ones with five hundred pieces?"

"Sure, those are good. But really any kind. I like figuring things out."

Win laughed and slid his phone out of his pocket. "I should get your number."

Since panic had erased those ten digits from my memory, I blurted out the first thought I grasped. "Whoa. Is that the new model? I guess we know who the favorite kid is, because Curtis doesn't—" I trailed off as his face clouded.

"I bought it myself."

My joke had done worse than bombed; it had hurt him. He covered the phone with his hand, but I could still see the corners of the case. It was the type that looked military grade, like it could be run over by a tank. And even though the phone had to be less than a month old, the case was already scuffed. All this, plus his reaction? Easy conclusions.

"That isn't latched correctly," I told him. "You should fix it before you drop it again."

Win's nostrils flared as he shoved the phone into his pocket. "It's fine."

"Yeah, except it's not. The sealing gasket is pinched in the upper right corner. And since you don't have a paycheck anymore, you probably don't want to have to buy another new one." One look at his face and I knew I'd said too much. Why did I always do this? I pressed a fist to my mouth. "Sorry. None of my business. I'm sure it's fine."

Win looked down at the hands he'd pressed into his legs. Then he sighed and handed me his phone. "No, it's probably not. Can you fix it? I really like the camera on this one—it'd be good if I didn't bust it."

Realigning the seal was the work of two seconds, but forgetting I'd screwed up would take me much longer.

Win slid closer as he took the phone back. He'd been doing that all morning: subtle shifts of half an inch when he thought I wasn't looking. We'd started on opposite ends of the couch, but now there was only half a cushion between us. And Win's latest maneuver hadn't been subtle; he'd wanted me to notice. His grin was toothy—a little bit swagger, a little bit nervous. A lot like he was trying to make us forget the last two minutes. "So, puzzles? Are you figuring me out?"

"Trying to. You're harder than most people." Win's mouth tightened and so did my stomach. He'd been expecting something flirty, and instead I'd insulted. I hurried to add, "All the best people are."

He moved closer. Now there was just a quarter cushion, and my mouth felt dry. Eight. Maybe nine? I could measure my anxiety in couch cushion inches. "So, um. Your turn."

Win blinked. "My turn for what?"

"To answer." Hadn't he just started a new round of the question game? "What do you like, Winston Cavendish?"

"Dimples," he said, then added. "Yours." He scooted still closer. "You."

Eight inches became five became two became none. And as he leaned in, my thoughts blurred: *Do I have coffee breath? Which way do I tilt my chin? What if we hit noses? When do I exhale?* Smeared across all these fears: *Am I ready for this*?

Clearly the answer was no, because panic and adrenaline had me bailing. Forget baseball; I should've told Curtis I was going out for track, because I climbed over the back of the couch like it was some sort of upholstered hurdle, almost kneeing Win in the face during my escape.

"I guess Curtis forgot our plans," I said from a safe distance away. "Tell him I stopped by, and, uh, I'll see you around."

My race out the door set land speed records in the cowardice-yard dash, but I froze on their stoop. What he'd done took courage—and it wasn't an impulsive decision. When I mentally reviewed the morning, I could see all the hints and groundwork. My reaction? Pure coward. *I'll see you around?* Not likely. Embarrassment this acute had to be terminal.

I smacked my hand against my forehead. "Stupid. Stupid. Stupid."

"Well, if you weren't before, that's a good way to kill some brain cells." Curtis whistled as he walked up the driveway. His lips were swollen, so clearly one of us had *not* run away from a kiss.

"Eliza's back?" I asked.

"Yeah, sorry I stood you up." He rubbed his mouth, and there was nothing apologetic about his grin. "She was supposed to get in last night but got delayed. Her flight landed this morning. I meant to text, but... I'll make you a batch of apology muffins."

I shrugged. It was no big deal, but I'd never turn down muffins. "How is she?" The question was polite but a waste of words. The answer was written on his smile.

"Exhausted from spending four days in transit and jet-lagged like whoa, but she says she'll be over for a run tomorrow. Mr. Campbell suggested she sleep in. We'll see who wins."

I knew he was betting on his girlfriend. That he'd always bet on Eliza. But what about Win? Why did no one—not his brother, not his parents, not his twin—bet on him? It was something I knew with certainty—but I couldn't point to a specific moment of *why*. It was a collection of subtle statements, unconscious observations. Of "cactus" and being unaccompanied to his Hero High interview. Of Wink running away when her brothers' bickering grew darker edges.

"So why are you stupid? Or you're describing Win, right? I warned you." Curtis raised his hands. "Remember, I'm Swisser than cheese."

The front door opened before I had a chance to lash out with angry words that likely would've cost me my Knight Light. "What are you guys talking about?" There was a defensive edge to Win's question, but based on what Curtis had just said, it was merited.

"How Huck is stupid, apparently."

That statement had never felt more accurate. "I was just—" I stepped sideways, like I could dodge my emotions by putting space between myself and both Cavendish brothers. It didn't work. I nodded at Curtis. "He's right, I was stupid."

"Because you bolted when I tried to kiss you? I'm not going to disagree with you on that one, Dimples." The laughter in Win's voice wasn't mocking, and I dared to lift my chin. His eyes were full of amusement, mine brimming with regret.

I would've forgotten we weren't alone, except Curtis singsonged "*sitting in a tree*" as he slipped by his brother and into the house.

Win shrugged. "So what now? I've been pretty obvious I like you. I'm less clear about how you feel about me."

"Seriously?" I felt like I couldn't be more obvious, and obviously inexperienced, if I carried around a neon sign that read "*Winston Fanboi*"—spelled with an *i* for maximum patheticness.

"Well, you did just vault the couch to escape kissing me."

"Yeah, but—" Which of my many humiliations did I offer up as proof? Now was probably not the time to bring up how I'd upset him by calling him a puzzle or accused him of being careless with his phone. "I'm not good at this," I mumbled.

"Answering questions?" One side of his mouth twitched, but he cut off the smile by biting his cheek. "Because you still haven't."

"Do I like you?" I rubbed the back of my neck. "Yeah, because who likes tall, dark, and snarky? No one ever. Must stink to be you."

He laughed again. "I'm going to assume that's a yes. Also, you're taller and you've got these—" He reached out like he might touch one of the divots bracketing my smile but pulled back. "Between the cheekbones and the dimples and the way you pout when you're thinking—which is always—cameras must just hate you."

The next move had to be mine—but the thought of intermingling our personal space made my heart race in contradictory ways. He was amazing and I was . . . a lot. Did he know me well enough to know what he'd be getting into?

Because unlike his phone, I had no protective case. What happened if he dropped me?

"Can I . . ." I ground out the words slowly, like I was testing their stability.

"Get your number?" he prompted. "Yes."

Well, sure, I wanted that too. But also more time for my head and heart and body to sync. I had all these facts, all these observations. Sherlock would scoff at my inability to add it all up. But this wasn't a place for subtlety or interpretation. This was a place for blunt honesty and no chance for misunderstanding. I took a deep breath.

"Winston Cavendish, I like you. Will you go out with me? On a date?"

6

I had a new shirt from Mom hanging in my closet. I had two tickets to a movie Dad helped pick on my desk. I had a hundred strategy texts with Rory on my phone.

I have a date with Winston Cavendish.

I held on to this thought as I headed down Hero High's long driveway on the Monday morning after spring break. Dad had dropped me at the curb, which meant I had a quarter-mile walk to convince myself not to turn around.

And a good reason *not* to was that I had a date with Win Cavendish on Wednesday. If I got caught skipping school I'd be grounded. If I got grounded I couldn't go on my date. With Win. This Wednesday.

It was the only night Showe Time Theatre—the local artsy place that took itself as seriously as the *e*-ending name implied—was showing *Dead Poets Society*. I'd never seen it, but Dad promised it was perfect, and Win's text about it had said You pick this time. I'll get next.

Next.

I clutched those four letters like a shield as I approached the main campus—where Clara was standing in front of the science building surrounded by friends. Their expressions were a variety pack of sympathy: pinched eyebrows, creased foreheads, and voices high and whispery, like someone had died.

Clara's hair was straight—even though it should be Monday curls. She had her chin up and her shoulders back, and she was shrugging off the eager squeezes of her entourage. "Thanks, but—I have to go talk to Lynnie."

She dodged out of the group, and I watched her exhale before dashing across the quad to catch her brother Penn's girlfriend.

All those enthusiastically sympathetic girls were left without a focus, and it took only a second for them to find a new one: me. They pounced with collective rage.

"I can't believe—"

"Do you even know—"

"How could you—"

None of them were wrong.

Last night I'd lain in bed and texted Win. Not about anything flirty or fun—about this. *I need to apologize in person. Her humiliation was public, should my apology be too?*

I owed her the chance to say whatever she wanted, however she wanted. And I had to accept it and listen without defending myself. Even if the whole school turned against me, it was less than a fraction of the attention she'd received.

I don't want her to hate me—I know that's not my choice. But still . . .

It had been a lot of vulnerability for eleven p.m. and pre-first date. I'd twisted in my flannel sheets as I waited for his response to light up my screen.

I get your urge to give her a chance to "get back at you" or whatever. But I'd do it privately so it doesn't look performative.

It had been the perfect advice. And "performative" was

the perfect word for the chorus of sympathy groupies who were trying to outdo one another with their indignation.

"How can you show your face here?" asked Mira. "I mean, after you showed *hers* to the whole world?"

There was one person in the group not nodding or chiming in. Rory detached from the others and came to my side. "It's almost time for art," she said, leading the way to our lockers and first class.

She filled the trip with anecdotes about Merri's decorating disasters: Eliza returning to all her clothes piled on the floor because the glue Merri had used to stick wallpaper to the inside of her drawers wouldn't dry. I smiled, but it wasn't because of the story; it was because of this toothpick of a girl who was attempting to act as my bodyguard.

"Hey," I said as we set up our easels in our favorite corner of Mrs. Mundhenk's studio. "Thank you."

She held up her wrist, showing off a lumpy lime-green, red, and electric-blue friendship bracelet. I'd promised it to her the first time we met, right after I awkwardly, half-jokingly asked her to be my best friend. I'd known immediately that we could be—it had been a moment's observation to deduce our personalities, talents, and interests were compatible. By the time I'd actually figured out how to make the thing—and I was never admitting the number of iLive videos I'd watched or the wad of tangled rejects on the floor of my closet—it was true. "I seem to remember a certain someone who's had my back every day in this room."

She snapped a piece of paper to her easel and picked up her pencil. This was the Rory version of saying *enough sappiness*, so I took her cue and turned to my own drawing. Luckily I no longer had to divide my attention between my art and safeguarding hers. We were the only two freshmen in Advanced Art, and I was good—great at pottery—but Rory was a once-in-a-lifetime talent. That hadn't gone over well with the upperclassmen. Especially back in the fall when there'd been a fellowship with Andrea Snipes on the line.

By now the class had calmed down. Rory and I even hung out with Byron de Grance, the junior whose twin sister, Lynnie, was dating Clara's older brother. Which, based on loyalty priorities, meant he probably hated me now too.

But I had a date with Winston Cavendish.

I'd looked up all the restaurants within three blocks of the theater. We could do Italian. Except, garlic breath. Based on past patterns, the Chinese place rarely had a wait on Wednesday nights, but it was noisy. Pizza My Heart had better seating, but the name might be too much. Pho Sure was an option, but service was slow. I might need to adjust our timeline...

I wanted Win here, now. Holding my hand. Which was both premature and selfish, but man, I hoped he got into Hero High so that on some future day he could.

"What are you thinking about so hard over there?" asked Rory.

Her eyes were on my paper, where I'd added so much shading to a drawing of a mug that the cup was indistinguishable from the coffee inside. I sighed and picked up my eraser. "This drawing is just like my mood and my coffee: black." It was meant to be a joke. Glib was what I did. Normally it was easy, because normally I could see through problems to their solutions. But I didn't see a solution to getting Clara off the internet.

Rory confiscated my eraser and smirked at the hole I'd

worn through my paper. "I think you're experiencing what we mere mortals call 'stress.'"

"I don't like it." English class was next and probably my best chance to apologize...especially if I could get Rory to run interference. "Hey, I need your help."

Rory was as private as Merri was public. If Merri could've drawn even passable stick figures, she would've handed out sketches like party favors, but Rory turned red and closed her notebook if anyone even glanced at the margin doodles on her class notes.

So the fact that she'd gathered Ms. Gregoire and the bulk of our English classmates around her desk and was talking book covers and showing them sketches—that was better than any friendship bracelet.

It gave me the perfect chance to poach Clara from the edge of the group with a soft "Hey."

"Hi." She lifted a bare-nailed hand to her hair, but there weren't curls to twirl.

Ms. Gregoire was praising something in Rory's drawing, but her eyes were on me. She gave a nod. I took a deep breath. "I don't know if you got my emails—"

"I did." Clara's cheekbones looked sharper—either she'd lost weight or was biting the inside of her cheeks.

"I really am sorry. I didn't mean for it—"

"I know." She retreated to her desk. It was a conversational red light. I read and respected her signal.

Ms. Gregoire clapped her hands. "Thanks for sharing, Rory. I think everyone in here benefits from a good reminder that what we see on a cover so rarely reflects the internal story."

As my classmates shuffled to their desks, she added, "Before we begin, I have a schedule change from the office. Next period you'll be having a Knight Lights meeting."

I doubted anyone heard the assignment she gave afterward. They were all too busy staring at Clara, at me. Next period—third period—was usually science.

Did Clara think avoiding that classroom and our new teacher was a reprieve, or, like me, just a prolonged purgatory?

I could've deduced this from a glance, but I refused to add mine to the eyes already on her.

Knight Lights meetings were held in a big open room above the cafeteria. It had chalkboard paint and all sorts of eclectic seating—floor cushions and foam cubes, tall stools and low chairs. Exposed Edison bulbs. Framed vintage pictures of graduating classes. It looked like there should be baristas with names like Kale and Vortex who made unbelievable foam art to go on top of the world's strongest lattes. Actually, I could've done without Kale and Vortex; it was the caffeine I really wanted as I approached the group around my mentor.

Rory and Toby were curled up in a giant wingback chair. Sera and Hannah shared a beanbag, flanked by their adoptees, Merri and Eliza. Dante was checking his phone, while his mentor, Lance, was digging through his backpack. When I reached them, Curtis pushed a stool toward me with his foot, then stood up from his own and held out his hands like he was about to give a sermon.

"Now that Huck's here, I want to say something. This room, this area right here: it's a safe space, a shun-free zone where we don't beat people up over their mistakes—no matter how much they deserve it."

Whether or not I deserved it, I'd gladly take his offer. Wren had approached me in the hall on the walk over—and they'd been right to do so. I didn't know them—other than that they were a senior and editor on the yearbook—but they told me they'd been hurt by my "exclusionary binary-gender analysis." I hadn't had an answer beyond listening and acknowledging their pain. I'd offered an apology and a promise to do better and gained a new reason to self-recriminate, a new group of people I'd accidentally injured.

"I won't tolerate anyone picking on my adoptee. Got it?" Curtis had clearly failed the part of kindergarten where you learn "indoor voice," but the rest of the room was oblivious, busy creating its own noisy chaos.

But when I scanned the crowd, I spotted Clara. She was tucked by the back wall, on a chair beside her mentor. Sitting on her hands. It was a thing she did now. And she hadn't volunteered all English class. I swallowed past an itch in my throat and turned to my group.

The Campbell girls were nodding. Eliza shrugged indifferently. Dante had an eyebrow cocked. "Milverton's a waste of mucus. I'm glad you busted him." He was looking at Clara too—only the Clara he was looking at was an iLive post on his cell. "This meme's a sick takedown of Hero High."

Lance swiped the phone. "C'mon. It's not like we haven't all done something stupid for a girl before. Hannah, you dyed your bangs green because it's Sera's favorite color. The red is way better. Toby's gone maestro for Rory. Curtis practically ate peanuts for Eliza. Who here hasn't done something like this? I . . ." Lance faltered. "Never mind what I did. My point is, we've all messed up."

"To clarify," said Curtis. "I didn't eat peanuts for Eliza. That was an accident."

"One you won't repeat," she commanded. "Let's be clear, there's not a single instance where anaphylaxis is romantic."

"I want to hear about this hair thing," said Sera. Her soft voice was the opposite of Curtis's; anyone more than six inches away had to strain to hear her. She turned to her girlfriend. "The green was for me?"

Amid the laughter and teasing, the red had faded from Lance's cheeks. His skin was as fair as Dante's was dark, and he didn't so much blush as splotch. He was a good guy; a heck of a lacrosse player and Curtis's best friend. If I were still meddling, I would've figured out the recipient of his mystery crush. I would've started finding ways to make their paths cross and talk him up.

Instead I did the mental version of Clara's sitting on hands. I shoved the idea to the corner of my mind. He hadn't asked for help. Not my place to interfere.

"I didn't do it for a girl." They were all talking, but if what Lance said about me was what they thought, I would need to correct that now. I spoke louder. "It wasn't about impressing Clara."

My back was to the front of the room. I didn't see Mr. Welch walk in, so as everyone else fell quiet, I raised my voice even more. "I definitely don't *like* Clara."

Maybe at some point I'd become accustomed to so many pairs of angry eyes, but not today. And my tall stool made me an easy target for the collective glares of the freshman and sophomore classes.

Curtis clapped a hand on my shoulder. "Phew. Because I really don't want to have that conversation with my brother." And maybe there would've been more laughter or whispers, but he pivoted toward the podium and boomed out, "Hey, Mr. Welch, what are we up to today?"

The soft-spoken media teacher jumped into an explanation. "You'll be working in groups to propose new ideas for the school's spirit days. We'll vote at the end of the period, so get started."

Eliza pulled out a notebook. "I'm all for options besides 'dress-down day.'"

"Anyone else not shocked that Eliza has a problem with casual?" Toby teased. Though "casual" and "dress-down" were relative terms. One Friday a month we were allowed to wear the Hero High sweatshirts with our last names on the back that we'd received with our admissions letters—but they still had to be paired with pants or a skirt that fit the uniform dress code.

"My problem," Eliza clarified, "is with the patriarchal and heterocentric tradition of girls wearing their boyfriends' sweatshirts. It's antiquated and sexist: a girl wearing a guy's name to prove she's his . . . his property? And if that's *not* what that indicates, why don't guys ever wear girls' sweatshirts?"

"I hear you," Curtis said. "But, Firebug, your sweatshirt would be a crop top on me."

"So? Yours would be a poncho on me." She raised an eyebrow. "This tradition was never about making a fashion statement."

Curtis paused. "That's—that's a good point."

"Do you ever wear each other's? I've never noticed," Merri asked Sera and Hannah.

They shook their heads. Though, to be fair, Sera didn't participate in dress-down day. Neither did her brother, Fielding. I wondered if being the children of the headmaster meant they weren't allowed to go casual.

I opened my mouth to ask, then glanced at Clara, still sitting on her hands. Never mind. I was done meddling.

"See? Problematic." Eliza waved a finger at Curtis.

He caught her hand and kissed the fingertip. "Fine. Bring me your sweatshirt on the next dress-down day. I'll prove I can rock a crop top while bucking the patriarchy."

Eliza smiled. "That's all I ask."

My eyes shifted from them to Sera and Hannah, to lovelorn Lance, to Clara. I chewed my lip and stayed silent.

7

Monday night I texted Win: Can I call? Because I didn't have the patience to correct autocorrect, and I wanted more clues than my screen provided: tone of voice, pauses, inflection.

He answered immediately: Talk on the phone? For you, I guess. But you owe me.

I exhaled my relief and dialed. He answered with "How'd it go?"

"Not well. Do you think I should try again?" I was asking a lot of him, especially since Win and I hadn't even started yet. We were in the prologue of whatever our story would be. But I was certain he wouldn't mind. If anything, he'd be flattered I was trusting him, because based on my observations, his family didn't.

Which was stupid on their part, because he gave empathetic advice. But first, he paused. Normally I hated "downtime" or "think time" or whatever it was called now, but since I didn't have an answer for this question, I appreciated him being thoughtful as he constructed his.

"I think you try one more time. If she doesn't want to hear you, you respect that and let it go. Otherwise you're making the apology *for you*, not her."

"You're right." His words had been slow, but my response was immediate.

He snorted. "I should record that and make it my ringtone. But no one would believe it'd been said about me." He was trying to sound like he was joking, but his voice was tight, the chuckle forced. If he were here—and man, I wished he were—he'd have the pinched line above his eye.

"Thanks." I shoved as much sincerity as I could into the word. "This helped."

I could hear the smile when he said, "I'll see you Wednesday."

It rivaled mine when I answered, "It's a date."

In the meantime, I was looking for my chance to get Clara alone and try again.

It was harder than it should've been. Tuesday was a dud. The only positive being our new science teacher, Mrs. Vogelsang. She had a masters in biochem, a background in pharmaceuticals, and a smile for *every* student when she greeted us at the classroom door or called on us—equally—during class.

Wednesday. Date day! I woke up hopeful and determined. Clara and I had two classes together before lunch, but her friends were still acting like bodyguards—oblivious to her posture, the flickers in her smile, or the dozen other signals she was giving off that screamed *Back up. I need space.*

Somehow she managed to escape them during lunch. I saw her slip down the dead-end hallway with the water-bottle-filling fountain and followed, only to second-guess. Was it selfish to steal her hard-won private moment and force an apology on her? Win was right: the only person who'd feel better if I intruded was me.

I lurched to a halt, my shoe squeaking on the tile floor.

Her head jerked up. "Huck?"

"Hey. I don't want to bother you. It seems like everyone's bothering you."

She shrugged but didn't deny it.

"I want you to know how sorry I am. If I could take this back, I would. And if you want, like, horrible photos of me, or to tell me off—"

"I don't."

"Clara, I just want to fix this."

She looked down at the floor. "But you can't."

"There you are!" We both turned to see Mira and Elinor charging down the hallway. "What are you doing, Huck? Haven't you done enough?"

Clara squared her shoulders. Anyone who underestimated this girl was a fool. That included every one of her friends who thought she needed or wanted to be coddled. "You have to leave Huck alone. I've forgiven him, which means there's no excuse for anyone else."

Elinor simpered an insincere "Of course. Anything you want." Mira stayed silent.

Clara met my gaze and nodded. She'd heard me, and I'd heard what she didn't say: *Give me space.*

Normally my mind worked in plans. Figuring an end goal, then reverse engineering the steps to achieve it. I looked at a lump of clay and saw a tall, graceful vase. I'd met a stranger in art class and saw a future friend. I'd observed Rory and Toby in an auditorium six months ago and known that with the right prodding they'd be the mega couple who inspired the most #relationshipgoal posts on iLive's Hero High freshman forum.

I thought I'd feel better after apologizing. I didn't. Nothing had changed. Clara had to live with what I'd done. I had to live with the knowledge that I couldn't fix it.

Ms. Gregoire stopped me during my race to be the first one out of Convocation—Hero High's daily end-of-the-day whole school assembly. "Huck, come by my room. I want to check in about your video."

I stifled a groan. I was supposed to be heading home so I could change and have a predate strategy session with Rory. I needed to finalize my restaurant decision, and she was pushing hard for something called a "lip mask." But Ms. Gregoire was doing me a favor with the project, so I nodded and knocked on her door after stopping at my locker.

"I'm sorry," I told her. "I'm not sure how productive this meeting will be. I haven't come up with an idea yet."

She shrugged. "Grab a seat and let's brainstorm."

There was a reason English was my favorite class—and it was the teacher, not the material. When she taught, she moved around the room, engaged us all. Rory called her "dramatic," and she wasn't wrong. But whatever label you pinned on Ms. Gregoire, she made it easier to focus. I'd never gotten in trouble in here or had to borrow someone's notes because I'd gotten so lost in my head that I missed a discussion.

So it killed me to have to tell her, "I can't."

"Oh?"

I rocked back on my heels and blurted out the words I'd been mentally replaying all week. "I have a date."

"Really?" She laughed in delight. "That's a good excuse. Do I know them?" She held up a hand. "To be clear, you do *not* have to tell me. I'm just being nosy."

I wasn't offended. Ms. Gregoire's connection with the student body bordered on supernatural. It was the sort of thing I would've laughed at, until I realized how seriously those involved took it. And I hadn't really understood the whispers around campus about Ms. Gregoire being magic until Rory explained. Like she had told me, it was all about books. Rory, Merri, even *do-you-have-a-citation-for-that* Eliza all attributed their relationships to novels our teacher had assigned them.

Which had made me nervous about *Sherlock Holmes*—except now that I was a few hundred pages into the collection, it was clearly not romantic. And hopefully her meddling was unnecessary, since I'd already bumbled into a date.

But just in case there was any truth to the rumors, I said, "Winston Cavendish." Superstitious or super-stupid, it couldn't *hurt* to get her endorsement.

"Winston Cavendish? Why do I know that name?" She tapped her lip. "Oh, wait! From admissions committee. He's on the list of transfer applicants we'll discuss at next week's meeting."

"Next week?" She was on the admissions committee?

"Yes, but no decisions are final or official until the end of the month."

Logically I knew his fate wasn't up to her, that she was just *one* person on the committee. But I wished I could unlearn this. If I stayed in this classroom another thirty seconds, I was going to start begging for "unofficial" decisions or ask if she took bribes.

I pulled out my phone to check the time and make my excuse. Then stared at the screen. The text message had been sent hours ago. It'd been waiting like a land mine for me to click so it could detonate. I sank into a chair. "I guess I have time to work on the project after all."

"Oh?" She sat at the desk next to mine. "Everything okay?"

"He canceled." I was no stranger to oversharing, but normally I did it with a smile and carefully curated truths slipped into jokes. Now I was serving up rejection on a bare plate, too disappointed to add any garnish.

I'd thought Win liked me. No. I *knew* he did.

I had a mental list of proof. We'd texted and talked, and tonight we were going to do more: dinner, take a walk, see a movie. Flirt, talk. Maybe coffee. Maybe a kiss. Who was I kidding? Definitely coffee. And I'd been equally hopeful for my first kiss.

Five words had ruined it all: Can't make it tonight. Sorry.

No mention of rescheduling. No rain check. No hint of why or what or how. I'd already read twenty-one Sherlock Holmes stories, but there was nothing here—no clues for me to figure out.

"Hmm." Ms. Gregoire mused. I'd expected more sympathy. I mean, wasn't that request clear in my self-pitying statement? The only reason for disclosing my pain was so she could do her love-guru-magic thing and make me feel better about it. This was a social construct established back when toddlers held up boo-boos for healing kisses. I was even wearing my best pathetic expression.

"Cavendish? Is he related to Curtis?" She tilted her head. "I wonder if this is connected to why he ran out of class early. I hope everything's okay."

Curtis had left early? I did a mental rewind of Convocation. Rory and Toby had sat in the back with me. Eight rows up had been *Hannah-Sera-Fielding-Merri-Eliza-Lance*. No Curtis.

Half my things fell from my unzipped backpack as I scooped it up. "I've got to go."

"You'll want to hang on to this." Ms. Gregoire passed me a book I hadn't realized was even *in* my bag—I thought I'd left it at home on my dresser. *Sherlock Holmes*'s black cover felt cold beneath my fingers, or maybe it was my hands that had gone icy.

I tucked it under my arm and shoved notebooks back into my bag. "You don't know what happened?"

She shook her head. "Sometimes life is a lot like one of Sherlock's mysteries—you get the problem at the beginning but don't find out the answer until the last page."

I froze. How often in the past three days had I mentally compared Win and me to a story? *We're in our prologue. This date's our first chapter*. She couldn't know that.

"Think back to those elementary school book reports where everyone uses the same closing. It might be trite, but it's actually good advice." She tilted her head in an encouraging smile and singsonged, "*If you want to know what happens, you have to read the book.*"

8

It was a ten-minute walk to the Cavendishes' house. I spent them second-guessing. Was Ms. Gregoire saying I should go home and read *Sherlock* or show up for a date that'd been canceled? Both? Neither?

The afternoon was gray. Not rainy, but something more than cloudy. It made the spires of the fence posts I was dragging my fingers over damp. This wasn't the fence where Win had hung up the toddler mitten, but that memory made me close my fist and shove my hand into my pocket.

Can't make it tonight.

It could be nothing. Homework. A migraine. A family commitment he forgot. Or maybe something good had happened—a surprise vacation or concert. He'd had to rush off and would fill me in later.

I wanted answers, and they were close—just up the walk and behind his front door. His parents' car was in the driveway. The hood was still warm, so they'd come home early, not been here all day. Their presence escalated things—they would've had to cancel appointments and leave work—and that had me hesitating on their welcome mat.

I could hear voices through the door—raised, emotional, but not loud enough for me to learn anything. So, I knocked.

All noise hushed. The knob rotated and the door opened wide enough for Curtis to lean out. "Huckleberry, hey." His smile was flat. "It's not a good time, man. Let's talk tomorrow."

"I'm not here to see you." I stuck my foot in the gap before he could close the door. I was tall, but he was taller—and not above bobbing and weaving to block my view as I tried to peer past him. "Is Win home?"

"Hi." The voice that came from beyond Curtis was muted and stuffy. So there was my answer: Win was sick. I exhaled. No big deal. Not the drama I'd imagined. Who wants to go on a date when they're snotty and congested? Good on him, keeping his germs to himself. We'd reschedule once he was feeling better. You probably needed to be able to breathe through your nose to kiss. "Curtis, let him in."

After hesitating like he expected his brother to be overruled, Curtis stepped aside. Win was standing by the back of the couch with his chin tilted down, his head angled away. He shoved a crumpled tissue into his pocket. And sniffed. Both of which supported my cold theory. As did the reddened skin around his nose.

But it wasn't germs or allergies. His eyes were red too, his lashes clumped, the skin around them splotchy.

"I sent you a text." His voice was choked and his head still averted. My chest tightened. If he thought I hadn't figured out he'd been crying—or that I'd judge him for it—then he didn't know me that well.

I stepped past Curtis, not bothering to remove my boots—even though this was definitely a shoes-off house—and crossed to where he was studying the rug. I was standing so close to him. Too close for people who weren't yet dating. But it still felt like canyons of distance to cross with hushed words and a soft hand to his upper arm. "Hey, what happened? Are you okay?"

Win inhaled sharply at my touch, his muscles rigid beneath my hand. Then they trembled and he melted toward me, like the last of his resolve was gone. He closed the half step between us and rested his forehead on my shoulder. My fingers tightened around his bicep, my other hand automatically coming up in a fierce grip on the back of his neck. My fear of being unwelcome dissolved in the shuttered breath he took against my skin, but in its place was gutting dread.

I tucked my chin against his shoulder, registering for the first time that there were other people in the room. Not just Curtis, but Wink—whose face was even splotchier than her twin's—and Mr. and Mrs. Cavendish, who stood together by the kitchen island, their postures and expressions tight.

I'd abandoned any hint of a plan the second he'd reached for me. I didn't know what was going on, but I knew no one else here was comforting Win. That was enough for me to narrow my eyes and brush aside any bashfulness at this embrace being so public.

Win took another steadying breath before pulling back. "I didn't get in."

"Get in?" I kept my eyes on his family, my hand on his arm, watching him from my periphery and trying to offer him as much privacy as I could while still being present.

"To Hero High." Curtis looked guilty. Maybe he was remembering all his jokes about our school's superiority? They'd just gotten a whole lot less funny. But I'd have to come back to that because Win's dad was clearing his throat.

"We appreciate you stopping by, but another day would be better. We need some time to process this news as a family."

I frowned, facts connecting in my mind. "That can't be true."

"And yet, it is." His mom had to stretch to put an arm around Win's shoulder. And maybe there was supposed to be support in the gesture, but she was also drawing him away from me.

I shook my head. "Acceptance and rejection letters aren't being mailed until the end of the month."

"Clearly some went out early." His dad sounded less patient now.

I doubted it. Otherwise Ms. Gregoire was a liar and Headmaster Williams's video deadline made no sense. "Even if some did, Win's wouldn't have." I turned to him. "Yours wouldn't. You're on the agenda for *next* week's committee meeting."

Curtis's smile was weak as he stepped between his brother and me. "Huckleberry, dude, I see what you're trying to do, and if I thought it would cheer up Win, I'd help—"

I swallowed a frustrated growl. "Please, listen to me. I *know* I'm right. Can I see the letter?"

"It's an email," said Wink. Her parents were both shaking their heads. Win's chin was still down, his left hand shredding the tissue in his pocket, but his eyebrows were up. He was listening.

Curtis pressed his palms together like he was praying, then pointed the tips of his fingers at me. "I know after the whole Clara thing, you're trying to atone, but—"

I flinched but didn't back down. "I'm telling you, Headmaster Williams said letters were being *mailed* on March thirtieth." Since they didn't believe me, I needed more. "Did Wink's come too? Was hers an email? Because I got a physical letter when I applied last year. Doesn't any of this strike you as odd?"

"Lincoln's already in. She got in last year and deferred," said Mrs. Cavendish.

"Please let me see the email." But why would they? No one had invited me here or asked for my opinion. No one believed it. I could see their answers forming on four sets of frowns.

Win ducked out of his mom's grasp and pulled his phone from his pocket. An email was still up on the screen, and his voice was gravelly. "Here. Here's where they say I'm not good enough."

I wanted to read it slowly so I could methodically collect all its clues, but even from a skim I'd gleaned enough to know I was right. Now I just needed to convince them.

"This is fake."

"Huck!" Both Curtis and his dad said my name in barely cloaked exasperation. They were seconds from bodily removing me, so I hastily explained.

"One: there's a typo in the first sentence and another in the third. Headmaster Williams wouldn't confuse 'peak' and 'peek,' and he knows when to use a colon. Two: rejections are normally supportive and sensitive; this is condescending in a way that's inappropriate. Three: the letterhead is missing the school motto. They throw that Latin nonsense anywhere they can. Four—and this is the big one: look at the sender's email. Whoever sent this doesn't think of the school as 'Reginald R. Hero Preparatory School,' or isn't very observant—because all Hero High addresses end in RRHPS dot edu, and they've set up their email to come from 'Admin at Hero High dot com.'"

I curbed the urge to forward it to myself for analysis. There had to be more clues in the final paragraph: We recognize this is Winston's second attempt at applying to Hero High and would not recommend doing so again. Our answer won't change. It's our belief that Winston would not benefit from or contribute to the school–

Whoever sent this wanted him not only rejected but crushed. They also didn't know the difference between "or" and "nor."

I held out the phone for someone to take, but they were all frozen, mouths agape. Maybe I'd gone too fast? I dropped my hand. "Uh, do you need me to explain it again?"

My question thawed his parents, but instead of answering me, they pivoted toward Win.

"Did you send this?" his father asked. "Is it some kind of joke? Because I don't get it."

"Win, buddy, I know you're anxious about getting in, but this is not funny." His mom shook her head. "Poor Lincoln was really upset. We all were."

Win's shoulders hiked to his ears. "Did I miss the part where I was laughing or acting like any of this was amusing?"

"We've talked about this—the difference between being nervous and self-sabotaging." His dad's voice gentled. "I thought you were starting to learn that."

"I didn't send it." Win's words were desperate, but his posture was already defeated.

He rested a hip against the island and slumped so he was the same height as his mom, who was patting his back and saying, "Come on, bud, talk to us."

Curtis backed me up a step and dropped his voice. "Huck,

go. This is classic Win. Eventually he's going to confess. You don't need to be here for that. He wouldn't want you to."

I disagreed with so much of what was happening, but Curtis wasn't wrong; Win wouldn't want me witnessing this. And I was *right*—but I wasn't helping.

I wanted to hug him again, but there was no way through the wall of his parents' shoulders. "Win, call me later if you want."

"Not tonight," said Mrs. Cavendish.

It was obvious to me that his reaction to the email had been genuine, that he'd been devastated by the rejection. That he was equally devastated by his parents' reaction to it. Somehow that wasn't clear to everyone else in the room.

"I don't know who sent that or why, but I'll figure it out. I promise." It was a stupid thing to say. Even Sherlock Holmes didn't make promises. He made statements about likelihoods and possibilities, but not promises. And what was I even basing mine on? I had zero evidence or leads.

But I also didn't care about that, because amid his parents' disapproval, Wink's sniffles, and Curtis's conflicted expression, Win's red eyes were raised to mine. It was the first time since I walked in the door that he'd looked directly at me, the first time he'd looked relieved. I hoped my eyes said everything my lips couldn't: *Even if they don't, I believe you.*

9

Curtis tried to walk me out, but I waved him off. I hadn't come to see him, and I wasn't leaving with him—not in front of the brother I had come for. Win would feel that like a slap; he'd worry about what was said behind his back. I wanted no part of it.

The mist from earlier had given way to a stupidly gorgeous mid-March night. Instead of walking home alone, I wanted to be enjoying the weather while strolling the sidewalk with Win—waiting for the theater to open so we could pick seats in the back corner. Not because we'd be the clichéd couple making out, but because I liked watching the audience as much as the movie. But maybe—hopefully—we would've kissed too. Actually, no. I didn't want our first kiss to be in a dark theater. When we kissed, I wanted there to be enough light to see every facet of his expression. I wanted every detail to sear in my memory. I wanted.

And I wanted to know who sent that email to Win. And why.

I unlocked my front door with a sigh. There was an unrelenting restlessness that came from facing a problem I couldn't fix. It was a feeling I'd become familiar with since the Clara debacle, but leaving the Cavendishes' house with their not believing Win had doubled the sensation.

No one was home at mine. My parents had taken my date night as an excuse to plan one of their own. If I called, they'd abandon appetizers and candlelit cocktails and be home as soon as the speed limit allowed—but for what purpose? To watch me pace?

I had the stupid punishment project and a thousand-page book to keep me company. Given those choices, I picked *Sherlock*, because maybe Ms. Gregoire was onto something and there'd be a clue among those pages. Or at least a distraction.

But it's hard to read while checking your phone every ninety seconds. There were so many questions I wanted to ask Win: *Do your parents believe you yet? Did I make things worse? Can you forward me the email? Let's talk enemies…*

I squeaked like one of the dog toys at Haute Dog, the Campbells' pet boutique, when my phone finally buzzed.

FYI—I'm expecting a date report the second you walk in the door.

I rolled my head back and groaned at the ceiling. I couldn't tell Rory the *why* without Win's permission, so I typed up what I hoped was the truth: Something came up. Had to take a rain check.

Her response was immediate: You okay?

The two words encompassed more than just Win; she was checking on my general well-being, and I wouldn't lie. But the truth was muzzy. I hesitated, then answered: Hanging in.

Want to come over?

The invitation was tempting for the wrong reasons. I wanted to go over in case Eliza was home. In case Eliza had talked to Curtis and had more news. But that wasn't fair to Rory or Win. I'm good. Thanks.

The email was fake, and I'd convinced Mr. and Mrs. Cavendish as much. But until I could offer them an alternative explanation, it seemed unlikely they'd believe Win wasn't the sender.

I didn't have answers—yet—but I'd start finding them tomorrow.

Technically students weren't allowed anything but water inside Hero High classrooms. In the lunchroom, sure. Juice, smoothies, soda, cold brew, and even Rory's favorite—gag, kombucha—flowed freely. Pink cardboard Cool Beans cups were a common accessory in car cupholders and in the halls, but they were recycled before bridging classroom doors.

I was completely disregarding this rule. While Mom was in the shower, I'd brewed a covert second pot and filled two metal water bottles with coffee. One was in my backpack for later, the other in my hand as I paced in front of the administration building, waiting for the door to be unlocked. Unless someone was close enough to smell my coffee, they'd think I was super concerned with hydration. And maybe someday in the future, I would be. Today I was focused on staying alert.

The doorknob jiggled as it was unlocked from the inside. I hastily twisted the cap on my bottle and shoved it into my bag.

"Oh," said Mrs. York as she opened the door. "Good morning, Mr. Baker. Do you have an appointment?

"Good morning!" I went full dimple—pulling on the smile that's been known to elicit parental comparisons to "cherubs." This was pretty easy to pull off with all the caffeine thrumming in my bloodstream.

I may have also had two cups at home. Dad okaying the second out of pity, patting my back as he refilled my mug. "Okay, Puck, what do we do with disappointment? We actionize it. So your first date with Win won't be at that movie—not a big deal. I've already started coming up with options for when you guys reschedule. I looked up pinkeye, and it's usually contagious for—"

Yeah, I'd lied. I figured Win already had enough parents doubting him. I wanted mine to be firmly Team... Hunston? Wick? Bakerdish? Whatever. I wanted them on his side. Our side. And boy were they ever.

Despite Win's not having seen the shirt Mom bought for our canceled date, she'd gone online-shopping for "next time." Dad offered to make Win soup. Even Miles had vid-called to tell me about a time his date *should've* rescheduled and instead had stuck him with a cleaning bill after she'd thrown up in a cab.

My family: they were *a lot*, but they were mine. And in a different scenario, maybe I would've gotten snarky or pushed for privacy, but after seeing the Cavendishes with Win, I'd hugged Dad and listened when Mom spent the drive to school explaining the colors she thought best suited me.

"Let me just boot up my computer," Mrs. York said after I followed her into the office. She paused to sip from her travel mug, and I gave my backpack a wistful pat that made the two coffee canteens clank. "But I don't remember an early meeting on the headmaster's schedule, and he isn't here yet."

"I had a question for you, actually," I said, helpfully taking the trash can off a chair, where it must've been placed so the janitorial crew could vacuum. "It's about transfer students."

She frowned and pulled off her reading glasses. "I can't comment on students' applications."

"Oh, of course not." I upped the dimples and busied myself with straightening stacks of flyers on the table beside her desk. "I mean, *yes*, I am interested because of a certain student..." I glanced at her with exaggerated sheepishness. "But I don't need specifics. I just want to make sure I'm ready. Have any acceptance or rejection letters gone out yet? I'll be buying ice cream either way—I'll have to wait to see if I'm pairing it with a bow or tissues."

"You young people and your crushes. The timeline is on our admissions page, so I guess it can't hurt to answer." She smiled as she confirmed what I already knew. "All letters get mailed on March thirtieth."

Not for sixteen days. I now had it from three sources: Headmaster Williams, Ms. Gregoire, and Mrs. York. Would that be enough to convince Win's parents? "So there's *no* way a student would hear sooner? Not even if they're the sibling of a current student? There's no exceptions or accelerated process for students reapplying? Or when one's twin's already in?"

Her eyes widened with recognition at my hints. "Well, no. Not from us." Mrs. York glanced around the empty office and leaned forward before dropping her voice. "But if a student decided to withdraw their application, he could do that at any time. And there was no need for such theatrics. It's a shame."

That—that was definitely information she wasn't supposed to give out. It made my stomach clench as I said goodbye, ignoring the tissues she'd nudged my way, like I was now the one in need of consoling. I had my phone in my hand before I was down the building's stone steps. You need to call Hero High. Ask about your application.

I watched the screen until my fingers got cold and stiff from holding it so tight. When other students began to arrive, I stormed to the sophomore wing and paced, dodging hallway traffic and chugging my coffee.

Curtis strolled in with his arm curved around Eliza. A less observant person might see a breathtakingly beautiful girl and a blatantly smitten guy. But anyone who spent five minutes in their orbit knew they were a pair of brainy opposites: Him dark, her fair. Him comedic, her serious. He was sentimental; she was skeptical. Their flirtation was one part argument and four parts science. They were perfectly matched and perfectly content in their nerd bubble.

Which I was about to pop.

"Hey, Eliza." Was I happy for them? Sure. But their conversation on "quark-gluon plasma" could wait. Curtis had been a brother for fifteen years and a boyfriend for four weeks. Win came first. Literally. "Curtis, we need to talk."

Their attention didn't snap to me but lingered in a gaze that made the corners of her mouth tilt and him grin. They didn't touch, but it felt like a PDA. Eliza's eyes were still soft when she turned to me. "Huck, make sure he doesn't google 'heavy ions.'" She touched his arm before leaving. "See you in bio, Cupcake."

He called after her. "Remind me, Firebug: Which of us has the fancy science medal?" His grin faded as he faced me. "I don't know anything new. And even if I did, I don't think I should talk about Win's business when he's not here."

"Fine, then you can listen. I already texted him—"

He spun his lock. "Not going to work. My parents took his phone."

The loud clang of my bottle against his locker made everyone jump. Curtis put down his backpack and met my eyes. "Then you need to call them. They need to call the school. Mrs. York told me something was up with his application."

He frowned. "Really? She said, 'Something's fishy about Winston Cavendish's application'?"

"Not in so many words, but—"

"Stop. I know you like my brother and you're trying to help, but Win sent the stupid email. He panicked and sent a fake rejection because he didn't want to wait until the school sends a real one."

"He said that?"

Curtis shoved his coat on a hook. "He hasn't exactly confessed yet, but what else could it be? At least it's fake so no real harm done."

I shook my head. "There's something more going on. Tell your parents to call the school and check his application."

While I hoped it went deeper, my and Curtis's was a friendship based on banter. During September heatwave practices, when the inside of our lacrosse helmets had been sweat swamps, we had made joking bets about the first person who'd puke. I felt like vomiting now, but there was no humor on our faces as we stared each other down.

Curtis looked away first, reaching into his pocket to pull out his phone. "I hope you're wrong."

I wanted to answer "Me too," but my parting words were more honest: "I'm not."

For the rest of the day, my focus splintered like Dad's windshield that time it got hit by a rock—only I had dual points of impact: Winston *and* Clara, who in science class whirled on the two girls fighting over accompanying her to the bathroom.

"Enough," she snapped. "Seriously."

Mrs. Vogelsang had been chatting with Dante about last night's homework, but she stood up. "Is everything okay, girls?"

"No," said Clara. "I need you all to give me some space. This meme isn't going to break me. I'm fine. So everyone can just back off and treat me like they used to."

I hoped everyone heard her, respected her request. And I hoped no one else noticed her words were false bravado, that her knees were turned in and she was hiding bare, bitten nails in her pockets. Regardless of what she wanted people to believe, this *was* impacting her deeply.

"Do you want to talk about it, Clara?" asked Mrs. V. "We could have a class meeting—"

"No. I just want to go to the bathroom. By myself." Her eyes were starting to gloss.

I felt slightly guilty when I tipped my chair back on two legs because Mrs. V had stopped me after class the other day and told me it gave her a heart attack when I did that. What

I felt *extra* guilty about was pushing off my toes while saying a prayer to the gods of gravity and classroom floors that this impulse didn't end in a concussion.

There's a myth that drunk drivers are more likely to survive accidents because they keep their muscles loose. It's false. Drivers—sober or otherwise—sit in the most protected seat of the car. When you know an impact is coming, it's better to brace for it. Anyone watching me could've noticed my tensed muscles and known this was intentional. But all eyes were still on Clara—until I hit the floor.

"Huck!" Mrs. Vogelsang and Rory's voices blended in my ringing head. "Are you okay?"

"Atticus, go get Nurse Peter!" Mrs. V hovered over me, but I glanced at the door. Clara had slipped out. Solo bathroom break achieved. "Huck, what hurts? Don't move."

"I'm okay." I rotated my shoulders and checked my neck to make sure this was true. I'd have a heck of a bruise behind my knees from the chair, but no worse than a hard hit in lacrosse.

Getting myself, my chair, and my desk back in place was a noisy, clumsy production. But whatever. People could laugh and stare at *me* all they wanted.

Gemma smirked. "Too bad no one got *that* on camera. Maybe we could've made a new meme."

If only.

Mrs. V insisted I talk to Nurse Peter, but I reassured him I hadn't hit my head, I wasn't dizzy, and nothing was broken. I turned down his offers of ice or Advil and ducked back into class with a bow. "For my next trick, I will—"

"Sit in your seat with all four legs on the floor and complete your outline of chapter eleven?" suggested Mrs. V.

"That sounds about right."

Rory's eyes were shrewd. The problem with best friends knowing you is that they *know* you. She didn't bother making an accusation, but she did mouth, "You okay?" at least twice an hour for the rest of the day.

And while I regretted rejecting Nurse Peter's offer of Advil, I wasn't lying when I told her I was fine. A little sore, but totally worth it.

Though I winced when someone grabbed my arm at dismissal while I carefully crouched at my locker. I turned with my whole body—because that was a thing I'd be doing until I got a heating pad and maybe a hot bath—to see Curtis standing there.

His omnipresent smile was absent. "I just talked to my parents." He reached past me and grabbed my backpack. "I need you to come with me."

10

Curtis didn't say where or why he wanted me to follow him, but Sherlock was always ready to hop on a train and investigate—I could let my curiosity lead me down a sidewalk or two. Especially if it also meant a chance to see Win.

I figured we were headed to their house, but instead he circled toward the woodsy back side of campus and the visitors' parking lot. Mr. and Mrs. Cavendish were standing on the driver's side of their car, leaning down to talk to—no, argue with—whoever was seated in the back.

I assumed it was Win and was proven right when, in response to Curtis's loud "Hey, I found Huck," he slid across the back seat and opened the passenger side door.

His dad muttered, "Oh, *now* he gets out," but I stayed focused on my side of the car where Win was emerging with reddened eyes. He kept the open door between us like a shield as we traded soft "Heys" and softer looks. Mine searching for answers to if he was okay, his trying to fake it.

Mr. Cavendish shut the back door on his side. "How did you know?"

"Know what?" I asked. "I *don't* know what's going on. Curtis hasn't filled me in."

"But you told him to have us call Hero High about Winston's application," said Mrs. Cavendish.

I shifted my bag on my shoulder. "Did you?"

"They called us. To make sure we were aware Win emailed last night asking to rescind his application."

"I didn't send it," said Win.

"Obviously," I said, at the same time his father added, "We're just trying to get to the bottom of this. If you *did*, it's not too late to admit it and fix things."

Mrs. Cavendish paused by the trunk, absently tracing the H-shaped logo while studying me. "We have to ask: are you involved with this?"

The question probably would've staggered me if I hadn't anticipated it. If they thought Win was guilty, then my protests meant I likely was too. "No, but I want to help. Mrs. York implied something was off—now I know what. Can I see the new email?"

His father frowned. "We didn't think to ask for it."

"Win, pull up your sent box," I suggested. "Show it to your parents."

"They have my phone," he said. "And my laptop."

"Hmm." I tried not to let the triumph show in my voice. "So, an email Win supposedly sent last night went out while he didn't have access to any means of emailing?"

"I'm old, not ancient." Mr. Cavendish's eyes sparkled, and for the first time I saw some of his sons' humor in them. "Even people my age know there are ways to delay sending things."

Oh, right. Yeah, that was not the big victory I'd imagined. Dang.

The momentary hope in Win's eyes dimmed.

"He hasn't even mastered 'reply all.' I doubt he'd know how to do that," interjected Curtis, but they weren't listening.

Win wasn't as tall as Curtis or me, but he wasn't short. Right then he looked it. Like the power of their combined disapproval had shrunken him.

"Why are you here?" I gestured at the visitors' lot, which was mostly empty this time of day—just a substitute teacher getting into her car and a few students passing through on their way to the theater.

My parents liked to joke that there was no instruction manual for parenting, but I had my doubts. How else did they all learn that passive-aggressive technique of talking about you, in front of you, without including you? Dad liked to use this method for things like asking Mom, "Does it seem like we're going through coffee faster than we should be? I hope we don't have to remind Huck about our two-cup rule again. I'd hate to have to take away his coffee privileges."

For the Cavendishes it was, "We were hoping Win would use this opportunity to show us he was taking his future seriously by apologizing."

"We were going to go with him, of course," added his mom, before breaking role and addressing him directly. "We're on *your* side. We can fix this."

"I'm not apologizing for something I didn't do," said Win.

His dad puffed out his cheeks and exhaled slowly, but his words were still gritted. "Then looks like this was a waste of time and we've got a stalemate. You've never been excited about coming here—I guess you get your wish."

Mrs. Cavendish looked torn between going to her husband and her youngest. "Just talk to us, Win. We're here. We'll listen. There's no need for this."

His mouth gaped like the word "but" was stuck between his lips.

"I believe you, Win." I wanted it said aloud, because there'd been so many statements to the contrary. "And I'll prove it." It was the second time I'd gone all big declaration. And it was the second time I'd felt stupid in the aftermath, because... *how*? All I had was a copy of *Sherlock Holmes* and an unshakable certainty that Winston Cavendish wasn't lying.

"Can I—can I talk to Huck alone?" Win's voice was rough and hesitant. This was the second day he'd been talked about and around without being allowed to say much. "Please?"

His mom frowned and opened her mouth, then looked more closely at her son. Maybe it was the way he'd tacked on manners, or how his hand drifted across the top of the car door like it was reaching for mine.

She nodded. "Ten minutes." His dad's head jerked up like he was going to object. She poked him. "That's plenty of time for you to walk home. We'll meet you there. After that, you're grounded."

Win shut the car door, and we scrambled across the parking lot like it was a footrace. But the air felt crowded with everything accused and unknown, and neither of us spoke until we followed the woods' trail around the corner.

Win stopped walking. "You know I'm into you."

"Me too," I blurted, my thoughts spinning wild. Were we really doing this now? After *that*? He stepped closer, so we must be. I ticked down a mental checklist: Chin angles. Breath check. Lip balm? Was ten minutes enough? It'd have to be, right? I couldn't mess this up again. I took a step toward him, my pulse hitching. First kiss, let's do this.

"But I'm grounded," he said. "And it's not like I expect you to wait around for my parents to believe me or get over it."

Oh. So clearly we weren't on the same page and I could stop worrying about how my deodorant was holding up. Or, rather, failing to. My throat loosened. "But... you *didn't* send the emails. I said I'll prove it."

Win gave a wry half smile. "You were serious about that? How?" He kicked an acorn and started walking. "I mean, I'm glad you believe me and all, but... what would you proving it even look like?"

I hesitated, because I wasn't sure what my solving it looked like either. But maybe Hero High did have some magic in the English department after all, because Ms. Gregoire had given me the perfect solution in Sir Arthur Conan Doyle. It all came down to a four-word question: *What Would Sherlock Do?*

Holmes was always so confident, and the only thing I was confident about was that Win was being wronged. So WWSD? Win was watching me out of the corner of his eye and we were one street away from his, and the answer was both obvious and brutal. Holmes had spelled this out in no uncertain terms in *The Sign of the Four*: "The emotional qualities are antagonistic to clear reasoning."

Sherlock would not get romantically involved with the subject of a case.

"I can't..." Two minutes ago I'd been worried about chapped lips and bad breath, and now, I gritted my teeth. "We can't—we can't date while I'm figuring out who's behind the emails. I need to have clarity and perspective. I can't be worried if a question is going to upset you or, like, hold your hand while I interrogate you." *Or be distracted by the shape of your mouth while trying to pay attention to the answers coming out of it*. Luckily I didn't say this last part out loud.

"Interrogate me?" Win chuckled uncertainly. "Wow. Um, yeah. What if you *don't* play detective? Can we date then?"

I was trying to pull out the right words, not the first ones. The ones that wouldn't hurt and also provided clarity—because I didn't think I was wrong. Into that delay, Win dropped another doubt. "I don't want you to be finding out all my screwups and then be stuck wondering if you still want..." He shrugged. "Me."

Yeah, he so didn't need to be worried about that, but with every delay I made him a little less confident. I needed a better response, and I needed it thirty seconds ago.

"I'm going to figure this out," I announced as we turned onto his block. "You know I love puzzles."

Was that a little too close to *I love you*? I didn't mean it that way. But Win was frowning, so maybe it overstepped.

"Puzzles," he said slowly, jabbing a crosswalk button while refusing to look at me. "Okay. Right. Sure."

Those words all meant the same thing and all implied approval, but each had been accompanied by another jab at the button, and I didn't believe any of them. "Do you have any thoughts on who would do this?"

Win smirked over his shoulder as he crossed the street. It was his try-hard smirk, the one he wore when he was projecting that he didn't care, not when he actually didn't. They differed by angles and the light in his eyes. It wasn't a face he'd aimed at me before. "Got a notebook? I'll make you a list."

"Time's up," his dad called from their stoop as we approached the driveway. "Say goodbye."

Win didn't argue and wouldn't look at me. "If that's your choice—I guess, let me know if you need anything. And thanks . . . for believing me."

My stomach sank as the door shut behind him. I'd messed this up. I'd failed to communicate that this was a rest stop, not a dead end. Somehow he couldn't tell I'd decided to start with the temporary role of detective, because I wanted to be his boyfriend for much longer.

11

I headed straight for the pottery wheel in art class the next morning. I wasn't ready to explain this to Rory yet. Not that she wouldn't understand—the road to her and Toby had had roadblocks and boy-faux-rend detours—but I couldn't put this into words: How it had felt like a mistake *and* my only choice. How I had only two weeks until the *last* admissions committee meeting of the year, only fifteen days until acceptance letters went out. How I wanted to make sure he got one.

The pottery wheel was my form of meditation: centering clay, making it spin, watching shapes rise tall and graceful beneath my steady hands. Only they weren't steady today. I sent more than one bowl collapsing. As I went to the table to wedge my clay—again—I almost laughed. Building and crushing—this felt like a metaphor for what I'd be doing to Win's hopes if I failed.

My thoughts chased the clay dizzily around the wheel, but unlike it, my fears weren't easily rinsed down the drain at the end of class. They shadowed me across campus to English and burrowed in deeper. I was just a boy playing detective. I had no special skills or training. It was no different than when I'd read *Harry Potter* and wished I were a wizard. No amount of finger-crossing got me a Hogwarts letter on my eleventh birthday. There was no point in running around on a broomstick and calling it quidditch. Sitting in English class plotting clues and stakeouts was equally worthless.

"You with us, Huck?" Ms. Gregoire had paused by my desk. I shook off the daydream of Win and I sharing a magnifying glass. Everyone else in the classroom was typing. My laptop wasn't even out.

"Sorry. What was the assignment?" She started to explain, but I interrupted. "You know how you were talking about mysteries the other day? Not knowing the solution until the end?"

Her expression melted from instructive to intrigued. "Yes."

"What if you had a real-life mystery to solve?"

She tapped a silvery nail against her lip. "Well, I guess I'd ask myself what Sherlock would do."

My ribs were too tight—they were cages around my lungs as I gulped air. *How had she . . . ?* Those were my *exact* thoughts on the walk to Win's. And I'd spent all the hours since then wishing for an alternative—someone else to be detective so I could be the date. But this confirmed it: I'd done the right thing. Even if it sucked.

"He'd go to the scene of the crime," I said.

"Sure. Or ask questions of the victim. Often Sherlock only traveled to confirm what he already knew."

"Right." Because Holmes solved some of his cases at first glance, then the rest of the story was a slow unfurling of his solution.

"Does that help?" After I nodded, she smiled and tapped my desk. "Good. Now get to work."

She meant on whatever today's assignment was, but I could only focus on the case. It didn't really have a *scene*, but there was a victim. So once school was over, going to see Win was the best place to start.

There were no cars in the driveway today. No family huddle behind the front door, which Wink answered with wide eyes. "You can't be here. Win's grounded. My parents would—"

"Is it Morris?" Win called. "He can come in. We'll just say he's here to see you if..." He trailed off as he saw me. "Oh. Huck. Why are you here? I mean, besides giving Wink a panic attack."

"I thought I told you yesterday..." I rubbed the back of my neck. This wasn't the welcome I'd been expecting. "I'm going to solve this."

"Oh. Right." He snapped his fingers. "Because I'm *a puzzle*."

My stomach sank. Okay. I *had* said that. But I hadn't meant it that way. And I *had* hoped to compartmentalize, to keep my feelings for Win shut away from my pragmatic thoughts about the case. So clearly I was failing all around. Sherlock would be so proud.

"Once this is over," I told him, "you can pick whatever you want for our first date—restaurant, movie. Anything, everything. Your choice." We locked eyes, and I could see him warily measuring the sincerity of my words, judging my motives.

"Is he staying?" Wink asked, and we looked to her. "If he does—maybe I should go?"

"Take a breath," Win said. "You're fine. I'm not going to get you in trouble."

Wink visibly followed her brother's suggestion, and I tried not to let my fascination with their dynamic show as she turned to me. "What's your plan? Do you have one?"

"Remember when you offered to make me a list of suspects?" I asked Win. "Let's start there."

"Oh sure. My list of nemeses. I keep that with my cage match invites."

Wink smacked him, but if my options were sarcastic or withdrawn, I'd vote snark every time. Also, *valid*.

So I wasn't Sherlock yet. This was my first try, and Ms. Gregoire wouldn't have assigned the book if I couldn't handle it. I stood up straighter. "Do you have last year's yearbook?"

"Wink does," he said. She hesitated then turned and walked out of view. Win stepped back to let me in. "Pizza," he said. "Bowling. Maybe ice cream too. From the new gelato place. Milk It."

I laughed. "Is 'milk it' the name of the gelato shop, or what you're doing right now?" Either way, it sounded like a perfect date. Now we just needed to get there. I took a deep breath and tried to channel my inner Sherlock as Win led me down the hall toward his bedroom.

But Sherlock didn't think of his clients or Watson in the dry-mouthed way my thoughts circled Win as he pushed open the door. I followed him into a medium-size room with a pair of twin beds, dressers, and desks. The side near the window was neat. The other half was not.

I grinned and gestured to shelves overflowing with Legos and random screws, those metal bottle caps with sayings.

Two broken pairs of swim goggles. So many camera pieces and printed photos. "*Tidying Up*, huh? Favorite show?"

"What can I say, everything 'sparks joy.'" His grin was fleeting as he threw himself down on a rumpled bed, bouncing a stack of folded shirts to the floor. I wanted to pick them up and tuck them inside a drawer. Sherlock would so he could examine the contents. But I just wanted to inhale the laundry soap that smelled so much better on him than his siblings.

I kept scanning the room, not sure what I was looking for: *Whodunnit for Dummies*? Hate mail? A doll modeled after him, stuck with pins and conveniently labeled "Made by X"? I didn't find any of these things, but on the floor by his closet was a half-rolled cheeseball poster of the bleach-blond swimming dynamo who came home from the last summer Olympics with another gold medal. He wasn't wearing it in the poster though; his chest was on full display. If you photoshopped muscles—okay, *lots* of muscles—onto me, we could be brothers. Blond, tall, dimpled. Granted I couldn't swim, but it looked like Win had a type. The fact rattled in my head as he watched me inspect his room. Was that why he liked me—or just why he'd given me a second glance?

And was there some magic trick for banishing these intrusive thoughts and focusing on the case?

I turned to inspect the cage on his dresser. Inside was a wooden house made with crooked nails and decorated with the guinea pig's name in lopsided cursive letters—based on that and the wear patterns, he'd made it five, maybe six years ago. A spotted guinea pig waddled out, equally curious to meet me. "Hey, Hudson."

"He doesn't have a carrot, Hud," Win called from the bed. "But if you promise not to spend the next hour squealing, I'll give you one later."

"Why not give it to him now?" I asked.

"The vet said he can only have one a day. I have to save it for when Curtis is doing homework. Otherwise he gets cranky—Curtis, not Hudson. He's at baseball practice. You need to be gone before he's home to tattle."

I stuck a finger through the bars and rubbed Hudson's nose. It was easier to look at the pet than at the guy. I needed to be objective and open to *all* possibilities—even the one of Win being guilty.

But I refused to believe that. Win worried about disturbing his brother's homework, he talked down his panicking sister, he rescued toddler mittens from snowbanks, and he was direct and honest about the fact he liked me. No way he'd go through all this subterfuge and deception just to get out of applying to Hero High. And if he *was* going to go through all that trouble, why not do it *before* his interview? No, it didn't add up.

Focus. Sherlock—clues. He always found them on people's shoes, but Win was in socks. I looked over my shoulder to where he was sprawled on the bed. Gray athletic socks with a logo of a single bee on the heel. Curtis wore bright printed pairs that coordinated with our school colors. Were Win's remarkable for being unremarkable? His pants: dark jeans. I couldn't see the brand, but I doubted they were fancy. They were worn in ways that artificially distressed denim never got right.

"Huck?"

"Hmm?" I forced my gaze up to meet his.

"While you were checking me out, I asked what your favorite planet was."

"Oh. I—" I cleared my throat. "I was, um, taking observational evidence."

He grinned. "Is that what we're calling it?" Before my face could burn hotter, he shrugged. "So, planet?"

It took me a second to register that Win had started a round of the question game. Then another second to think. "Pluto? I can never remember, is that still a planet?"

Win laughed. "Are you joking?"

"I'm horribly at astronomy. I bet I couldn't name all seven. Nine? How many are there?"

"You think you can prove I'm innocent, but you don't know how many planets are in our solar system?"

I shrugged. Sherlock didn't think it was important either. Of course Sherlock was fiction, but it's not like this would be a question on the SATs or Win relevant.

"Careful," I teased, then swallowed the rest of my sentence. I'd been about to say, *"or I'll ask your favorite sonata,"* but I knew how that'd play out: him feeling ignorant. My unfinished warning hovered in the air. It was all too appropriate. We were both being so *careful*. We had to be.

"Mine's Pluto too," he said. "I always identify with underdogs." He shifted, and vulnerability peeked through the cracks in his snark. "You really think we can figure out who sent them?"

I was saved from answering by Wink bustling in with a handful of yearbooks. "Here's sixth, seventh, and eighth. This year's won't be out for months—which is a problem since last year we were at Mayfield Middle Academy and there's not much overlap between there and Chester High."

Mayfield was where Curtis and Toby and Clara and most of Hero High had gone. And at some point I was going to need to ask about the elephant in the room—the *why* of Win's rejection last year. But not right now, when his posture was coiled and Wink looked like any question would spook her.

"Thanks," I said.

She nodded. "I'm going in my room and shutting the door. If you get caught, I'm saying I didn't know Huck was here and have no clue how you got my yearbooks."

"That's one option," said Win. "Or...you could help? I'm not calling you a gossip, but you know everything about everyone. Besides, Mom and Dad won't be home for hours."

"Unless they leave work early to check on you." She reluctantly sat down on the bed. "What do you need to know?"

I flipped the yearbook open to the first page of student photos. "Anything. Even if it's small and doesn't seem relevant."

Sherlock Holmes said, "The little things are infinitely the most important," and I was starting from scratch—well, not *quite* from scratch. The first person pictured was Bancroft Adams.

"How is Banny?" Win asked. "Miss that guy. We haven't stayed in touch since Mayfield."

I thought about Susie and Phil and everyone in Ohio. "Yeah, I know how that is."

"Um." Wink raised a hand. "Except you used to tell him his name was backwards."

"It is." Win reached over and ruffled the pages, his hand an inch from mine. "Adam Bancroft sounds better. But it was just a joke. He didn't care."

"Yeah, I feel like maybe people can't always tell when

you're joking?" Wink said slowly. "Or you don't know what other people find funny."

Win pulled back and frowned. "You're always saying that—but people laugh."

She tilted a hand back and forth. "Not always." They'd both adopted defensive postures, but I couldn't tell which of them was overreacting.

I pointed to the book. "Moving on. Colleen Allen?"

"She's at Aspen Crest," said Wink. "Though, did you see her iLive post about wanting to transfer?" She was looking at Win for a response, but he was studying me.

And I was making a mental note: Competition as motive? How many transfer spots were there? "Thoughts on Colleen?"

"She's not my favorite person, but I honestly don't think we ever had a conversation." Win was rubbing his bottom lip with his thumb and pointer finger, and I wondered if he knew how much that gesture distracted me.

"But..." Wink trailed off when he shot her a look.

"What?" I prompted.

"Um." Wink's eyes kept flicking to her brother's stony face. "She was in the science class where Win released a tank full of crickets. And I heard she hates bugs."

There was more here, but pressing might trigger a twin throwdown. I moved on. "Kiara Amar."

"She's at Chester High with us. We're cool," said Win.

He glanced at Wink, waiting for her confirmation, but she shook her head. "Not since that thing you said about her hair."

"Her hair?" Win squinted. "I have no idea what you're talking about."

"Yes, you do! About the dye? Do you want me to look it up and show you? This is what I mean about the unfunny jokes."

He leaned forward. "Still no clue what you're talking about. Look it up? Why would I say anything about her hair? I don't even know what it looks like."

I tapped loudly on the yearbook. "Franklin Arnold?"

He glared at his sister. "I don't know—ask Wink."

If he thought she was enjoying this, then he missed the way her fingers were knotted or how she braced herself each time she spoke. At some point I'd need to get her alone, because her need to be helpful was at war with her conflict avoidance. "Frank's fine. At least, as far as I know? I'd have to check iLive."

Win flipped the yearbook closed. "You know what, clearly this is hopeless and everyone hates me."

"I didn't say that." Wink stood. "I'm not helping, so I'm going to—" She exited the room before finishing.

We hadn't even made it off the first page.

Win looked like he was being stuck by a million misplaced acupuncture needles. I wanted to put an arm around his bowed shoulders, but any touch would probably feel like pity and drive the pain in deeper.

"Two days ago, you and I were going on a date. I had a chance at Hero High—maybe a slim one, but a chance. Everything seemed okay." Win lowered his head into his hands. "Now, it turns out I've got all these secret enemies, my parents have given up on me, Hero High is long gone, and you've decided to play Inspector Gadget."

I cleared the yearbook out of the way and sat down. I had no clue what to say, but looming over him couldn't be helpful.

"I don't know what's happening and I don't know why." He lowered one hand and looked at me sideways. "I just—I need a chance to catch up."

I didn't do quiet. I was pretty much allergic to sitting still. But I remained silently beside him until he lifted his head. "Okay, let's—let's keep going."

But I didn't pick up a yearbook, because maybe quiet contemplation wasn't the worst thing ever. While I'd waited, I'd had a thought. "What about your iLive page? That's probably easier."

"It might be," he said. "If I had one."

My chin shot up as shivers gathered at the base of my spine. "What do you mean you don't have one? I friend requested you."

He shrugged. "Must be another Winston Cavendish. I hope that dude's luck is better than mine."

I was cataloging his posture, his expression; every cell on him seemed nonchalant, which was the opposite of how I was feeling. "It—it has your picture."

"What? Show me." He whirled toward his desk, then growled under his breath. "My parents took my laptop and phone."

"I can pull it up on mine." Hopefully he wouldn't notice it was already up, because clearly I hadn't learned that lesson.

Win's knee grazed my hip, and his hand landed on my blazer as he leaned in to look at the screen. "That's my school picture from this year." His grip tightened on my shoulder. "But I didn't make this page."

12

Click on my profile," Win said.

"We're not friends." The pressure from his hand lightened, like he was about to pull away from my shoulder. I covered it with mine and clarified. "On iLive. I sent a friend request, but it hasn't been accepted."

This had gotten a whole lot more complicated—and seeing what was on that page more important. "We need a real computer—or at least a tablet with a bigger screen so we can both look."

"Right." I followed him across the hall to Wink's door. He knocked.

"You done?" she asked. "Is Huck leaving?"

"No, we're looking at iLive."

She wrinkled her nose. "Oh, I should've thought of that first. You have no filter on there."

I couldn't look at Win and watch that comment land, because if *I'd* felt it like a gut punch, how would he react? But there was a plus side here as well. I stepped into her bedroom. "You're iLive friends? I need your computer."

She jumped at my brusque tone but pointed at her desk. Her walls were pale purple, the bedroom furniture white.

Everything about the room coordinated, and she'd clearly inherited the organizational and tidiness genes that'd skipped her brother, because her desk was neat and dust-free. Even her pens and pencils were sorted into cups that looked like the pipes from Mario Brothers.

I stepped out of the way so she could sit down and log in, but Win was still standing in the doorway. It wasn't until she pulled up his profile that he came over. The bio below his picture contained his age, his school, and one line: `If you can't take a joke, leave.`

"Like I keep telling you: you're really not funny." Wink began to scroll. "Like, not even a little bit."

I cringed. I'd said those same things to Miles, but it was all about context—and once Wink knew, she'd feel as wrecked as she was currently making him. Also, Miles really *wasn't* funny—so it was my duty to tell him.

The top post was a familiar gif with a caption I hadn't seen yet. But one I realized Headmaster Williams and Dante had: `Who can name the worst private school in PA?` As Clara's hand shot up, glowing arrows circled the Hero High badge on her blazer.

"You..." Win opened and closed his mouth several times. His throat bobbed, and the muscles of his jaw tightened. Wink wasn't watching him; her eyes were on the screen. I moved mine there too, because I doubted he wanted either of us to know how close he was to crying.

"This is what you meant about Kiara?" He pointed to a photo captioned `Most likely to think hair dye makes her *edgy*`. "She hates me because of this post?"

"Can you blame her?" Wink's shoulders crept up. "This

whole series of fake superlatives you're doing is—" She mimed a finger across her throat. "Except for the one about Ty being 'most likely to win a Darwin award'—the rest are a hot mess."

"*That's* why you keep telling me to join yearbook?" he asked. "I thought it was because they needed a photographer."

"Yeah." She squinted up at him. "I mean, I doubt they'll say no to your photographic brilliance, but also, *clearly* you need a better outlet for superlatives."

"And this is why you keep telling me I'm not funny?"

"I mean, obviously."

"*Not* obviously!" He seethed. "This isn't mine! None of it. I've never seen this post or this page before. I didn't even know it existed. And you *believed it*?"

I reached out, then pulled back. Maybe my holding his hand would be comforting, but maybe it'd be confusing. He didn't need mixed signals.

Wink spun her chair around to face him. "What?"

He took advantage of her shock to seize control of the mouse. "I didn't write any of this." Win winced as he scrolled to another post. I couldn't read it, but whatever it said made him pinch the bridge of his nose.

"But we've talked about it," she said, blinking rapidly.

"No, we haven't."

"We have! Beyond stuff about your jokes and joining yearbook, we had that whole conversation about how iLive is where people go to forget their manners and let out their inner jerks. You agreed."

"I agreed the site sucks—because it does. Which is why I don't have one."

"Oh." She chewed her bottom lip. "How was I supposed to know?"

"Because you're supposed to know me!" His voice was explosive. The guinea pig in the other room squealed and scurried. "And you never thought—like, to just tell me directly about any of this? Like, there was no point in calling me a jerk after any of these posts and telling me why, because that's just who you think I am?"

"I... I..." Wink's eyes were glassy, but Win was oblivious. He'd turned his back and was studying the collage of smiling classmates on her wall.

"How many of them are on this page?" he asked.

Subtext: *How many of them hate me?*

"Can you go one day without yelling? Hudson is freaking out and getting wood chips all over the floor," Curtis called from the doorway. "Whoa, are you making Lincoln cry?" There was so much condemnation in his voice, but he dropped it as he asked, "You okay, Wink? Do I need to preheat the oven?"

She sniffled. "I don't deserve baked goods."

"Don't be dramatic," snapped Win. "It's fine. Go make cookies. But I'm borrowing your laptop to look at this."

"It's not fine," I said as Curtis stepped into the room.

His eyebrows shot up. "Huck can't be here. What part of 'grounded' don't you get? How do you always find a way to make things *worse*?"

"Talent," Win said flatly.

"They're not here flirting." Wink sniffled and crossed her arms, squaring up beside her twin. "And I mean that in the *real* way, not the oh-we're-not-dating nonsense you and Eliza pulled. If you tell Mom and Dad, I'll... set up the router to block your IP address."

"Harsh and unnecessary." Curtis raised his hands. "Why are you defending him? What's going on?"

"Nothing for you to worry about," said Win.

Was he protecting *them* or himself? Maybe he didn't want to know if Curtis had seen the page, had believed it was his too. Even if that meant taking the blame for upsetting Wink and being the bad guy.

It was the role they'd cast him in, one he always played—sometimes by choice, sometimes by force, sometimes for necessity.

I pried the laptop from beneath Win's white knuckles and shut it. "Let's take a walk. That's not going anywhere."

"Yeah, but *you* need to. Within the next hour, before my parents get home," said Curtis.

Win nodded and stormed out of the bedroom, out of the house. I grabbed our coats and followed. Everything about him was tight. His posture, his footsteps, the way he shoved his arms into his jacket. He stomped to the corner, then stopped. Whirled on me with eyes that blazed.

"I live in this constant state of just wanting to scream." His voice was so low, I had to step closer to hear him. "I don't expect you to understand, but it's *not in my head*. All year I've been saying... But I didn't make it up or imagine it. People really are pissed at me. And I had no idea why. And my parents, Wink, and Curtis, they've all—they've all made me feel like I must've done something to deserve it. And I'm not perfect, but I didn't do... *that*. But Wink thought..." He shook his head. "I'm angry. I'm so..." He broke off to search my face. "Do you get it?"

I nodded. "It's gaslighting. And it's not the same—not nearly the same magnitude—but I spent the whole drive from Ohio to Pennsylvania trying not to lose it each time my parents told me moving was 'no big deal'—that my friends were 'just a phone screen away.' That it would be easy to make new ones. Their casual dismissal of my whole life, while I had no say. I get it."

Win kicked at a hardened snowbank. "I know who I am. I'm the kid who spoiled the tooth fairy for his kindergarten class. Who switched the caps on the markers in art. Who decided to stick out his tongue in the one photo from his grandma's birthday party where everyone had their eyes open." He rubbed the back of his neck. "I know who I am in my family—and it doesn't matter what's true. It matters what they believe."

I took a step toward him, then paused. His posture was closed; my entering his personal space, even to offer comfort, wouldn't be comforting. He wanted someone to listen. I could do that.

"What if my parents won't believe that's not my page?"

"Then that's their fault, not yours." I clenched my fists. "Just like my parents' disappointment that I'm not Big Man on Campus at the new school is on them. Their expectations, but my life."

"What do we do?" His eyes were searching, like he thought I might have an answer.

So I gave him one. "We find places it's safe to scream. We find people who'll listen."

"You?"

"Me," I agreed. "And anyone else I can make hear us."

He nodded slowly and turned back toward his house, but I halted his progress with a hand on his sleeve. "I didn't ask—and I should've. But...do you *want* my help?" I held my breath because I'd learned from Clara. If he said no, I'd respect that.

It'd kill me, but I'd respect it.

"It's not like anyone else is lining up to help me." Win's words were bitter, but then his expression turned as soft as the hand he grazed across the back of mine. "What I mean is, thanks."

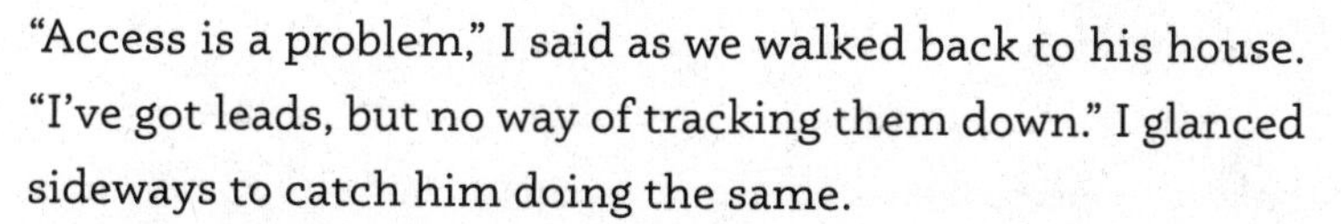

"Access is a problem," I said as we walked back to his house. "I've got leads, but no way of tracking them down." I glanced sideways to catch him doing the same.

He grinned. "I like it when you talk detective."

I made a grumbly old man noise. Flirting was fun, but I had to focus. "Do you think I could go undercover at your school?" Sherlock had successfully done that several times, and I wouldn't even need a disguise. I could wear pretty much anything in my closet *but* my Hero High uniform. "I could pose as a transfer student—" Win's laughter interrupted my planning, and I frowned.

"Oh wait, were you serious?" he asked. "Then, no. No, I don't. A new kid can't show up without paperwork."

"Could I fake it?" I was half serious, but vamping it up because he'd laughed. And I think we both needed to hear that sound after this afternoon's revelations.

Win bumped his shoulder against mine, and I cursed our coats and layers and the mysteries that kept us apart. "I like the enthusiasm, but let's put that idea on hold."

"For now," I conceded. "But not forever."

He might have been talking about me visiting his school, but I was talking about me and him.

When we reentered his house, Wink had her laptop on the kitchen island. Curtis hovered behind her, wearing oven mitts and cursing whatever was on the screen. The kitchen timer was counting down from eight minutes. I wasn't sure if that was for when I needed to leave or for whatever baked good was making the house smell like mint.

Curtis turned toward us, his face drawn and sober. "Wink told me about the page. I've already looked up how we report it. They'll take it down."

Win's hand clutched my arm as he kicked off a shoe. His balance hadn't wavered, so it was emotional support, not physical. His shoulders sagged with relief, and it killed me to have to say, "Don't. You can't."

He let go and stepped back. "Why?"

"It's our best lead. That page needs to stay up. No one outside this room can know it's fake."

"You can't be serious," said Curtis. "Have you seen all this?"

"No. And that's exactly *why* I'm serious." Had Sherlock cared when his actions made him hated? Because I wouldn't make it a full day as a detective if it always felt like this.

"Every one of those posts is a garbage fire at Win's expense," said Wink.

"They're also all clues. And we *need* this person to keep posting. Whoever's behind this page and the emails, they can't know we know. It's better if they think you all agree with your parents—that Win self-sabotaged at Hero High."

They stared at me, angry, annoyed, betrayed. The silence was brutal, the timer counting down.

Curtis nodded first. "This stinks."

"I'm going to fill out the reporting form now. As soon as you say go, I'll have it ready to send," said Wink.

Win squinted past her to the laptop. "Is that Reese?"

"Wink's friend?" I asked, thinking back over our conversations—the one who either liked or loathed Win's friend Morris.

"Yeah. And it's not like we're besties, but I like her. We get along. At least we *did*." Win groaned. "Her whole family is just... cool. Her dad's middle name is Thor. And, like, when Craig and Shannon go away, they pay Wink and me way too much to watch Zoe and Ziggy."

"Is that another set of twins?"

"No." They all laughed before Win clarified. "They're dogs. English bulldogs. Her little brother's Sam, and that kid is chill. Ugh. What did 'I' say about her?"

Wink read quietly. "People who treat dogs like people are freaking weird. Hashtag: No dogs at the dining table. Hashtag: Unsanitary. Hashtag: Dog hair for dinner."

"I didn't post this," Win said.

"I know," said Curtis. "We believe you."

It was the most important thing they'd said all day, but Win didn't notice. "No, but here's the thing—I did have this conversation. I said a lot of that."

Wink nodded. "I was there—it's why I thought this was real."

"But I wasn't being mean, I swear." He turned to me. "I'd sat at their table and Reese made me move because I was in 'Zoe's seat.' I made a joke—they laughed."

Wink turned the laptop away. "It was funny—no one was mad... then."

I was all for Win and Wink working things out, but they could do that later. I had less than three minutes on the timer. "Who else was there for the conversation?"

"A lot of people." Win shrugged. "The Kimmels always have people over. That time was a football game."

"NFC championship," Wink added. "I'll make you a list of who I remember."

"Thanks." I clicked screenshots of the top few posts—there were more anti-Hero High versions of the Clara gif. "Can you email me these?"

The timer beeped and I looked up from the computer. Win was stoic. His face so wiped of any emotion that I knew he must be feeling them all. Sherlock might not have the detective equivalent of "bedside manner," but clearly neither did I, since the best I could offer was a solemn nod. Words felt hollow, and the temptation to make grand promises was too strong.

"You should go," he said softly.

I looked back when I reached the corner, saw the Cavendishes' Honda turn onto the block. I prayed to the gods of current events and office snafus that there was some engrossing topic that would sail them through dinner conversation on a current of oblivious self-absorption.

And that wish came true—at least in my house, where my parents chattered about midterms and grading. I devoured my spaghetti and escaped to my room before they noticed it was Friday night and I had no plans.

The only thing waiting for me was an email from Ms. Gregoire.

Hey Huck,

Headmaster Williams asked about your video project. I promised him an update next week-so I need one first. Stop by my room before first period on Monday. If you're still feeling stuck we'll come up with a plan together.

Enjoy your weekend.

Ms. G.

I flopped back on the bed and put a pillow over my face. I didn't want to scream into it or smother myself—I just wanted the outside world to go away so I could force my brain to find the answers that must be in there somewhere.

My parents wanted me to ascend the summit of popularity—or at least expand my social circle beyond Rory and Curtis, who were both currently out on some "triple date" Merri had coerced them into attending with her and Fielding and Toby and Eliza.

Ms. Gregoire—well, Headmaster Williams—wanted me to somehow repair Hero High's reputation. Despite the fact that things usually went viral for negative or scandalous reasons. I couldn't replicate the reach of Clara's video with a positive puff piece.

The Cavendish offspring wanted the solution to Win's mystery, but since he was grounded I lacked access to both him *and* the iLive page.

I gripped the pillow tighter and ordered myself to think. Three problems, zero solutions. What I really needed was an espresso, but there's no way I could turn on the coffee maker without Mom hearing.

Friends. Video. Access. Friends-video-access. *Friendsvideoaccess.*

I threw the pillow aside and sat up. They weren't three separate problems. I grabbed my phone. Emailed Ms. Gregoire: Sounds good. See you Monday. Then texted Curtis: When will your parents be gone tomorrow? I'm coming over.

13

I didn't know if Win was an early riser. He'd been asleep that time Curtis no-showed for our run, but was that typical? If my parents weren't the loudest humans on the planet—singing show tunes while weeding the flower bed below my window at eight thirty—I would've still been snoring.

I consulted Rory. She said showing up before ten a.m. on a Saturday was "obscene," though it's possible her feelings on the subject were influenced by Lilly dragging her to an eight o'clock goat yoga class.

Goat.

Yoga.

It wasn't an autocorrect; I'd checked. It was genuine barn animals in class. Clearly I'd need more details after she'd showered off the old McDonald smell.

Since I was up, I started reading "The Speckled Band" while watching the clock. I turned pages and drank coffee, getting out my contraband French press after I'd finished my first cup. This was the second Holmes story I'd read about dastardly plots to prevent people from getting married. I refilled my mug. I knew there weren't direct parallels between the stories and Win and me, but that didn't make it any easier to accept that someone was toying with his life, manipulating and sabotaging his relationships.

I shut the book's cover—9:41 was late enough—and headed down the sidewalk while my parents serenaded me with "So Long, Farewell" from *The Sound of Music*.

In a lot of Sherlock's stories, the motivation was money. Was that relevant here? Hero High tuition wasn't cheap. Curtis was on a decent scholarship, but would that be tripled for the twins? And since the financial aid pool was limited and competitive, was that a motive? Should I focus on other applicants? The school financial officer? Neither seemed likely, but I lacked Sherlock's ability to differentiate between dead ends, red herrings, and leads.

Self-doubt was burning through my caffeine buzz as I knocked on the Cavendishes' door. Win answered, freshly showered, hair still wet. The collar of his plain gray T-shirt damp where it'd dripped. "Hi? Did you figure out who's behind this?"

His faith was a blow, and it hurt to answer. "No, but I've got a plan. Well, a plan for a plan if I can get Ms. Gregoire to sign off. I think she will."

"A plan for a plan?" His shoulders slumped as he shoved a hand into the pocket of his jeans. "Gee, I feel so much better."

"You're being sarcastic," I stated. "You're angry."

"What gave me away? The glare, or that I punched a wall last night when my sister headed out with a group of our classmates while I stayed home and wondered how many of them had been insulted on my page?" He held up his left hand, bandages across the knuckles. "Is that a demo of your super-sleuthing?"

I didn't even have to be above-average observant to see he was shoving me away as hard as he could—and that it was hurting him to do so. But there was an easy solution: I wouldn't let myself be shoved.

Though physically, I shoved him. Well, not really a shove, but I maneuvered around him and into the house. "We've only got until one before your parents get back. Let's get started."

"Started with what? I've got stuff to do." He pointed at a magnetic whiteboard on the fridge. I couldn't read the subscript from here, but the heading was clear: *Winston's Chores*. "My parents will be pissed if they get home and those aren't done. And you don't have to watch me change Hudson's cage or fold laundry or clean the inside of the kitchen cabinets."

"Watch? No." I shrugged off my jacket. "I'm going to help."

"I'm not making you do my chores." His face and voice were aimed at the floor, his shoulders drawn in.

"You're not making me, I volunteered." I crossed the kitchen to read the list. "Better chores here with you than at home. My parents are singing *Sound of Music*. They'll make me play *all* the von Trapp kids."

One corner of his mouth lifted. "Can you sing?"

"Not even a little. And my mom is determined to train me. Seriously, save me from lectures on 'breathing from my diaphragm' while weeding."

"You don't have to be here."

I exhaled. There wasn't anything inviting in his voice or body language, but at least he was no longer aggressively pushing me away. "I want to be." I said the words firmly, waiting for him to meet my eyes. "Though I have no clue how to change a guinea pig cage, so you'll have to tell me what to do."

"I can do that. But Curtis is still sleeping, so we should start out here."

"Sounds good." First I fetched Wink's laptop. She'd told Curtis we were free to use it and had put a sticky note with her password on the lid. *I'm trusting you, Win* scrawled underneath. I crumpled it and tossed it into her trash. She'd also left a few pages of notes about the posts. These, I pocketed.

iLive messenger was open on her screen. I skimmed the conversations as I closed their windows.

Reese Kimmel: When will you get here?

Lincoln Cavendish: Not soon enough. It's been A DAY

Reese Kimmel: Isn't it always in your house?

Lincoln Cavendish: Truth

I frowned. It was *a* truth, but not all of it. Granted, she couldn't share *all* of it, but she'd slanted her words to become the victim.

Morris Henderson: Win grounded? He's not answering my texts.

Lincoln Cavendish: Yup. Want me to give him a message?

Morris Henderson: No point. Was asking about plans. What are you doing?

Lincoln Cavendish: Sleeping over Reese's

Morris Henderson: :(

Morris Henderson: Heads-up, I talked to Nunes about starting a coding club next year.

Lincoln Cavendish: ?? You don't code

Morris Henderson: You can teach me.

Morris Henderson: Won't you?

There could be a hundred reasons why Wink hadn't responded: She'd been called to dinner; she'd left for Reese's; Morris had BO and the thought of sitting near him made her gag. Sherlock could probably figure out how to get that answer without revealing he'd snooped, but like Morris, I felt left hanging.

I placed the laptop on the kitchen island like it was some strange centerpiece we stacked dishes around while spraying and wiping down the cabinets. Win was flustered, apologetic, wincing when the cuts on his hand stung. "Your fingers are going to smell like vinegar."

I shrugged. "So will yours. So will Wink's computer." As we worked I scrolled to the bottom of the page, figuring I'd start when it did. "This is only five months old. Can you think of anything major happening in your life around Halloween?"

He was stacking mugs in a precarious tower of mismatched bases and rims. Before they crashed, I reached over and moved the handprint one and the mug below it. For a second I was adrift, imagining one of *my* mugs among his; how I'd shape and glaze and—

"Halloween was the opposite of interesting," he said. "I was studying and retaking the SSATs that weekend."

I frowned. The first post was of a girl dressed as a witch, captioned: `I thought the point was to wear costumes.` I clicked on it and sighed, because the photo's source wasn't a clue. The caption was new, but the picture linked back to the girl's—Ava's—own feed. Turning away from the digital dead end, I grumbled and glared at the stacks of plates blocking the coffee maker.

"Sorry," said Win. "I'm trying to be helpful."

"No, you are. I'm just thinking." And it was hard to do that here. Because of him. Because I knew I came across as annoyed or angry or distracted when I got lost in analysis. Rory laughed about it. My parents tolerated it. Other people didn't notice when I checked out, or didn't care enough to care. If I wanted Win to, I should prepare him.

Especially since I knew he'd interpret my behavior as personal rejections. And the only way we'd make any progress with this case or *us* was if I laid things out in the open—explained what was going on in my head and gave him clues and context to decode me.

I rapped a knuckle against the counter and waited until he turned around. "Something you should know about me: I'm going to space out. I'll sigh and huff and likely start pacing. I'll miss things you tell me, or think aloud without giving context." I spoke slower than normal, watching to make sure he was *hearing* me, monitoring the way each statement landed. "People tell me it's annoying, but it's how I think. And it's not—I'm not mad at you, or ignoring you or anything. Even if it seems like it."

Win nodded and rubbed his bottom lip between bandaged fingers. It was still hot, but I now recognized it as a gesture he made when he felt vulnerable. "I hate this—I feel like all my screwups are on display. And lots I didn't do. You're cleaning my kitchen, writing lists of my enemies—how could this possibly not make you run away?"

The room stank of vinegar. I still couldn't make coffee, and if all his past failures were on display, so was my inability to pay attention to the realities outside my head *or* connect the distracting facts inside it into something useful. Despite all this, my answer was honest. "I'm where I want to be."

"Because I'm your latest puzzle and you like figuring things out? What happens when you do? Is a puzzle still interesting once it's solved? Or if it can't be? What if I don't get into Hero High?"

Hero High. I frowned and held up a finger. Moving a stack of bowls, I pulled the laptop closer, clicking to the admissions page of the school website. "There has to be a connection between this iLive profile and Hero High. You said you took the SSATs that weekend? Talk me through the timeline of your application."

"Um, sure." Win's back was to me as he dried a shelf. He was more comfortable answering while facing away, and I wasn't about to tell him that his body language and tone of voice were as transparent as his expressions.

But—I'd *hurt* him somehow. I lifted my fingers from the keys and realized I'd skipped over his questions to chase my own answers. "Wait. You're not a puzzle and—"

"It's fine," he said. It wasn't, but I let him continue because facts were more comfortable than feelings. "Anyway, it was last October when Wink and my parents talked me into reapplying. I had to start from scratch: new essays, letters of recommendation, SSATs—'cause there are so many adults waiting to say great things about me and the test was super fun to take twice."

"And SSATs. You took them the week of Halloween? You're sure?"

"Yeah, Mom and Dad dropped me at Mayfield on their way to work."

The testing company's website confirmed there'd been a

test that Saturday morning at Mayfield Middle Academy. I clicked back to iLive—the Halloween picture had been posted at 10:17 a.m. I highly doubted Win's proctor had provided social media breaks. "Hmm."

"Got something?" Win put down a paper towel, his voice rising hopefully.

"Not yet," I told him. "But I'm working on it."

14

"Can I ask you something?" Win said.

Curtis had woken up and was in the kitchen making muffins, so we were tackling Hudson's cage in the garage. Not that we would've cleaned it *in the kitchen*—hello, salmonella—but picking a garage chore gave us privacy.

I grinned. "That seems fair, since I've done nothing but question you." And it was getting easier. Win talked more while working, like tasks distracted him from what he was saying. I was distracted too—case in point, my shoes were covered in a layer of wood shavings because I was watching him, not where I was scooping.

He passed me the broom. "At least they're the clean shavings."

"True. What's your question?"

"You think whoever made the page wrote the emails, right? So why do the people in the posts matter? I mean, I know they matter, but why ask me about them?"

"There's two possibilities." I hung the broom back on its hook. "Either there's one person with a vendetta who made the iLive page *and* sent the emails. Or it's two separate puzzles: some jerk made the page and someone insulted on it sent the letters as revenge.

"If it's the first scenario, I'm looking for patterns or motives or connections to whoever is behind it. If it's the second, I need to know who would be so upset by iLive that they'd lash out at your application."

"So either one person hates me an extreme amount, or two people hate me slightly less extremely." He scrubbed his hands across his face. "And I have no idea who. I feel like I'm walking into school with a target on my back."

"Fess up," I said, waggling my eyebrows. "My undercover plan is sounding better. I could be your stealth bodyguard."

He gave an unexpected bark of laughter. It was like poorly brewed espresso: short-lived and slightly bitter—but right now, I'd take it.

While Win carried the crate into the house and resituated Hudson, I consulted the chore list. "Only one task left," I said as he reentered the kitchen.

He stiffened. "You do *not* have to help me clean the bathroom."

"It's just a bigger guinea pig cage, minus the shavings," I joked as I followed him down the hall. Except, when I slid into the room beside him, I realized how small it was. We were practically jeans-to-jeans, eye-to-eye. My mind mapped all the ways we'd fit better—if one of us sat on the toilet lid or edge of the tub, stood in the shower, or shuffled onto the bath mat. Instead we were both crowded between the wall and the sink. I kicked the door shut, which opened up some room to my right, but neither of us stepped into it.

My wide eyes and flushed cheeks were reflected in the

mirror behind him. I ignored them and fixated on the guy leaning against the sink in front of me. Win was watching me assess the scene like a fly caught in the sweetest trap. His foot was separated from mine by just a line of tile grout.

I swallowed, forced myself to mirror his posture and lean back, which meant taking a towel bar to the kidneys and knocking the towels to the floor. There wasn't room to bend and pick them up, so they now lived in a puddle around my feet.

"Have you got more questions for me?" Win uncrossed his feet. "Or have I earned a break?"

Right. Questions. Case. I sucked in a huge breath, hoping the oxygen would clear my head, find some of the objectivity and focus that had scattered within this room.

Last time he'd been this close, I'd run—literally. And right now my heart was pounding like my feet had already obeyed that muscle memory to flee. "I—uh. A break. That sounds good."

"You okay?" His eyes roamed my face with dizzying intensity.

"Just a little light-headed from the smell of the cleaner. We should turn the fan on; bathroom solvents are especially toxic."

There. That sounded logical. Not at all like there should be a cloud of heart-eyed emojis circling my head. We both reached for the fan switch at the same time. I shivered when our fingers touched. Win grinned.

"I'm going to get . . ." I floundered. "A drink. Water."

"Sure." He nodded. "There's really not room in here for both of us. But while you're getting your drink, could you get something for me too?"

I nodded, maybe a little too enthusiastically. "Cranberry juice?"

"No, the bathroom spray. It's under the kitchen sink. I forgot to grab it." He smirked, and my face turned the same color as his juice. Juice I would not be fetching. He could get his own cleaner too. He hummed and raised an eyebrow.

I laughed and told him, "Shut up."

He continued smirking. "I didn't say anything. It must be all those fumes—they're really getting to you."

I returned his grin and leaned forward, bringing one hand up to flick the center of his forehead before ducking out of the room.

I was fully aware, fully willing to admit that flirting was Win's domain. One where I clearly and frequently failed. But analysis was mine. As long as I kept a minimum of eighteen inches between us and didn't look directly at him when he was doing that smolder-grin or that thing where he tugged his lower lip, then I could be focused. Logical. This hydration break was just what I needed.

I situated myself on the couch with Wink's laptop and notes, then jumped when the door opened. Wink set down a bag and pointed to the pages. "Hey. Have those been helpful?"

"Very." It was an exaggeration, not a lie. "Do you need your laptop?"

"No. I'm only home to grab a book on coding. I'm headed to record Eliza's podcast."

"Coding." I raised an eyebrow. "Like the club that's starting at Chester? It was up on your screen, I couldn't help but see it."

She shrugged. "Morris means well, but..." Her eyes panned the room and I said, "Cleaning the bathroom," before she dropped her voice and finished. "I won't *be* at Chester next year."

"You'll go to Hero High without Win?"

She flinched but nodded. "Does that make me evil? I haven't told him yet, so—"

The bathroom door opened, and she shot me a pleading look. I nodded, because I'd keep her secret. But between this and Curtis's "Win can't know I approve of you two," I wondered if anyone in this family ever communicated.

"Hey," Win called. "When'd you get home? Did you say hi to Zig for me?"

"Of course." She pulled a huge book from her backpack. "But I'm not staying. I'm a guest on *Science Party*."

"Cool. Tell Eliza I'm in to talk photography when I'm ungrounded."

I frowned, slightly offended I'd never been asked to be on her podcast.

"Will do. She said to ask if you guys had any science questions for future episodes." Wink had her hand on the door, so she wasn't expecting an immediate response, but Win had one.

"Huck's not clear on how many planets are in our solar system. Could she have a first-grader come on and explain it for him?" His eyes shot sideways to me, tight in the corners until I laughed, then relaxing as he joined in.

Wink muttered, "Ugh, inside jokes," then left while we were still laughing.

"You've been busy out here." He nodded at the laptop and notes, which I'd strategically arranged on the couch to ensure we'd get that buffer zone between us.

"Tell me about this guy." I pointed to a recent post and

thanked the gods of all things social media and sabotage that whoever was behind this vengeance spree had started slow. The first posts were a month apart, then it was less than one a week. They'd only recently become more frequent.

Wink's notes about it said, While Win can absolutely make a gif, there's no way he went to a baseball game.

Because that's what the post was—a gif of a guy dropping a ball then staring at his empty glove in extreme disbelief. It was the sort of thing that *could've* gone viral. For Win and the outfielder's sake, I was glad it hadn't.

"Erick? He went to Mayfield and now Chester. He plays baseball." Win flopped onto the couch and scrubbed his hands over his eyes, then frowned. "My fingers still smell."

He'd replaced the bandages on his knuckles with fresh ones while in the bathroom. The sight sliced at me and I clenched a fist. When I figured out who was behind this, I'd hold them accountable for every bit of his pain—both physical and mental. "Anything else?"

"We don't have any classes together this year." He chewed his lip. "Honestly, the only thing that stands out was in sixth grade he went around pantsing everyone and we had to have a whole assembly on 'no-no zones' and 'bubble space.'"

"Did he pants you?"

"I dunno. Probably?" Win tucked a throw pillow behind his head and propped a foot on the coffee table. "It only lasted, like, two days before they shut it down, but it became this big thing because one of the guys was going commando."

"Not you?" I silenced the part of my mind that wanted to register I was asking Win about his underwear preferences. This was case pertinent.

Or not, actually, because he shook his head. "I'm trying

to think of anything else about Erick. He plays drums?" Win shrugged. "Sorry, the dude just hasn't been on my radar."

But he *was* on Win's fake iLive page—so either someone wanted Erick to have a grudge against Win, or someone wanted to target Erick. I frowned. "I'll see what else I can dig up from his profile before I talk to him."

"Wait." Win's foot dropped to the ground, and the pillow slid sideways as he sat up. "You're going to talk to people on the page? About me?"

"Not directly about you—I can't say the page is fake or reveal you know it exists." And I couldn't tell him my plan until I got it approved. I didn't want to be another person who disappointed him.

He sighed and tilted his head toward the ceiling. It was a vulnerable posture, one that'd vanish in an instant if Curtis walked out of their bedroom. His trust was an almost painful ache in my chest.

I looked away. "There's only two weeks until Hero High letters go out—and I want to..." I wanted to get him *in*, but I didn't have the power to do that. I didn't have a full two weeks either, since decisions were probably made sooner. Hopefully I could at least prove he hadn't rejected *them* by sending those emails. "I need all the clues I can get."

The noise he made was closer to a cough than an acknowledgment. Like he was literally and metaphorically choking under the pressure. Maybe Wink's drained laptop wasn't the only thing that needed to be shut down. We needed a break from scrutiny and some balance—a time where he got to do the asking and I offered up answers. "What's your favorite pizza topping?"

His mouth turned up instantly, and my chest warmed

with the knowledge I'd read the situation correctly. Read *him* correctly. "Who says I like pizza?"

"Um, you did?" He blinked, and I pretended to stagger back against the couch. "'Pizza, bowling, gelato'—did you forget your plans for our first date?"

He snorted. "Can't we fast-forward to that part? But I like it boring: cheese and sauce."

"Not boring; classic." He raised an eyebrow, like he was measuring the sincerity of my response. "It's my favorite too."

"Yeah?" Was it wrong that I leaned forward to read the microwave clock? Not to see how long until his parents came home—seventeen minutes—but because I wanted to note the moment he'd started smiling.

I sat back, smug satisfaction changing to something else entirely when my hand brushed his as I moved Wink's notes. His smile flickered as his eyes dropped to my mouth and lingered. Then his brows pulled inward as he deliberately leaned out of my personal space.

"My question," he said. "Favorite sport?"

I blinked like a toddler waking from a nap. I hadn't misread Win's thoughts a moment before—he'd wanted to kiss me. But he was playing nice, respecting the boundaries I'd set, which only made him all the more attractive. I cleared my throat and still sounded hoarse when I answered. "Um, lacrosse to play. Hockey to watch, which is good since I pretty much grew up rinkside at Miles's games."

"Same. Only with Curtis and lacrosse and I don't like watching it."

"Ouch."

He shrugged. "Mine's swimming."

I snapped my fingers as neural pathways finally started

cooperating. All day I'd been trying to figure out what was familiar about the scent of these cleaners. Chlorine. Like in pools. The sharp smell I'd sniffed on him during our first walk home but hadn't detected since. Also, the shirtless dimpled eye candy. "So, Lochte, huh? I saw the poster on the floor by your closet."

"Ha. I forgot about that." He chuckled and shrugged. "He was hotter before I heard him interviewed."

I wondered if *I* was more appealing before I'd turned all our interactions into interviews. *Question: Do I ask too many questions?*

The clock was getting uncomfortably close to when I'd calculated I'd have to leave. "Are you on your school team?" If so, maybe I could go to a meet. See how he interacted with his teammates. See him in a swimsuit.

He raised an eyebrow. "Do I look like a team player?" I refused to take the bait. If I waited, he'd elaborate. The eyebrow dropped. "I couldn't be even if I wanted to. They practice before school, before the busses are running. I don't have a way to get there. But sometimes—when I'm not grounded—Coach lets me swim after school if he's hanging around."

"So you're good?" That wasn't the sort of favor a coach would grant without recruitment hopes.

He crossed his ankles. "Yeah."

I liked that he was unapologetic about his talent, but I hated everything else about this scenario. "Have you asked your parents if they can work something out for practice? Or can you carpool?"

He shrugged. "What's the point? It'd be a hassle for everyone, and I'd probably end up kicked off for, like, academic probation, and then everyone would be pissed."

"The point would be you love it." He hadn't stated that explicitly, but he didn't deny it. "You know, Hero High's walkable. If you transfer, you can do their team."

I immediately wanted to suck the words back in, because that "if" hinged on answers I was the only one pursuing. And his acceptance hadn't been a sure thing *before* the faux-email drama.

"I know." His voice was quiet, but not angry or wistful. Resigned. "If there was any possibility I'd get in, that'd be the second best thing about the school."

"What's the fir—" I trailed off as he gave me a pointed look. "Oh." But our silence wasn't heated; it was bleak. I couldn't offer him reassurances, so I changed the subject—volunteering some of *my* vulnerabilities to counterbalance his. "I can't swim. The last time I took lessons, they were still telling me to think of my hands like ice cream scoops."

Win sucked a breath between his teeth. "Yeah, we're going to have to change that."

I laughed nervously. "Oh, you think so? I don't." Because the idea of doggy paddling while Win watched made me feel...likely the way *he* did every time I asked about enemies. Overexposed and dangerously defenseless. "Sorry, I'm no Lochte. But, you're, uh, picturing me in a speedo right now, aren't you?"

I'd meant it as a joke, but he nodded. "Sure am."

"Oh." I dropped my chin as my face burned.

Win tilted his head. "On a scale of one to fake fumes, how embarrassed are you right now? Because I like making you blush, but I don't want you to feel uncomfortable."

My face was sunburn hot. *This* was why no one should ever have believed that was Winston's page. He didn't hide behind jokes; he faced things head on. Called me out on vaulting over couches, fleeing imaginary fumes. Baldly told me he liked me. Respected and checked my boundaries. "I'm…okay. But I have to go."

Win cupped the back of his neck and sighed. "Sorry. I didn't mean—"

"No." I pointed to the clock. "I *really* have to go. I'm a minute past my must-leave time."

"Oh." Win stood as I shoved my feet into my shoes and snagged my coat from the hook. I rolled Wink's notes into a messy cylinder and shoved it into my pocket. "I have one more question."

We didn't have time for him to ask or me to answer, but I nodded anyway.

"Why do you think no one reported the page? Not to iLive, but, like, no one told on 'me'?"

My hand slid off the door as I considered. "Tattletale or person-who-can't-take-a-joke isn't a good look on anyone. Plus, when the first posts went up, no one was following the page. It's still set to private—*my* friend request hasn't been accepted. I'm not sure how many of the people in the posts even know. And those that do—well, people in new posts probably feel pressure not to make a fuss since no one else has. And people in the old posts probably felt like it was too late to do anything."

It sounded clinical and probably wasn't what he wanted to hear, but it was honest. It was also foolish, because while I stood there trying to find words to make the truth less caustic, the garage door went up.

We locked panicked eyes as Curtis came sliding down the hall in his socks. "Huckleberry, what are you still doing here? Come on, back door." He grabbed me by the sleeve, tugging so hard my arm came out. The slider squeaked as he shoved it open, and he was still shutting it as his parents entered. "Hey, boys."

I ducked under the kitchen window as his dad asked, "Letting all the heat out?"

"Some of it," said Curtis. "Along with cleaner fumes. Can't you smell how hard my main man Winston's been working?"

I pressed my back against the bricks and waited for the rest—the part where Curtis undermined his support with some joke that cut a little too close to a nerve, or Win lashed out preemptively, or his parents expressed skepticism.

Mr. Cavendish said, "It looks great, Win."

I did a celebratory fist clench. Curtis and Win's interactions almost always defaulted to antagonism, but Win had no choice but to be vulnerable with his iLive secret, and Curtis would jump all over that opportunity to force his brother to let him in. I had no clue what would happen with Hero High or iLive—but if this reset their dynamic from rivals to partners, that'd be its own victory.

I exhaled and began a slow creep toward the gate. Winston Cavendish had had enough losses. It was time for him to win.

15

Rory called to fill me in on goat yoga during a dead shift at Haute Dog on Sunday night. I still didn't understand. "So, it's just a regular yoga class . . . only there are tiny goats roaming around? Why goats? Why not cats or dogs or scorpions? Why any animal at all?"

"Just because I was there—and I have hoof prints on my shirt to prove it—doesn't mean I get it. But I'll gladly volunteer you to take my spot if Lilly goes back. Then you can see for yourself."

"Hard pass." I drummed my fingers on the covers of *Sherlock* and Wink's seventh-grade yearbook. Since I'd left the Cavendishes' house yesterday, I'd been alternating between reading and taking notes for my Ms. Gregoire meeting and reading and taking notes about Win's case. "Hey, do you think my nose is hawk-like?" It was how Holmes's was described, and I'd spent a stupid-long time trying to decide if it matched mine.

"Huck-like? Who else would it be like?"

There was a barking noise in the background, which I guess was to be expected at a dog store. I raised my voice to be heard over it. "No, hawk-like."

"Huck-light?"

"Hawk. *Hawk*. Like the bird. You know, beaky?" I had no clue how a hawk sounded, but my impression consisted of a *caw-squawk*.

She laughed. "Oh, I heard you the first time. I just wanted to see what you'd do. And, no. Are you about to go all Amy March on me?"

"I don't know what that means." Though I knew it had to do with her favorite character from *Little Women*. Rory had been obsessed with the book since Ms. Gregoire assigned it to her, and based on my current nasal fixation, I had zero grounds for mocking that.

"She was always worried about her nose, but it was fine and so is yours."

"Thanks," I said. "By the way, do you know anything about Ava Jones? She's a grade above us." Thanks to Wink's yearbook, I'd ID'd the girl in the witch costume post.

"Dark hair? If she's who I'm thinking of, Merri says she's full of herself and mentions how her dad's on the Hero High board in *every* conversation. I think there's more to it than that—something about Monroe and Fielding, but I don't know the whole story. Eliza's not a fan either."

"Hmm." The part about Merri's ex probably wasn't relevant, but the other part definitely was. It connected the first post on Win's iLive page to Hero High.

"What are you up to?" Rory asked, but the barking had escalated. I predicted her next words before she said them. "Actually, I have to hang up. I've got to go do Botox."

Okay. I didn't predict *all* those words. "Um, *what*?" I could hear her sister calling her name, and while Merri was mostly awesome, she wasn't exactly a paragon of common sense—so I was searching for my shoes to go intercede between my best friend and botulism.

"Pug! Botox is a pug," she clarified, before calling out, "*Be right there.*" She dropped her voice and added, "A super-spoiled one that Merri's currently getting all sorts of rowdy. So if I don't start this drawing soon, it's pretty much going to be a pug-shaped blur."

"Oh." I laughed. "Right." Her side hustle of doing pet drawings at the store had become incredibly popular, which was good because she was saving to spend part of her summer in New York shadowing her favorite artist. Which meant I'd spend those weeks begging to live on Miles's couch, because if things didn't go right with Win and she was away, I had very little anchoring me to this town.

While Rory wrangled a hyper pup, I called my brother. It was more phone time than I typically logged in a week, but Miles was a Generation Z with Generation X tendencies. This meant he liked to *talk* on the phone instead of texting and got a newspaper delivered instead of reading the *Times* app on the subway; he was twenty-three going on sixty.

"Hey Puck, what's up?"

"Not much, Half-G." His nickname came from an eighties song by the Proclaimers about being willing to walk five hundred miles to get to a person. I knew Curtis had a reputation for bad nicknames, but he could get in line—my parents were the OG cheeseballs.

I heard Miles mute a podcast. "I need a date update. Did you reschedule for post-pinkeye?"

"Something like that," I mumbled. Mom and Dad were at the grocery store, and my bedroom was starting to feel like an impossible escape room, full of puzzles I couldn't solve. So I headed downstairs, turned on the coffee maker, then leaned against the counter while it did it's warming-up thing. On the other end of the line I could hear Miles moving around, a door opening, and then a steady stream of liquid. "Are you peeing?"

"No, getting water from the fridge." He laughed. "I thought we had a no-bathroom-breaks-on-the-phone rule? Or at least an agreement to mute." Right. That was his cabinet, not a door. I should've known. And he would've had to be holding the phone much lower to get that sort of acoustics while—

"I gotta say—" He slurped water too close to the receiver. "I'm glad you're putting yourself out there. I was getting sick of Mom and Dad's panicked phone calls. They kept worrying they'd turned you into a—I need you to visualize the air quotes I'm about to make—'latchkey kid.' I've been telling them they moved one state east, not time-traveled back to the nineties or whenever that was a thing."

"Yeah. Dad's practically volunteering to cold-call classmates' parents and arrange play dates—because *that* would make me so popular."

"I'm also relieved your first date won't be a movie."

"Why?" The warm-up light on the coffee maker had stopped blinking, but now I was. "Dad said it was a good one."

"Yeahhh. For starters, why are you going to Dad for dating advice when you have me?"

"Good point. Who wouldn't want tips from a twenty-something geezer? Please tell me all your secrets for finding shuffleboard and bingo nights." I opened a cabinet and grabbed the biggest mug.

"Cute. But *Dead Poets Society* is a sobfest and you snot-cry. Also, you are the most obnoxious person to watch a movie with. Let's save that for people you *don't* want to want a second date."

"What?" But even as I asked, I anticipated his answer, and my "Because I figure them out?" jumbled with his "You make predictions the whole time!"

Miles laughed. "You point out every clue and red herring. And worse, you're right ninety-five percent of the time. The few times I've seen you stumped, you deconstruct the whole movie to explain why the twist ending defied logic or had plot holes."

I made a noncommittal noise and hit the Brew button. While it percolated, I mentally reviewed the last few movies I'd seen with Rory. Had I done this? There was that time she'd whacked me with a pillow and told me we were playing "the quiet game." So, maybe?

If only I could apply the same logic to life—if only all side plots were filtered out and simplified, the important details highlighted with mood lighting or musical cues. "Noted."

"Are you sulking?" Miles asked. "You sound like you are."

I was mid-sigh when he said this, and I scowled into my coffee. "Am not."

"Maybe stick to movies you've already seen? You don't feel the need to spoil them on your second watch." I could hear him banging around his kitchen, which was his night-time charade: pretending he was going to cook before he gave up and had something delivered. "Anyway, there's nothing in my fridge, so I got to get dinner. But keep me posted on the date stuff. And let me know when you're coming to visit."

"A little late for the early-bird buffet," I joked. "You missed first crack at the Jell-O."

"Hardy, har, har," he said. But he was actually laughing when he hung up.

I dumped my half-full mug down the drain. Maybe tonight I'd sleep instead of bang my head against the same facts. Maybe tomorrow things would be clearer.

16

From the door of her classroom Ms. Gregoire's dress looked red striped with beige, but as I approached her desk before school on Monday, it became clear it was a beige dress, encircled by a print of red snakes. It made me think of "The Speckled Band." It made me smile.

Or maybe it was hope that pried out my dimples, because standing in this room with our matching Cool Beans cups and the promise of her help on my project, I felt the buoyancy of possibility. I just needed to sell her on my idea.

"Good morning." She lifted her pink cardboard cup in salute. "Pull up a chair and let's come up with some ideas to get Headmaster Williams off your back."

"Actually, I have one." I dragged a desk over and sat. "I know he expects me to just film people saying good things about the school. But what if instead of Hero High propaganda, I did something deeper about the school's reputation internally and externally?"

She leaned forward. "What would that look like?"

"I'd ask people a list of questions. 'What's the first thing you think of when you hear "Hero High"?' That sort of thing. And then I'd do an overlay with the facts versus perception." I was assuming a certain guy with mad photo skills would be willing to teach me how to do that. "For example, if someone says it's a school for rich kids, that would be countered by a caption listing the percent of students receiving financial aid."

"Who are you asking?"

I put on a poker face. "A variety of people: current students, alumni, teachers. Kids from other schools: Aspen Crest, Mayfield, Chester High..."

"I like it." She clinked her coffee against mine, and I almost dropped the cup in relief. Luckily I held on to it. I wasn't sure if breaking the "only water" rule was bad enough to be Headmaster Williams's third strike, but I had no desire to find out. Also, it would've been a tragic waste of caffeine.

I drained the rest of my coffee as Ms. Gregoire asked, "What do you need from me?"

I grinned. "First, a phone call."

"Hey, Bancroft! Banny!" He was ahead of me in the hall, and there were still a few minutes before first period. It was "Banny" that made him turn, eyebrows raised in amusement.

"Hey Huck." He held up his hand for a high five, then proceeded to make it all sorts of complicated by adding a press of the back of our hands, a fist tap, and a tug into a one-armed bro hug. I would've felt awkward not knowing the parts, but all I'd had to do was raise my hand; he did the rest of the work. And when he finished, I felt like I'd been initiated into some sort of club. Maybe this was all it took; maybe the only thing holding me back from making friends at Hero High had been *me*. My lack of engagement or initiative. He grinned. "I thought I left that nickname back at Mayfield—who spilled?"

"The Cavendish twins." I was keeping careful watch on his body language, but he just nodded.

"Man, Wink and Win." He shook his head. "How are those guys? I need to stop by and see Win. It's been too long."

There wasn't any malice in his nostalgia, so I pushed ahead. "They might transfer here."

"Get out. That'd be cool. More of the old gang back together. Is Wink still a complete monster at games? Like, that girl takes competition to a whole new level. We used to fight over whose team she'd be on whenever we played anything with remotes or gameboards. She was a card shark on field trip busses too."

"I've never played with her." But I was filing that information away for future use. "I'm closer with Win."

"Oh. *Oh*. I got you." Bancroft grinned—and fine, he might still be a suck-up in class, but he was cool with me and seemed to be cool with Win too. He looked so pleased by the idea of us together that I didn't correct him.

I tried to sound casual. "He said he might've annoyed you by joking about your name?"

"What? Nah, it's all good. Middle school stuff." Bancroft shrugged. "I got to get to class, but tell him I say hi. And no more of that 'Banny' business, 'kay?"

"'Kay." I mirrored his speech to create a sense of inclusiveness and was the one to initiate the handshake sequence.

"You're a cool guy, Huck," said Bancroft as he walked away backward. "We should hang more. Bring Win."

Was this a sign that I really hadn't given this school a chance to let me in? Regardless, Win would be relieved that Banny had shown zero signs of resentment. I nodded. "Let's do it."

The Cavendishes' front door was cracked open when I walked over after orchestra practice. And clearly I was reading too much Sherlock, because my first stomach-clenching thought wasn't "carelessness," but "crime scene." Like an idiot, I'd gotten out a pen and nudged the door open without touching—like I was a character in a police drama, avoiding contaminating a scene with fingerprints. Instead of blood or bodies, I got boys. Two. Seated on the couch. For an irrational half second, that seemed worse. One was Win, but the other person holding a controller wasn't Curtis. I frowned. So much for being grounded. And if Win wasn't grounded, why hadn't he texted to let me know? At least when he broke the rules with me, he did so for a purpose. We didn't sit around and play video games.

A white guy who was medium tall with a medium build and medium brown hair hit Pause. He leaned over the back of the couch and held out his hand. "Hey, I'm Morris. You've got to be Huck."

The nod and thumbs-up he gave Win weren't nearly as subtle as he thought. I grinned. "Yup. Hi. You're the friend, right?"

Morris playfully puffed out his chest. "*The* friend? I like the sound of that."

"Dude, who says that?" But Win was pleased. Ducking

his chin into the collar of his gray pullover to hide a smile. "You want a friendship bracelet? Ask Wink."

"Hey now." Mad hot or not, I wasn't letting Win's casual sexism slide. Also, I hadn't spent hours learning fancy knots to skip a chance to brag about it. "I make a pretty mean friendship bracelet. Ask my BFF, Rory, to show you sometime."

Morris laughed. "Oh, I like this one. I hope you stick around."

Win raised a hand to his face, and I was glad he was down to one small bandage on his knuckles, plus a few mostly healed scrapes. "You two are not allowed to team up against me."

"No promises," I told him as I slid my shoes off. "You ungrounded?"

"Nope. If my parents catch him, we'll say he's here to see Wink. Super easy lie."

"It's not *un*true," said Morris quickly.

"Sure." Win held up his remote. "Morris's parents have confiscated all his games until next report card—but technically these aren't *his* games."

"Nice loophole," I said.

"And technically I'm only playing for Wink while she finishes something."

"What's she finishing?" If Wink was as competitive as Bancroft said, it was hard to believe she'd let anyone sub in.

"Her homework." Win unpaused the game. But instead of resuming play, he fired at the other avatar. The words "Game Over" showed up amid the bullet holes dotting the screen.

"You just shot me!" exclaimed Morris.

"Whoops." Win held up his hands—remote included—in an exaggerated shrug.

"Jerk," Morris teased. There were all sorts of good-humored implications in his eyebrows. "Was that a not-so-subtle hint to go bug Wink and leave you two alone?"

Win patted his shoulder. "You're a good friend, Morris. I'll have Huck start your bracelet right now."

"Yeah," he said with a snort as he got up. "I'm sure that's exactly what you'll be doing."

I waited until Morris was in Wink's room, then asked, "Rough day?"

It hadn't been in his words or his expression, but in his posture. He softened in the space of blinks; it was like watching a stop-motion movie of him lowering his guard. "I kept looking around my classroom, the halls, the lunchroom—and wondering how many people there hate me. And who hates me *enough* to do this? Who's going to hate me *next* based on whatever twisted post goes up? Who's going to be hurt next?"

I thought of his last question on Saturday—when he'd been wishing for a tattletale, because he feared punishment less than causing pain. And when I said, "I'm sorry," I meant it, but I knew he was looking for permission to take the page down, or asking me to—and I couldn't give him that. Without a villain to point to, he didn't get to stop playing that role and exonerate himself.

Win sighed. "Fine. Let today's questioning begin."

But the door opened first—and I watched Win go pale, so clearly he wasn't as blasé about his grounding as he pretended. It was Curtis, mud-caked and whistling. "You're here again?"

Instead of answering, I asked, "How was practice?"

"Slippery." He must've removed his shoes outside, but

now he peeled off his sweatshirt as well as whatever layers he had underneath. "Are your visits going to become a daily thing?"

I let Win be the one to field that question. He shrugged. "Get used to it. And put some clothes on."

"Jealous?" Curtis patted his chest—he was taller than Win, but thinner. Lean, with runner's muscles, while Win had the broad shoulders of a swimmer. He threw me a wink before schooling his expression into a very fake scowl and turning to his brother. "Personally, I don't care if you're playing doctor or detective—I just don't want to walk in on my Knight Light adoptee making out with my brother."

Win was glaring, but I was biting back a laugh. Curtis was a *horrible* actor. He was barely containing his own grin—how could Win not know this was all fake disapproval? And what could I do to make it so their relationship functioned in a way where Curtis's *approval* wouldn't make Win like me less?

"Good thing you're so busy overachieving that you're never here." I doubted Win meant for his retort to be so telling, but I filed away those echoes of resentment and envy and loneliness. I could work with that.

But maybe I didn't need to—because the glance Curtis threw my way as he bent to strip off his socks looked a lot like we were on the same page. "All I can say is, Huckleberry better fix this, or—"

Win braced himself for the threat to come, his toes turning in and his jaw hardening as he prepared his counterattack.

Curtis made a fake whip out of a wet sock and lashed the air in front of him. "Or he should find himself a new Knight Light."

Win waited for me to laugh first—and his was soft and

hesitant, like he was worried he'd misread his brother's joke and was double-checking it wasn't the setup for him being the punchline.

"Just saying," added Curtis as he bundled up his clothes. "And if you need another incentive, you get him in Hero High, Huckleberry, and the two of you can spend all your time together—even when he's grounded—without having to duck out back doors."

"Working on it," I said, and he answered, "Good."

Win blinked back his surprise. While Curtis teasing him about Hero High wasn't new, I wondered if he'd ever explicitly stated that he *wanted* Win there—or had Win spent the time since Curtis's enrollment feeling not good enough *and* not welcome?

Curtis bowed at us. "Now, if you'll excuse me, I'm off to make the shower Win just cleaned super dirty."

I gave zero cares if he was being supportive because he felt bad about the iLive page or because Win was finally letting him. All that mattered was that Win was looking at his brother's retreating back like he'd saved the day.

When he turned to me, I pivoted my plans. "Want to go for a walk?"

"Where to?" But he was already grabbing his sneakers. "I have to be back before six."

"Hero High." His hands paused on his laces, and he looked up at me for more answers. "I need still photos of campus for my video. I was hoping you'd help."

"Oh." He nodded slowly. "Okay, let me grab my camera."

The shower was already running, so I asked, "Should we let Wink and Morris know we're leaving? Would it be weird to interrupt them?"

Win snorted. "The only thing we'd interrupt would be him not helping with math. She's better than he is."

I wasn't sure Morris would agree, but I didn't have enough data points to be certain. And I hadn't seen Wink interact with him, so I had zero idea if there was anything reciprocal. Either way, this seemed enough like Miles's complaining about me and movie spoilers that I opted to keep my fledgling prediction to myself, pending further evidence.

I did need photos, but I also knew Win felt more comfortable with a task. So I let him hide behind lenses, waiting until we'd reached the end of the avenue leading to the campus before I tackled today's topic. "I should've asked this earlier when we were first talking suspects, but... exes—do you have any?"

The steady clicking of his camera paused, but he didn't lower it. "Isn't talking about exes a dating taboo?" He turned away to focus on the school sign. "Good thing we're not, huh?"

Yeah, there was absolutely zero chance I was answering that. "So, no ex-boyfriends?"

"No, of course there are."

My cheeks flushed, and I started down the sidewalk, knowing he'd catch up after he finished his shot. He was "of course" and I was "none." The closest I'd come to a relationship was pretending to date Rory to make Toby jealous. In my defense, it had worked.

His camera was lowered when he came up beside me, his voice calmer. "The only one I was serious about—well, eighth-grade serious—was Mackenzie Smith."

"How long were you guys together?" My chest tightened, and it loosened only as I watched him have to think about that answer. But if he'd had it ready would that mean something different, or just mean he *was* someone different? Not everyone's life was a catalog of data.

"Six? Seven—no, eight. Maybe eightish months."

I swallowed. Clearly all my fears about the difference in our experience were valid. He might not have an exact number, but it was long. I looked around the campus, which I'd watched change from a sweaty September to a picturesque-foliage fall, through a snow-capped winter, to now, when the lawn was coming up green, the trees were budding, and tulips were starting to emerge. He'd been with Mackenzie longer than I'd been at Hero High.

"Huh." Win tilted his head. Snapped a picture of whatever my expression looked like. "I'm just realizing that you're somebody's Mac. You're somebody's guy-who-moved-away."

I tried to keep my voice from sounding as gruff as I felt. "Mac moved?"

"Yeah. Last summer. I thought he'd be at Chester with me, but then his parents separated and his mom moved back to Chicago to live with her sister. He went with her."

"Do you guys still talk and stuff?" I turned away from his lens, wanting to sound casual, but I didn't remember what casual sounded like.

"Not really. We broke up before he left. We texted a little in the fall. By December it was just 'Merry Christmas' and stuff. You know how it is."

I didn't.

"You don't think..." He straightened from where he'd been crouched, taking wide-angle shots of the stone buildings across the quad. "Is there a way to look at the friend list? I don't want him to—"

"We'll check." I was making mental comparisons to his

tone from earlier. Did he care more about Mac seeing "his" page than he had other people? I reassured myself that if there were residual feelings, he'd be awkward talking to me about his ex. Right?

"So..." He fussed with his camera. "Who's Mac for you? Or whose Mac are you?"

Boomerangs' original use were as hunting weapons, not as Nerf backyard toys or Australian souvenirs. And that question was definitely the OG type of boomerang, because it came back around and clobbered me. I picked my way around the circle drive toward the administration building, wondering if I could offer Win these facts instead of an answer. Because even if he thought they were off topic and weird, at least he wouldn't find *me* so.

I licked my lips and put my hands in my pockets, too aware of his camera and that he could be capturing all my hesitance and insecurity. "I don't have one."

He lowered the camera so it rested on its worn strap around his neck. "Get real."

"I am."

The line appeared above one eyebrow. "But—look at you. You're like corn-fed cover-model dimpled all-American poster boy. How is it possible—"

"Small town, big personality." And a tendency toward unrequited or celebrity crushes.

"No exes?"

Maybe I would've lied, but his voice wasn't judgmental. I shook my head. "Do you have others?"

We circled the library, caught the first glow of sunset on the science building's greenhouse as he answered. He'd had one: Shiloh—who was now at Hero High. "It was end of seventh grade. He lives a town over—and then summer vacation happened. It was one of those things where we could never get our parents to drive us, so it was like a month between the time we did mini-golf and then the next time we saw each other at Morris's pool party." He shrugged and sat on the low stone wall outside the science building. "When Mac and I got together in the fall, things ended with Shi—not badly. But I doubt it was the greatest. I mean, I had no idea what I was doing. He was my first boyfriend. My first kiss. We didn't talk for a few weeks until we ended up getting partnered for something in social studies. And then it was... whatever. Normal?"

Back in Ohio no one seemed to care who I liked—maybe because I never dated. And maybe that gave them permission to forget I wasn't straight, or maybe they felt progressive for being my friend. Or maybe they truly liked me as a person and would've been happy for me if I found someone. But, Win had two exes. If someone wanted an outlet for their bigotry, he was an easy, brown-skinned target. I sat beside him. "Can you think of anyone who was upset that you were dating guys?"

He flicked a button on his camera and began to scroll through the images he'd taken. They were gorgeous. I knew he wasn't ignoring my question; he was processing it, giving it the serious focus it deserved. "What do you think of this one?" He leaned closer so I could see a photo of the Convocation Hall that seemed to glow.

"Wow."

"Yeah, they don't call this the 'golden hour' for nothing. This light is amazing." He lowered the camera and tugged his bottom lip. "It's not like I didn't consider homophobia, because how could I not? But I don't think so. The posts you and Wink have shown me have nothing to do with me being gay. Do others?"

"None of them." I'd searched the first time I had control of her laptop. But maybe the things the idiot behind the keyboard *hadn't* mentioned were more significant. "What about race?"

"I mean, it could be?" Win spun some setting on his camera, then took another few shots of the statue of Reginald R. Hero. "It could be *anything*, but...I don't know. Why pick *me*? My school's pretty diverse. Both Mayfield and Chester have lots of Brown kids. And it comes up, sure, but it's less 'go back to where you came from' and more people asking if I have family that'd be impacted by travel bans. Or elementary school family tree/heritage projects."

"I hate to ask..." Because here I was again, making him relive his past traumas. "But are there any awful experiences that stick out?"

He tugged at his hair. "The one that hurt most isn't even that bad. I think I was just young and surprised."

I pulled my knee up on the wall and turned to face him. I didn't need to do either of those things to follow every nuance of his body language or the story, but it was a perception thing, a respect thing—I wanted to emphasize my giving him my full attention. "What happened?"

He was still clutching his camera, but his fingers were stiff, and his eyes looked unfocused as he gazed at the campus, so I knew he wasn't scouting more shots. "I was, like, ten. Nine? We were all on the playground. Not just my grade, because Curtis was there too. Maybe it was a fire drill? And this girl asked if I rode a camel to school. She said, 'That's what your people do, right?' and made some crack about dung beetles. Everyone laughed."

I could picture it too well. The scrawny boy from the family photos in their hall standing in a line by a swing set while some girl showed off her best Egyptian stereotypes. What I couldn't picture was his reaction. "What did you do?"

"Nothing," he admitted. "I froze. But Curtis said, 'Nope. But do *you* ride a broom? That's what *your* people do, right?'"

I snorted. "Of course he did."

Win shook his head, rolling his neck back to look at the sky. "I was so mad at Curtis. Like, why couldn't I come up with that comeback? Why did I need my big brother to defend me?"

"Wait—" Something pinged in my memory. This might be a stretch, but I fumbled in my pocket for my phone. "The girl—the camel girl—was it Ava Jones?"

Win's eyebrows shot up. "Okay, I know you're good—but how'd you know?"

I found the screenshots I'd taken of the iLive page and scrolled to the one of the first post from Halloween: the girl in a witch costume. "Check out this caption. Who else was on the playground that day?"

His lips moved as he silently read the words: *I thought the point was to wear costumes*. It wasn't exactly the same as Curtis's retort, but it traded on the same theme. Win's eyes were wide. "Everyone was on the playground. The whole school. I don't have a clue who would've heard or remembered—I hadn't thought of that in years."

But clearly someone had. I stared at him, trying to find answers in his stunned expression. While he didn't think his race or sexuality were motives, they couldn't be ruled out either.

"Huck Baker? What are you still doing here?"

I spun around to see my favorite teacher headed toward us. She was carrying a bag and had a green coat buttoned over her serpent dress.

"Hey, Ms. Gregoire. I was just—or rather, *he* was just—taking pictures for the video."

"Ah, very good." She smiled and shifted her gaze to the boy who'd stood up beside me and was straightening his coat. "May I see?"

"This is Winston Cavendish," I said. "Win, this is Ms. Gregoire. I'm working with her on the video and Sherlock..." I trailed off, just in case the magic theory was right. I didn't know if there was a jinx in acknowledging it.

"Hi." He awkwardly held out his hand, then offered her his camera. "Curtis talks about you a lot. So does Lance. And Eliza. Everyone, really."

She'd taken the camera but kept her focus on him. "I'm going to assume they're saying only delightful things. But coincidentally, I'm coming from a meeting where we were just talking about *you*."

I watched Win's throat as he swallowed. "Oh."

"There's been some confusion on the admissions committee about the status of your application." Her eyes dipped to the camera to give him a moment, then widened as she scrolled. "These are stunning. I always say the campus is the ugliest in March—mud everywhere and nothing's blooming—but you've filled these shots with such care and beauty. It's possible they've answered my question."

"What is it?" I asked, because I'd rather she save the

dramatic pauses for the classroom, not afternoons when I'd already put Win through an emotional gauntlet.

"Has your application been rescinded?" she asked. "Or would you still like to be considered for admission next year?"

"He would. He definitely would." But she didn't acknowledge me and instead looked from the photos to Winston.

He was shifting his weight, looking overexposed without his camera. "Yeah," he said slowly. "Yes, I would."

"Good. I'm glad to hear it. There are still two meetings left and a few roster slots we're dithering over. I'll make sure your interest is noted next time the committee meets."

It took a beat before Win accepted either thing she offered: the camera she was holding out, or the hope. He clutched the first to his chest and sat on the wall, sounding breathless when he said, "Thank you."

She nodded and pulled her car keys out of her bag. "Good night boys. I hope you both find whatever you're looking for."

Win's half smile had faded before her footsteps. It was gone entirely before her car had pulled out of the lot. "Let's not tell my parents. There's no reason to get their hopes up."

More Cavendish secrets.

I held out a hand to help him up. "We can wait if you want, but I don't know that I'd *ever* bet against Ms. Gregoire."

17

While Ms. Gregoire had happily coordinated the visits I needed for my video project, she'd warned me that the heads of the other schools had all been various degrees of smug when they'd agreed. It wasn't one of *their* students who'd cause a viral scandal.

I was keeping this in mind as Mom pulled up in front of Chester High. "This feels a little like a first day of school, doesn't it?" she asked when I hesitated with my fingers on the door handle.

I nodded, not taking my eyes from the brick front of the massive school.

"Well, you'll do great. Knock 'em dead, and I'll pick you up at noon." She patted my knee, and I took a deep breath and pushed the door open.

I hadn't realized how dependent I'd become on my uniform. Hadn't realized how much it felt like armor. Or how uncomfortable I'd feel without it. Walking into this school in jeans and a Henley was like changing out of pajamas for the first time after being home sick. Maybe I shouldn't have worn my blue oxfords? It's one thing to have shoes with presence when they're your only piece of flair in a sea of dark blazers and school ties, but I wasn't sure I wanted to stand out at Chester.

Officially I was here to talk to a few classes about the perils of social media. That was my entrance fee for getting access to ask students about Hero High for my project. I'd already emailed the video permissions waiver Ms. Gregoire and I created, and hopefully there'd be overlap between the students who'd gotten theirs signed and the group I wanted to talk to. If not, I'd have to get creative. Because unofficially, I had a list of the eleven Chester High students mentioned on the iLive page. If I had to talk off-record, that should be fine. The upside of a memory like mine was that while video would be proof for others, I didn't typically need it. Except, nothing about this was *typical*.

I mentally reviewed my three official questions while waiting in line at the main office.

What do you think of Hero High?

If you had to describe it in one word, what would you say?

How did you form your opinion, or what influenced it?

Principal Nunes stepped out of his office as I signed in with the harried woman at the front desk who was trying to juggle late passes and phone calls and a badge printer that kept jamming.

He grinned, and Ms. Gregoire's warning proved instantly apt when he said, "It's Hero High's own Michael Moore."

I kept my face neutral. "My name is Huck Baker, sir."

"No, I know." His smile faded. "You know, Michael Moore? The documentary filmmaker?"

I did know, but I continued to stare blankly. I'd figured out long ago that nothing deflated criticism faster than feigned confusion. It was hard to make a joke at someone's expense if you had to explain the critique. Or maybe it was that giving someone a moment to reflect on their words or asking them to explain an insult to your face flipped the script so they had to take ownership of their meanness, and it suddenly didn't seem so funny.

"Anyway. Mrs. Evans is expecting you. Second period starts in three minutes." He gave me directions and a stern "I hope you've learned your lesson and are making better choices." Then I was turned loose in Win's school. Left to wonder if he was behind any of the classroom doors I passed, or which of the lockers held his belongings.

I knocked on room 205. Mrs. Evans had a loud voice but timid eyes. Her makeup was too pale for her skin tone—making me wonder if the tan was new or if her bathroom lighting was too dim. I tried not to stare at the abrupt color change at her neck as she introduced me to her class. "Huck's going to talk about his experiences with social media. Then those of you who returned your waivers can speak to him on camera. I'll let him explain."

"Thanks." I stepped forward wearing a smile much brighter than the students' tepid applause warranted. But Erick of the dropped-ball gif was in here, so I aimed to charm. "A couple weeks ago, I got bored in science class..."

I'm pretty sure second period's takeaway from my talk was that a viral video made me famous. That I still got almost-daily calls and invitations from news media. It wasn't the message I'd been aiming for, but since the half of the class who hadn't already returned their waivers were texting their parents so they could be in my next video, I wasn't complaining. And maybe I should've felt worse, but I hadn't said anything they couldn't get from watching any of a hundred iLive VidChannels where the hosts confused cruelty and comedy in their desperate race to get followers and clicks. Anyone who thought my experiences were aspirational was missing an empathy gene.

Their interviews were good—good in the sense they were a perfect decoy, and I could edit them into what I needed to placate Headmaster Williams. They also provided me with an opening to meet Erick, who I conveniently assigned the last slot so I could run out of time and get his contact info to "follow up later."

But the hour also felt dishonest and was only half the story—it didn't include things like how I'd heard Clara tell Rory that on her last visit to see her dad, someone recognized her from the meme and shouted, "Do it! Raise your hand."

I'd caused that. So I changed what I said to the third-period class. This time focusing on the social cost for Clara and me. On the permanence of the video and our lack of control with how it was manipulated.

After class I waved off Mrs. Evans's offer to walk me back to the office. Because I wasn't headed to the office; I was going to the cafeteria.

Lunch was in full roar when I entered—emphasis on "roar." Chester High was triple the size of my Ohio school. Six times bigger than Hero High. Despite this, one of the first people I saw was Erick.

He stepped out of the lunch line. "Hey man, are we finishing that interview now?" He brushed his long hair out of his face with the same futile optimism I'd watched him display the twenty-seven times he'd made that gesture during class. And just like then, it fell back in his eyes within seconds.

"Nah." I shook my head and smiled. "We'll catch up

later—it's too loud in here. But I'm looking for someone. Do you know Winston Cavendish?"

There was zero malice in his eager nod. He scanned the room, pointed. "He's at that table by the window. The third one from the far wall."

Either Erick didn't know about his ball-drop gif or he didn't care. Either way, he spoke about Win way too nonchalantly for a grudge-holder. "I see him. Thanks."

"No problem." He paused, then added, "If there's anything you want me to do—you know, fall off a chair, spill a drink over myself, trip while holding my tray—let me know."

Yeah, if he was volunteering his humiliation in the hope of going viral, he wouldn't have minded the gif. Or maybe the thing he minded was that it hadn't made him internet famous? Either way, I was crossing him off the list. "Thanks, I'm all set."

His face fell as he stepped back into line, but I cared very little about his disappointment. He could become a famous fool on someone else's time; I still had ten people to track down and only half an hour left.

I knew who was next: Kiara—or, as I referred to her as I intercepted her on the way back from the trash, "Wait, are you hair-dye girl?"

She looked at me like I was more disgusting than the bin she'd just dumped her lunch in. "Excuse me?"

"From that iLive page?" I added. "I was named 'most likely to be forgotten.'" It was an easy lie, one that created a shared community and eased the tension out of her expression.

"Oh." She self-consciously touched her neck, where purple and green streaks had faded until they were barely distinguishable from her black hair. "That's . . . awful."

"I'm Huck, by the way." I flashed some dimples. "In case you've 'forgotten,' Kiara."

Using her name had been deliberate, a way to further establish our connection, and there was a flash of panic on her face as she tried to come up with proof that she remembered me. "Um..."

There was zero need to prolong her discomfort. She couldn't be behind the page. If so, she would've had a different reaction to my made-up post. I smiled again. "Anyway, I like the hair. Just wanted to say that."

"Thanks, uh, Huck?"

"See you around." I stepped back and she darted to her table, face lit up with amusement and a good story to tell. I pulled out my phone. It had been buzzing, and a person who'd been sitting by the windows had stood.

What are you doing here? I looked from my phone to him. The text was sent by "Wink," but since he was holding the phone, it seemed safe to assume he'd borrowed hers.

I texted back: I have all the appropriate permissions. No forgeries. Well, I sorta did. Technically those permissions had expired at the end of third period. Close enough.

But what are you DOING HERE?

I'd spotted the next person on my list. I tapped out my answer as I started toward her. Working on my project.

I could see his frown from across the room. He put the phone down. Picked it back up. Don't call me that.

"You're from media class." A red-haired guy had approached while I was looking at my phone. "My parents just sent in my waiver. I forwarded it to your email. Want to interview me?"

Based on the reactions of the people I'd interacted with

so far, there really wasn't any reason I couldn't walk across the cafeteria and talk to Win. But he could've done that too—and he hadn't.

"Uh, I can't right now. Sorry." I was still frowning at Win's last message and typing my reply. Call you what? Meet me in the bathroom.

"That's okay," said the redhead. "I thought your talk—"

Win marched out of the room, which was great, except...

I turned back to the guy who'd been chatting this whole time. "Can you tell me where the bathroom is?"

"Yeah, sure." He grinned. "And you have my email if you need anything. I—I put my number on there too."

I nodded. "Bathroom?"

When his grin faded, I realized his enthusiasm wasn't about the video—he was hitting on me. Oh. If Win weren't waiting, I would've found a way to ease out of the conversation more gracefully, but instead I stared at the door and shifted my weight like I really needed to pee. Which, actually, after finishing my full thermos of coffee, wasn't untrue.

I called thanks for the directions then darted after Win, glad for the immediate hush of the hallway. More glad for the guy waiting by the sinks. He was wearing a scowl that he'd pasted over the smile he couldn't force from his eyes. I grinned at him. "Surprise."

"Don't call me your 'project.'"

I took a step back. "I didn't." I said it with a shrug that was totally at odds with how the weight of his interpretation felt on my shoulders. "I'm here for my Hero High video. If I happen to learn some things while at Chester, well, that's a lucky coincidence."

"Oh." Win's face heated. "Right. Of course you're not here for me. I swear I'm not super conceited."

"Well, you're the reason I started at Chester and not Aspen Crest or Mayfield. And you might've had some influence on the people I'm talking to."

Win lifted an eyebrow. "This is going to backfire so bad."

"Maybe," I said. "But no one but Wink even knows I know you, so..."

"So I should stop wasting your special undercover time and let you go play Clue?"

"You're never a waste of time," I told him. "Except, yeah, I really should go." Mom would be here in eighteen minutes. "But maybe you can help me edit the footage later?"

"Sure." Win brightened and nodded to the door. "So, I'll let you..."

"Actually..." I pointed to the urinals. "I've got to go." I sounded like a five-year-old. When I caught my reflection in the mirror, my cheeks were officially the same color as the pink antibacterial soap.

Win was laughing as he left, which was at least a better mood than the one he'd had when I'd entered. I mentally reprioritized as I zipped my pants and washed my hands. There was no way I'd get through my list, but I knew who was next and strode directly across the cafeteria. I stopped at the end of a lunch table, beside a girl with curly brown hair. "Reese, right?"

She smiled curiously and waved goodbye to the girl who had been sitting next to her but was getting up. "Do I know you?"

"No. I don't go here."

Her eyes turned wary as she reached for the teal-and-purple water bottle in front of her. It had a sticker from a rock gym on it, and her arms were toned in ways that made it clear she actually climbed. "How do you know my name?"

I needed to slow down; I couldn't rush my way into anyone's trust, but with only fifteen minutes left, I didn't have time for finesse. Also, Wink could show up any second. "Listen, I need to—"

"Huck?" My shoulders stiffened. Hers did too.

Not Wink. I'd forgotten there was another person at Chester High who knew I knew Win.

Morris clapped a hand on my shoulder. "Hey. I thought that was you I saw talking to—"

"Hey." I echoed his greeting while cursing internally.

He patted my shoulder again before smugly telling Reese, "This is Win's new boyfriend."

Her mouth dropped slightly as she gave me a once-over. She wasn't the only one doing so, since Morris had used his best oral-presentation voice and now everyone at the surrounding lunch tables was listening. I tried to scan them all, catalog everyone's faces and reactions for future identification, but I knew it was futile and the effort was making me awkward.

I focused on Reese, putting my back to everyone else so I wouldn't be distracted by my failure to observe them all. "We're not dating. Not yet. But here's hoping." I held up crossed fingers and paired the overly cheesy gesture with some dimples and self-deprecation. "I mean, can you blame me?"

She laughed. Apparently Morris vouching for me had

been key, so maybe his interruption wasn't that unwelcome. But I remembered what Win had said about these two, and she wasn't exactly eager to include him in our conversation. So I sat on the edge of the table, forming a shoulder wall between them. Not that he'd noticed. He was engrossed in conversation with a guy a few seats down.

"No, I can't blame you at all. I had a huge crush on Win—before I knew he was gay." Her smile flickered and she turned pink. "I—I can't believe I just admitted that."

"It's the dimples," I reassured her. "I've been told they cause confessional reactions. But I won't tell Win, and I don't think he has any clue."

"Really?" She glanced up quickly, eyebrows quirked. "Because I said something to Wink about it a few weeks ago. It's ancient news, and I meant it as a joke, but..."

I could fill in that ellipsis: *But then the iLive post had gone up.* She assumed it was his way of saying back off.

I shook my head. "Whenever he talks about you, Win only has good things to say. He thinks your whole family is pretty cool. Seriously, I know about your dad's middle name, and how your mom's superpower is making everyone feel welcome, and your dogs, and your brother, and your trampoline. So, I guess even if Wink did tell him, it didn't faze him."

"What was that about Wink?" Morris leaned over to ask. "Are you looking for her? She's taking a math test, right?"

Reese gave a we-weren't-talking-to-you nod.

"Win's around though. Does he know you're here?" Morris's forehead wrinkled. "Why *are* you?"

"Measuring for friendship bracelets." The weak joke earned me a weak chuckle—and enough time to figure out a response. "It's for a school project. But I have no idea where Win is. This school is so *big*."

Morris laughed for real this time. "Want me to go find him? He'd kill me if he finds out you were here and I saw you and he didn't."

I nodded. "That'd be great. It's such a pain his parents took away his cell phone."

"Tell me about it." Morris rolled his eyes as he stood. "But you better get used to it. It's constant."

I waited for him to get out of earshot before sliding into the empty seat next to Reese and dropping my voice. "Listen, I want to tell you something, but you can't tell anyone." I wished we could go somewhere less public, but her posture had stiffened as soon as I leaned in. She was about two seconds from screaming *Stranger danger!* "That post from Win's iLive—"

"Oh, that?" She waved a stiff hand and almost knocked over her water bottle. "Pretty funny, right?"

"No, it really wasn't." I took a deep breath. This was a huge risk, but I hoped it'd pay off. Not necessarily in leads, but in making things right with at least one person. "Here's the thing: Win didn't write it."

She raised an eyebrow, looking around to see why *I* was looking around. "Who did?"

"We don't know." More people were packing up and starting to move. The lunch bell would ring soon. Morris would be back with a very confused Win. My mom would be arriving. I still had nine people I hadn't talked to, but this felt more important. "You can't tell anyone he didn't do it—don't even tell him or Wink you know. But... they were really upset you'd think he wrote that."

She tightened her grip on her water bottle. "I never believed it."

I allowed her the lie. It was only another second before she grabbed my arm then leaned in to whisper, "Wait, does that mean the whole page is fake? Poor Win."

I nodded. Smart girl. I could see why Wink liked her, why Win respected her. She'd drawn this conclusion much faster than anyone else had connected the dots.

Too fast? I narrowed my eyes and scrutinized her.

"Look who I found!"

Both Reese and I turned to see Morris leading Win our way. He was wide-eyed, and that forehead wrinkle was in full force as he tried to figure out how he was supposed to react to me. His voice strained as he said, "Hey, Huck. You're at my school?"

"Yeah." Morris laughed. "He's working on a project. So apparently that fancy private school can't have everything if he needed to come here."

Reese wrinkled her nose. "You go to Hero High?" It was the same sort of tone I'd heard in about half my interviews today. A common theme in the one-word answers had been "snobby," "stuck-up," "elitist." But Reese's disdain could also be Wink related. I wondered if she knew her best friend's plans for sophomore year.

Not that I could ask. There weren't many people still at the lunch table, but they were watching us, waiting for me to respond—which meant I needed to pay attention and do that.

"Yeah, I do," I told Reese, then turned to the guys. "Hey, Win. Thanks for tracking him down, Morris."

The timer on my phone began to buzz, and I exhaled

in relief. "I've got to go, but—walk me out? Do you have time?"

Win smiled. "Yeah."

My phone chimed as I lay in bed going over the events of the day and trying to sort them in my mind: What information had I gained? Which suspects had been exonerated, and who had climbed higher on the probability list? What mistakes had I made? What had I done right?

It was the mistakes I was dwelling on. How many people had heard Morris label me Win's boyfriend, and did that ruin my chances for future interviews or undercover work? Should I have warned Win about the visit? Did I make him late to fourth period? I didn't get to ask after school, because Curtis had warned me his dad was coming home early to take Wink to the dentist, so I shouldn't stop by.

Was it a huge betrayal that I'd told Reese after I'd made them swear to secrecy? How would he react if he knew?

I grabbed my phone from my bedside table and swiped to log in. The chime had been an iLive alert, and I almost ignored it. But some impulse or instinct had me clicking over.

`Friend request accepted: Click to see Winston Cavendish's profile.`

18

Baker!" Bancroft stopped by my locker Wednesday morning. "I meant it about hanging out. Let's do it. You in?"

My day had started with Mom shaking the empty coffee canister and asking, "How in the world did we go through a five-pound bag of beans in a week?"

That question had been tragic; this one was...suspicious? Or maybe that was the lack of caffeine talking. I'd been so irritable all morning that Dad had plundered the can of cold brew from his own lunch and handed it to me. "I'm only doing this for the sake of your poor teachers and classmates."

Bancroft's question was standing in the way of my having time to chug it before art. Even so, I hesitated before answering. "Sure."

"Cool. Can I catch your number? I'll text to set something up. The guys were talking about doing something old-school this Saturday because there's no game." He paused to grin. "Take that Mayfield. They cut me and Elijah and Morris from the team, now Lij and I are starting at Hero High."

"Baseball?" I asked, wondering if I should've tried out

after all. Though when would I have had time, with all this sleuthing and not sleeping?

"Yup. You're looking at Hero High's second baseman. Anyway, this weekend—maybe laser tag or go-carts. You in?"

He handed me his phone, unlocked and open to a blank contact. But I'd typed in only half my name before I looked up. "Actually, can I ask you a favor?"

"Uh, maybe?" He looked cautious, and I can't say I blamed him. I doubted my tie was on straight, I had no clue what my hair looked like. Instead of any sort of grooming, I'd spent my post-shower morning searching for the backup bag of coffee I kept in my closet for making contraband French press. I'd found it under my lacrosse jersey. Empty. "Hit me with it and I'll let you know."

"I'm doing this video—"

"Dude, *another* one? Maybe...don't." He was eyeing his phone like he was going to snatch it from my hands.

"Nothing like the Milverton-Clara one," I clarified. "That's *why* I have to do it. Headmaster Williams wants a video that makes Hero High look good."

"Phew." He turned somber. "I gotta say—I'm glad Milverton's gone. We all feel bad we didn't notice the not-calling-on-girls thing. It's solid that you did—you know, except for the whole Clara part. And this punishment."

I paused, wondering who the "we" in "we all" meant. Regardless, I was glad. "Thanks. But the problem is, no one really trusts me with a camera right now."

"Say no more. I got you." He twirled his phone and shoved it into his pocket. "I'll get a bunch of people together—like a movie night, only we'll be making one, not watching. Bring Win and Wink if you want."

"Really?" Suspicion or caffeine withdrawal sharpened the word. This was almost *too* convenient, and nothing had been easy lately.

"Sure." He shrugged and held up his hand for the handshake routine as the first bell rang. "I'm sick of laser tag anyway. Sounds like this could be cool."

I didn't know about cool, but my thanks was sincere. And only slightly tinged by the regret that I'd run out of time to gulp down my pilfered coffee before art.

My other school visits weren't scheduled until Friday (Aspen Crest) and next week (Mayfield Middle), but I spent my morning classes thinking about yesterday. About last night. About the iLive page.

What did it mean that my friend request had suddenly been accepted? No way was it random. Had I met the person behind the page yesterday—or had they simply seen me from afar? Was it one of the people sitting within earshot when Morris announced I was "Win's new boyfriend"? Based on the latest posts, probably.

Because someone must have been watching me closely. Must've seen whom I'd talked to in the cafeteria. Must not have been happy about my conversation with Seamus; I'd learned his name from a post that deemed him `Most likely to be shocked EVERY DANG TIME he gets a sunburn. #PSYoureARedhead.`

I was on there too. The latest punch line in this twisted vengeance game. I scrubbed my hands over my eyes and groaned.

"Something the matter, Huck?"

Ms. Gregoire's question made Gemma and Mira giggle,

but when I dropped my hands, the rest of my classmates looked concerned.

"Headache." It wasn't a lie. Mine was pounding. Lack of sleep and lack of caffeine was a killer combination. I still had ninety-eight minutes until I could chug the bottle of cold brew in my locker.

"You can go to Nurse Peter if you'd like," Ms. Gregoire began. "But most headaches are caused by dehydration. Why don't you grab the pass and go get a drink." She turned toward the electronic whiteboard where she'd been writing a list of poetry terms then pivoted back. "Of *water*. The fountain's that way."

I sighed. I'd been trying to figure out the shortest route from this room to my lunch bag, which was the opposite direction than the one she'd pointed in. I kept my head down during the walk, rubbing the pressure points at the base of my neck, only looking up when I heard the splash of the fountain already in use.

My throat went dry. "Shiloh?"

He turned, wiping his mouth on the back of his hand. I tried not to stare at it—at the lips that had been Win's first kiss. We looked nothing alike. Shiloh was short and muscular, built like the wrestler he was. He had freckles, brown hair, darker skin. And the type of sincere smile that probably made strangers feel like friends. "Hey," he said. "I'm done if you want a drink."

I shook my head, trying to ignore the throb at my temples. Was he a lead, or a suspect? I hadn't had time to prepare, and maybe there was a more subtle way to approach this, but I blurted out, "Did you see the post on iLive?"

"On Win's page?" He nodded and palmed his phone, holding it out to me.

I didn't need to look; I'd spent enough time staring at it last night. It'd been posted an hour after Seamus's, ten minutes after a picture of the Convocation Hall (Not sure which is more toxic, Hero High culture, or the lead paint on their walls), and immediately *before* my friend request was granted.

It was a photo of Shiloh from the Mayfield yearbook, captioned The moment when you come across a picture of your 1st ex-boyfriend and wonder if he's gotten any better at kissing. Then look at your future ex-boyfriend and realize he only seems better in comparison. #BarWasSetLow

"I responded," he said.

"Oh." I grabbed the phone I'd previously rejected and scrolled to see what he'd written. You can stop wondering. I have. He'd paired it with a pucker-up emoji. I let out a shaky laugh.

"Wait. Are you the 'future ex'?" He smiled. "Sometimes Win has a strange sense of humor."

"You're not—you're not mad?"

Shiloh snorted. "No. We were in seventh grade. I was bad at kissing. One time I bit him; I'd read online it was hot. It wasn't. We had no idea what we were doing. We're lucky we escaped without, like, stitches to the tongue or totally alienating our friends—that middle school jealousy stuff is no joke."

I narrowed my eyes, scrutinizing him with an intensity that infuriated my headache. But I didn't see any hints of inauthenticity or bravado. He truly didn't care. "Jealousy stuff?"

He shrugged. "Wink wasn't cool with him beating her to 'first boyfriend.' Then suddenly everyone wanted one: Reese asked out Morris and he said no, and they started feuding. Seamus announced some big crush on me and felt all betrayed because he thought Win knew. Banny was annoyed I was texting Win all the time. Stupid, dramatic seventh-grade stuff."

"Huh." I made all sorts of mental notes for when I was caffeinated.

"Just to be clear," Shiloh added, "Win wasn't any better at kissing. I hope he's improved since then too."

"Me too," I said woodenly, realizing too late I'd revealed that we hadn't kissed and the post was a lie. I crossed my fingers he wasn't paying too close attention—and also hoped that if and when the chance for kissing arose, *I* wasn't horrible. I made another mental note: no biting. "I'm Huck, by the way."

It was a weird thing to say because Hero High was too small not to know the names of pretty much everyone. But we'd made it to late March without having a real conversation, and it felt like introductions usually occurred before discussions of kissing prowess.

"Shi." He stuck out a hand, maybe to shake, but I handed back his phone instead. "Bancroft was just saying you're doing some sort of video project and need help?"

I blinked. Bancroft worked fast. "It's this punishment for Headmaster Williams. I need people to say good things about the school."

"Count me in if you want. And tell Win I say hi." My eyes narrowed again. I was no longer worried about the case, but if Shiloh seemed too interested in his ex. My expression must not have been subtle, because he added, "And if Win's really super curious, tell him to call up Elijah. My boyfriend will definitely vouch for me."

I exhaled. Shiloh was in a relationship. With Bancroft's best friend, Elijah. I hadn't known he was queer or whom he was dating—but now I got how Shi had heard about the video. And if he had his own boyfriend, I doubt he wanted mine.

Not that Win was mine. Yet. Despite what whoever wrote the post believed. I extended my arm for the handshake I'd brushed off before, adding, "I'm glad our paths crossed." And based on the Hero High Pride pin on his blazer, they would've much sooner if I'd ever followed Clara's suggestions to attend the meetings. I'd make the next one.

"Me too," said Shiloh. "But I gotta get back to class."

It took all my effort to keep my face neutral until he was out of sight, then I leaned over the cool metal of the water fountain and laughed. Okay. Fine. I was officially on Team Magic Teacher, because I never would've come here if Ms. Gregoire hadn't suggested it, and the timing was too impeccable to be coincidental. Sherlock, of course, would disagree. Would find some statistical probability or rational explanation.

All I knew was I headed back to class with a new connection, new clues, and a headache that had suddenly disappeared.

19

If Seamus hadn't appeared in an iLive post, I probably wouldn't have given him a second thought. But then Shiloh mentioned him too, and now he'd entered my mind like an invasive species, chasing me down rabbit holes—like whether he still held a grudge about Win "stealing" Shiloh, or if he was over the seventh-grade drama. The post about him had been unusually tame: clue or red herring? I added him to my list of questions without answers as I opened Win's door.

"Hey," I said with a grin. How long would it take for the thrill of Win to wear off? Just the fact that I could see him, just the shape of the back of his head—all these things that Sherlock would forbid me to feel but that for the first few seconds after I entered his house I couldn't stop feeling.

"Hi." Win turned toward me, and my stomach dropped faster than the book bag that fell from my fingers.

"What happened?" I pointed at his eye where red was bleeding into blue and purple.

"A fist," he answered. "Cole Martin's."

I'd heard that name for the first time a few hours ago, when I'd cornered Curtis before Convocation and shown him the latest iLive post.

He'd whistled. "Cole's got a temper." And if Curtis had known that immediately, had the person behind the page? Had they posted a picture of him with his finger knuckle-deep in his nose, captioned `Future archaeologist`, knowing he'd come out swinging?

"Not that I even knew about the post Cole thinks I wrote until *after* he hit me." Win shook his head, wincing a little. "But don't worry, even after the pummeling, I didn't tell him the truth."

I flinched. I'd told Reese. Had told her to keep it from him and her best friend. What gave me the right to play god with his safety, while telling him to keep his mouth shut? "Do you need some ice? Tylenol?"

"No. Morris took off for the nurse as soon as it happened. I've had ice on it for hours. And hours to think about how much more pissed Cole's going to be when he gets back to school after his five-day suspension."

"Then that's our new deadline. We'll either solve this by next Wednesday"—I tried to inject my voice with confidence as I shaved forty-eight hours off our timeline, tried not to absorb the lack of it on his face—"or if we can't, we expose the page as fake and take it down."

The relief that unknotted his shoulders was unmistakable, though he attempted to make his voice gruff when he said, "Good. That'll save *me* the suspension from when someone tells Principal Nunes why Cole punched me."

I hadn't considered the personal cost Win would pay from that page staying active. I'd focused on the posts as clues, not threats. I thought it would be easier for him knowing the reason for people's misplaced anger; he no longer had to internalize the blame. The gaslighting was over.

But the fallout was not. And my lack of foresight was cold. Sherlockian.

I turned to where he was sitting, forcing myself not to flinch or look away from his bruises. He was pinching his bottom lip again, rubbing it between his thumb and pointer. And it looked soft—

No. Focus. *Stop.*

"Stop what?" Win dropped his hand and looked at me sideways. Apparently I'd said that out loud.

"Stop with the—" I pointed in case he didn't know where his mouth was and in case I didn't already look like a complete fool. "It's just...you rub your bottom lip. And it's stupid hot and I'm trying to focus."

"Then maybe that's a sign you should take a break from doing your freaky super-observer tricks on me."

I winced. *Freaky super-observer* had to be the worst superhero name in the history of How to Make a Guy Lose Interest in You. "I can't. It's just how my brain works." Overactive enough to be exhausting for me and everyone around me, but not smart enough to solve this. "I can stop telling you what I observe if it helps."

Win groaned. "No. That's worse. Then you'll have this whole stash of info on me and I won't even know it."

Yeah, I already had that. But I wisely didn't point this out. "I promise not to use it for nefarious purposes."

Win's forehead creased before he looked away.

And it was only because of my "super-observer tricks" that I could reverse engineer the explanation. He didn't know what "nefarious" meant, and growing up with Curtis had made him sensitive to displays of intelligence. I needed a way to turn the tables—make him the expert. Make him smile.

I rubbed the back of my neck, then asked, "Does Hudson ever come out of his cage?"

Win blinked. "How is that related to the case?"

"It's not. Can he play fetch or something?"

Win's mouth slowly unfurled in a grin. "He's not a dog. But yeah, he can come out as long as we watch him and clean up after him." He stood. "Move the coffee table and roll up the rug while I get him."

I wouldn't have predicted I'd spend the afternoon sitting wide-legged on the Cavendishes' floor, trying to lure Hudson away from Win with apple slices. Him laughing at his pet's stubborn loyalty—or lack of spatial awareness, since it looked like Hudson was too brainless to figure out how to get from Win's lap to mine.

"If you could eat just one food or drink for the rest of your life, what would it be?" His answer was ramen.

Mine—coffee—inspired me to stand and make a cup. I selected a mug and loaded a pod into the machine before Win came up with his question, which he asked in a quiet rush.

"What's your coming-out story?"

Was it meant to be a loaded question? To make me expose memories as painful as those I was constantly asking him to reveal? If so, he was going to be disappointed. I set my mug in position and hit the button. Just the sight of steaming caffeine loosened my chest.

"I don't have any big moment. Not the type people talk about or that I've seen on TV. I mean, I was nervous—how could I not be? I sat my parents down three different times, but then chickened out of telling them. When I finally did, they were like 'we know'—and it was pretty anticlimactic." I gave him a sheepish grin, but his face was unreadable. "But

I'm lucky. My parents were always clear that all loves were equal. And I've always loved boys and girls equally."

I took a sip of coffee as I mentally replayed what I said, then choked on it as the implications of the sentence hit me.

Win moved to the other side of the island, Hudson held in one hand, tucked close to his chest. "Don't spew on us."

"Um, not that I've actually been in love." My voice was rough from coughing. "I wasn't saying that I—or you—"

Win bit his bottom lip, but the corners of his mouth were turned up in trapped laughter. "It's cool. I didn't think you were making a big declaration."

"Yeah, let's just..." I stared into my mug and debated whether it was possible to drown myself in the remaining two inches of coffee or better to gulp them quick and get a refill. The second option sounded better, so I swapped out the coffee pod while draining my cup. Win was watching me, head tilted in amusement until I said, "You didn't give your answer."

"Oh. Same. I told my family and no one cared."

But there were miles of difference between no one being upset and no one caring. I could point that out, push for more information than he'd volunteered—or I could ask a gentler question. But before I could do either, my phone dinged with the alert I'd set up. "There's a new post."

When Sherlock looked for clues, he found blood on windowsills, footprints in muddy fields. He analyzed tree growth and the hats of mugging victims. Just once I'd like to see how he'd handle digital evidence. Maybe he'd find that cyber footprints weren't as easy to follow as physical ones.

"How do you know?" Win pointed at the phone and

raised his eyebrows, or attempted to. The swelling on the left side of his face made them crooked.

"As of last night, we're friends. I mean, it's iLive official, so we must be." I held up the post. It was a group shot of a few dozen people in formal wear: the girls in white dresses and the boys in green Mayfield blazers, navy pants, and ties. It was the sort of post I should take to Wink, because in response to "Who's the girl whose face is replaced with a poop emoji?" Win had squinted, then shrugged.

"It's funny you think I'd have a clue. It's from graduation though."

Win put Hudson in his cage when he got Wink from her room. I tried not to read into the parallels: freedom time was over. Like the rodent, we were back to being trapped. She'd known immediately. "That's Colleen Allen."

I knew the name, it just took me a second to place it. "Goes to Aspen Crest and hates crickets?"

I got that they were twins; obviously fraternal, which meant they were no more genetically similar than Wink and Curtis or me and Miles. But there were times that felt untrue, like when they both turned toward me after she asked, "Need anything else?" Or how they'd leaned toward each other without looking. An eerie synchronicity.

I told her no thanks and watched her pass the plaster handprint molds hanging in the hallway. Curtis's was framed separately, but "Winston" and "Lincoln" shared one. They shared so much more than I could ever understand—including nonverbal communication in the glance they'd exchanged before she shut her bedroom door.

"What aren't you telling me about Colleen?"

"She isn't my favorite person." Win had used the same

wording when we'd gone through the yearbook. I'd let it go then; now I waited him out. "She accused me of cheating at the end of last year."

"Why?"

"Well, I guess technically I was?" He flipped his palms up. "Mac and I were copying Morris's social studies homework."

"So, not technically, but actually?" I teased.

"Yeah, but the teacher didn't collect or go over it. He'd just check off that you had it at the start of class." Win looked more annoyed by this time waste than he did by Colleen. "Because she told, we all missed the class trip to a Phillies game. I didn't care, but it wasn't fair Morris got punished too. He did the work. And Mac loves baseball."

"Why didn't you tell me this the first time we talked about Colleen?"

"Back then we didn't even know the page existed." He touched his face tentatively and groaned. "Look, I don't like Colleen, but right now someone is telling her about this post and she's crying or pissed or embarrassed. She's one more person who's upset because of this page. It doesn't even matter that I didn't do it—or that they think I did—it matters that they all feel lousy."

"It does matter," I objected. "And by Wednesday, we'll tell them you didn't." Hopefully sooner, because things were escalating. Last month it had been one to two posts a week. In the last twenty-four hours, there'd been five.

"Is that supposed to make *them* feel better? Or just me? Because it doesn't erase what was said about them. Whoever is doing this—they're hurting these people to hurt me. So, fine, I didn't type those words or post those pictures, but it's not *not* my fault."

I stared at him for a moment. What if it wasn't about Win? What if Win was just a convenient vehicle for other vendettas?

I followed his eyes back to my phone, which was lying on the kitchen counter, photo still on display. I hadn't looked closely at the non-poophead people in it. There were Wink and Win, Reese, Bancroft, Elijah, Morris, Shiloh, Clara, Mira, Elinor, Gemma, Atticus, Dante, and a handful of people I didn't know. Among them was a Black guy who was smiling at Win instead of at the camera.

"That's Mac?" I'd avoided searching iLive for him, hadn't wanted his face in my memory. But now I knew he had laughing eyes and shoulders that filled out a suit coat better than I ever would. "Swimmer?"

"Yup. And soccer and baseball." Win grinned, and my stomach twisted with the weight of a history I didn't know or share.

And also fear. Investigations were based on three things: motive, means, and opportunity. If Mac was on the Mayfield baseball team, he'd probably have been there when Erick dropped the ball. That was opportunity. And here was motive: revenge on Colleen. I needed to look up who he kept in touch with. Check how many posts were from this year versus Mayfield. And how many were like Ava's picture or Clara's gifs—pulled from others' social media? Was it possible the person behind the page didn't go to Chester or Hero High or even live in the state?

So many people had heard Morris call me "Win's new boyfriend" yesterday, and for a hot second I thought that plus my accepted friend request meant the page creator *had* to be in the Chester lunchroom. But news traveled—anyone could've reached out to Mac. Then the post about Shiloh and me would make so much sense.

"Did you—" I swallowed, because this was the sort of information I absolutely didn't want in my head, but absolutely needed. "Did you save your texts from Mac?"

"Why?" Win frowned and stepped back. "You think Mac—no. No way."

"You can't be certain," I said slowly, then rushed to add, "And I'm not saying it's him, but he could be a possibility."

"I can. For certain. I get you're on your scavenger hunt for clues, but this is my life and I'm making Mac off-limits."

"That's not how this works." Watson didn't get to hand out free passes for suspects or tell Sherlock to stop following leads.

"It is now. Sometimes it feels like you forget this is real. It's not some game or puzzle. Don't you care?"

I could feel my nostril's flaring. I knew Win used alienation as a defense mechanism. He provoked as a form of self-preservation. Well, congratulations to him; this time he'd won, and I practically spat out the words "If you really don't think I care, why am I here?" As soon as the words were out, I decided I didn't want an answer. Not with his ex-boyfriend's picture still on my phone like a reminder of all the fun memories Win and I *weren't* making. "You know what? Maybe I shouldn't be."

20

I didn't expect Win to call my bluff. To protest or stop me as I gathered my bag and shoes and coat. But I wished he would have. Instead he turned his back and hid any regret on his face. I felt like I was bleeding incompetence and wanted him to want me here anyway. To recognize I was trying—and that it killed me to be failing him.

I paused with my hand on the doorknob, searching for a way to rewind to the better part of the afternoon, or tell him I understood Hudson's loyalty. I didn't want to leave him either.

But the knob turned beneath my hand, the door swung open, and I just barely jumped out of its path.

His parents froze on the threshold—their eyes skipping from me to the oblivious boy in the kitchen. The one stoically not acknowledging what he thought was my exit.

"Winston Conan Cavendish!"

As his parents shrieked his name, he jumped and clutched his chest.

I silently mouthed a line from "The Speckled Band": *"How dangerous it is to reason from insufficient data."*

It was a quote that definitely referred to this situation, but as Win and his parents argued about putting ice on his face and whether they'd needed to leave work early after Principal Nunes had called, I realized it applied to so much more.

Win had respected my instructions to tell no one about the page, but it was time his parents had the full story. So I cleared my throat from my spot awkwardly hovering by the door. "There's something you need to know."

"Is it that Win's grounded and not allowed to have friends over?" asked his dad.

I watched Win for a signal of protest, but he didn't give one, so I said, "It's that someone's targeting your son. Not just the Hero High emails—they've also made a harassing iLive account using his name."

They looked at each other, mouths rounded, eyebrows raised. And really, if they'd been anything less than completely flummoxed, I would've been on DEFCON levels of suspicion. "*What?*"

Win groaned and covered his face with the ice pack his mom had gotten despite his objections.

"I don't understand," said Mr. Cavendish. "Someone's impersonating him?"

"Hey, Wink, can we borrow your laptop?" Maybe I was making myself too much at home by shouting down the hallway, but I'd cleaned their cabinets and almost helped with the toilets. Plus I didn't want to leave Win while we felt so precarious.

I wanted a Pause button so we could huddle up and get on the same page, because his parents weren't even reading the same book. Before they continued to cast him as the instigator and blame him for the black eye, they needed the SparkNotes version of reality.

"What's up?" Wink called, then she turned the corner and the color drained from her face. I grabbed her laptop before she could drop it. She stammered, "M-mom. Dad. *Huck*. I didn't know *any* of you were here."

Her parents were too distracted to pick up on her obvious lie—she'd carried the laptop out here because *I'd* asked her to. I set it on the island. "Can you pull up iLive?"

She whispered, "We're telling them? Good."

I walked around the island to stand beside Win. He wasn't saying anything, and since he usually had no issues voicing objections, I was trying to interpret his silence and decode his body language. I asked, "Are you okay with this?" but what I was really saying was, *I care—this is me caring.*

He shrugged but stepped closer to me. The action was stiff, and I finally got a read on his emotions: Not disinterested, not angry. Terrified. Which meant I was too.

"Okay, so this is it." Wink spun the laptop to face her parents and pushed a stool out of the way so she could join Win and me on the far side of the island.

They scrolled and clicked, but the comprehension I'd been expecting didn't surface. If anything, they looked increasingly confused. "This page says it's by 'Faker McFakepants.'"

I'd been watching them instead of the screen, but my eyes darted there now. Win's picture had been replaced by a digitally drawn stick figure wearing a shirt that read *Super Fake News*. His name was gone from the header and post attributions.

"Oh." Wink raised her hand. "I, uh, wrote a script to change that on my computer. I didn't like looking at it the other way. Hang on, I'll turn off the browser extension."

Win gave an asthmatic laugh; it faded before anyone joined in.

A few clicks later and the page was back to his name and picture being used to spew unkindness. Wink was right; her version was better.

And I'd forgotten Win hadn't seen it all—he didn't know about the exes post,. and he shot me a glance as it scrolled across the screen. It didn't feel like the right time to announce, *BTW, I met your ex-boyfriend today. He gave me a lesson on kissing, so don't worry, I won't bite.*

Especially since his parents had their own running commentary. "Is that poor Colleen with the poo on her face?" and "I'm not sure what this even means." And "Oh, *no*." They were a live-action reaction gif, cringes and gasps on repeat.

Curtis came home mid-scroll, the grin on his face faltering as he took in our grim moods huddled around the laptop. "So we're doing this? About time." He peeled off his muddy sneakers and socks, then hip-checked Wink out of the way so there was room for him between the twins.

I hoped Win recognized that they both had his back. That I did too. That the four of us were on the same team and any second his parents would be raising their hands and volunteering to be team captains.

Mr. and Mrs. Cavendish paused on an anti–Hero High meme and exchanged a weary look. I groped blindly for Win's hand, but all I managed to grasp was the ice pack. Even that didn't chill me as much as his dad's question. "And you're sure you didn't make this?"

It was good I was holding the ice pack, because at the words, Win let go.

"Geez, Dad!" Curtis's shoulders had gone back, his chest forward. It was an angry, aggressive stance—one I'd never seen him take. "You've got to be kidding me right now."

"We have to ask—it's not unprecedented. Win's been forging our names since second-grade reading logs. Is that any different from lying about a webpage or sending fake emails?"

"It's very different," Win gritted out. "Why won't you trust me?"

"Maybe we should talk about this privately, buddy," his mom suggested softly, but her expression tightened when all four of us shook our heads. "Fine. Win, trust is *earned*. And you've got a history. The reading logs, putting our signatures on failing tests—your fifth-grade permission slip for the science museum—"

Win closed his eyes—or *eye*, since the other one was practically swollen shut already. "You'd signed one slip and given us both money."

"We signed *Wink's*." His dad pinched the bridge of his nose. "When are you going to start taking personal responsibility? We become the behaviors we practice—what do your actions say about you?"

I was ready with a list of accolades and examples of how he made all their lives better, but Wink said, "Actually—" and lifted her fingers off the counter in the world's weakest hand raise.

Win opened his eyes. "Wink, don't."

She ignored him and whispered her answer to the counter. "It was his permission slip you signed. He switched with me on the bus when I realized I forgot and started crying."

"You shouldn't have told them." Win lowered his head so that their postures matched. The comparison was even more striking when Curtis took a step back so he was no longer separating them and Wink reached for Win's hand.

"Win's slip?" His mom sounded stunned, and I wondered if this was some lodestone memory, one they'd constructed their whole belief system about their younger son upon.

"It wasn't just that." Wink sniffed. "I know I shouldn't, but I let Win take the blame for other stuff too—I was the one who let the Kimmels' dogs get loose that time when we all had to look for them with flashlights in the snow. And I left the sink running when it overflowed and we had to replace the floor. It wasn't Win who cracked the old TV with the controller. But they were all accidents. I swear."

They would've been accidents when *he* did them too—but I bit my tongue so I didn't point this out. She was fully crying now, and I couldn't tell if it was from guilt or fear. Because for someone with such a deep phobia of messing up and conflict, she'd just exposed a minefield of mistakes.

"Let them believe what they want." Win said as her grip on his hand tightened along with his jaw. "They always do."

"Just—just give us a second here, Winston." His father was frowning but unsure of where to direct it—the computer, his youngest son, his daughter. When Curtis nervously hummed the *Jeopardy!* theme song, he got the full force of his dad's glare. "This is a lot to take in."

"You think?" Win said.

I looked around the kitchen, searching for the right words to interrupt this before it became a massacre. My eyes landed on my coffee mug. I'd picked a large blue one that read *Cavendish Physical Therapy*, but it had been nestled in the cabinet beside Curtis's kindergarten handprint. Another thing Win had owned up to for Wink.

"And that page..." His mom reached across the island for him and he stepped back. She flinched, so he rocked forward again, enduring her hand pat with rigid posture. "*Why* would anyone do this to you, buddy?"

Wink wiped her face and lifted her chin. "Are you seriously blaming *him*?"

Mrs. Cavendish pulled her hand back. "I didn't mean it that way. Frankly, with all these revelations, I don't know who or what to believe."

"Mom!" Curtis said.

"Oh, you're not blameless either, pal," said their dad. "You knew about this and didn't tell us."

"Why did we bother?" Win's eyebrows told whole volumes and stories. How could his parents not see the truth pinned between them? The betrayal balanced across them as they confirmed his deepest fear. He grabbed the softening ice pack and stormed to his room. But even full of the most justified anger, he shut his door without slamming it. I wanted to follow, but he needed an advocate out here. Someone who knew the whole story.

"Lincoln, you, Mom, and I will be having a *big* conversation later about personal responsibility, but let's put a pin in that for now and come up with a plan about how to handle... *this*." Mr. Cavendish waved a hand at the laptop and sank wearily onto a stool.

"How do we get it taken down?" Mrs. Cavendish aimed the question at Wink, proving that even if she missed a lot about her kids, she knew the techiest member of her family.

"We can report it," said Wink. "But..."

"Win and I agreed to report it on Wednesday if we haven't

figured out who's behind it by then," I shared. "My big fear is that if we *don't* know who made the page, what's to stop them from making another one?"

"What about the police? Isn't this a cybercrime or something?" their dad asked. "And the school. Someone needs to tell Hero High he didn't send that email."

That their belief was conditioned on proof and only occurred *after* Win was out of earshot had me forcing the words "We already did" from between clenched teeth.

"What I don't get is—how could this be going on and he wouldn't *tell us*?" Mrs. Cavendish's damp eyes swung toward the hallway.

I leaned over and shut the laptop, drawing all of their attention. "Respectfully, why *would* he tell you? He's spent months dealing with social fallout from fires he didn't set. People have been angry with him for reasons he couldn't know. You said it was in his head or told him to be nicer. You called him 'defensive'. . ." My finger was shaking as I pointed to the laptop. "You didn't believe him. How do you think he felt?"

"Huck!" We all spun toward the hallway. Everything in me that had been rage and powerlessness plummeted to the bottom of my stomach. Win was standing there, the dripping ice pack in hand. It was impossible to tell if any of the redness on his cheek was from crying or if the moisture there was from the ice. "Enough."

His voice was steady, but I wasn't. I'd been trembling with fury; now I just shook.

"I need to go," I said softly. Because if I stayed, I couldn't be sure I wouldn't say more or make things worse. Before he'd questioned *if* I cared; now I didn't know how to look at him without how much I felt being too clear on my face. He didn't need any more revelations today.

Curtis walked out with me and stood next to me on the stoop as I bent to tie my shoes. "I know you're judging my mom and dad right now."

I let my raised eyebrows answer.

"I'm not saying they don't deserve it, but remember when I felt like the worst brother alive for believing that was his page? That's how they're feeling right now—probably times ten, because it's got to be worse when it's your kid you've failed. Give them a chance to process."

"Tell Win—" I yanked my shoe's laces so hard that the plastic tip came off one side—it was called an "aglet," a fact as useless as I felt right then. "Tell him... I'm sorry."

There should've been a second part to that statement. An explanation of what I was sorry *for*: the way his parents hadn't listened, the way I'd gone too far, the fact that I didn't have the right words or disposition to be in there comforting him.

Curtis held out a hand. "Listen, I don't know what you guys are or aren't officially, or if you've put a label on it—but I'm sorry I tried to talk you out of dating my brother. There's no better guy, Huck. You're exactly what he needed."

Curtis was so rarely serious that I always paused to make sure he wasn't headed toward a wink-nudge-eyebrow waggle. This time he was stone-cold somber. I put my hand in his and let him pull me up to stand. "I need him too."

I read "A Scandal in Bohemia" that night... or at least I read until the line "It is a capital mistake to theorize before one has data. Insensibly one begins to twist facts to suit theories, instead of theories to suit facts." Then I put the book down.

It didn't feel possible to ever have all the facts here. I was never going to understand all the personal entanglements or motives or histories of the people involved. The more I learned, the more I learned what I *didn't* know.

I scrolled through iLive, hoping patterns would magically appear between the pictures and posts. But the thing that stood out was the lone positive message on the page. It was a birthday tribute to Wink.

`HBD to the only person I'd let treat me like a dog.` The attached picture wasn't one Win would've voluntarily made public, so I needed to know who had access to it. Was it in a frame somewhere in their house? Hidden away in an album? Had Wink or Curtis or their parents ever posted it online? It featured Wink in overalls and lopsided pigtails, barefoot on their back lawn. She was holding a leash. Winston was on all fours on the other end of it, the leash's clip attached to the back collar of his T-shirt. His tongue hanging out, fake-panting and revealing a gap-toothed smile. Someone had colored his nose black, drawn whiskers on his cheeks. It could've been eyeliner or face paint, but I bet they were courtesy of the Sharpie hanging out of Wink's pocket.

The most interesting part of this post was that it wasn't true. Wink wasn't the *only* person he'd do extreme favors for. To make his family happy, he'd have played Rover for *any* of them.

She was just the most likely to ask.

21

Miles called Thursday morning and asked if I wanted to come to the city for the weekend. Someone had given him a pair of Rangers tickets they couldn't use. It felt a little traitorous to my beloved Blue Jackets, but I'd gladly take a rain check on plans with Bancroft and a break from feeling like a broken detective to binge on rinkside nachos. And give *Win* a break too.

I didn't know the outcome of yesterday's mayhem, or if Win was okay, or if I'd be welcome at the Cavendishes'. But I was going right from Convocation to the train station tomorrow and didn't want to disappear for the weekend without giving him a heads-up.

As I trudged down the sidewalk to his house after school, my phone rang. It was a New York area code, which meant it was either Miles, a telemarketer, or—most likely—a news station. I'd spent the last few weeks sending them to voicemail and deleting the messages. But today—mostly out of procrastination—I answered and let a production assistant named Charles pitch me a segment about how it was "so admirable you noticed your teacher's sexism and took action."

"Stop," I said. "I'm just a guy that made a horrible mistake. If I could do it again, I'd make different choices."

Charles countered, "Then come on our show and talk about *that*: how you've learned to be a better feminist ally. Give advice to other guys about—"

"I pointed a phone and pressed a button. It was literally the least I could do." And getting praise for it made my stomach twist. "Mine is the last voice you need. Get people of color, get *women*. Anyone other than a white dude who messed up, saying he did it in the name of feminism."

"But you meant well—"

I groaned against the receiver. "My intentions are not a selling point. I observed. Clara experienced. If you want to talk to someone inspirational, why aren't you calling her?"

There was a pause. "That's—that's a good question. Will you give me her number?"

"Not a chance." I hung up before Charles could pitch his "Yeah, but—"

They all had a "Yeah, but," and they all infuriated me. My only consolation was that Clara *wasn't* getting hounded. I'd had Rory ask. But... maybe she should be? Not hounded, but asked. Given opportunities and platforms. I mulled this over as I knocked on Win's door.

"Hey." We said it simultaneously. Followed by a synchronized, "I'm sorry."

I elaborated first. "I'm sorry if I overstepped with your parents. It just made me so—" I paused and took a deep breath. "I want them to believe you."

"They do. I have my phone back. I'm ungrounded and probably have a few Get Out of Jail Free cards for future groundings." He shook his head, like he was disoriented by this shift in family dynamics. "If you didn't come over, I was going to call, because yesterday was a lot."

"Everyone okay? You and Wink?"

"Yeah, but I'm—I'm talked out. I'm really glad you're here though."

"Me too." Sometimes his honesty was so real it made me ache, made me uncomfortably aware of all the filters I fed my words through.

"We can work on your video." He bypassed the kitchen and led me straight to his room. "Maybe today I can help you for once. What'd you use to film the interviews?"

It was a clear request for a break from all things iLive, so I pulled out my phone and cued up the first video. "This."

"Probably stick with that then. Let's see what you've got to work with." He watched the first few seconds of the interviews. Each time he shook his head, I cringed. But his voice was soft and supportive when he said, "So, let's start with the basics. We can fix what you have here with filters and settings and cropping. But going forward, film horizontally, like a TV screen. And try to have the people all take up about the same room on-screen. Typically about a third. You're going to want to work on steadiness. Don't hold the phone; use a tripod or prop it against books or something so it's not moving."

I nodded, locking each of these facts away.

"You want to avoid backlighting—when the light source is behind your subject, it makes it hard to see their faces. So, no more filming people in front of windows. It's kinda ridiculous that no one in media class thought to tell you this." He pointed at the screen. "You wanted to do some text overlays, right? Put facts on there about the school?"

"Yeah, like statistics on diversity or sports or class size."

"Okay, then we need to make sure you leave space for those. The easiest way would be to shoot with a blank backdrop, against a bare wall or blackboard. And see if you can go in a quiet classroom so there's not so much background noise to scrub."

"You can really help me fix this?" I asked.

He laughed. "Isn't that supposed to be *my* line? I'm the screwup, you're the fixer."

"I disagree. Vehemently." He looked away, and I reached out and *almost* touched his face but pulled my fingers back. "Your eye looks better."

He smirked before sinking onto his bed. "Liar."

But it wasn't a lie. He always looked good to me. Was that the sort of thing I could say? It seemed like the type that he might. I shifted my feet. *Say it, swallow it, admit it, repress it.*

"Here." He tossed me my phone. "Send me the interview files and I'll fix them up this weekend. But first, show me you've been paying attention."

I frowned. "You know I have."

"Prove it. Where should I sit? Set up the shot."

I directed him to the end of his bed, away from the closet doors so I'd have a blank wall beside him. I dimmed the lights on the ceiling fan and opened a blind. Positioned the phone on his dresser and took a test shot. "That would work."

"So, ask me your questions."

"Right." I pressed Record. "Uh, what do you think of when you hear 'Hero High'?"

"Snazzy uniforms," he deadpanned, then glanced away. When he faced the camera again, his expression was serious. "It feels like Hero High is a safe space..."

I was glad I'd given his dresser the job of keeping the camera steady, because there's no way I could've. I asked my questions and he kept talking, earnest, honest. I couldn't look away. I didn't move, even after he said, "So, yeah. All that and snazzy uniforms."

I swallowed, but my mouth stayed dry. "Please tell me that's the answer you gave in your interview. Because good luck rejecting that."

He snorted. "Feel free to use it in your video. The eye will add a classy touch."

He was being sarcastic, but I paused to consider. "Do they make filters for that? There are dog ears and makeup and Santa hats . . ."

"Please—" His snort had ballooned to full laughter and he doubled over. "Please make me a black-eyed Santa. Or, like, the eyelashes—" He pantomimed batting his.

Win was still laughing when his phone rang on the bed beside him. He glanced at Wink's name on the screen and hit the speakerphone button. "It's not my fault if I'm being too loud. Someone"—he grinned at me—"is being unintentionally hilarious."

"I don't know what you're talking about, but whatever. I need your help," Wink whined. "I'm having a toilet paper emergency."

"You clogged the toilet?"

"No. Gross. Ugh. Brothers," she huffed. "I mean, there is none."

He was spectacularly nonchalant, leaning over the drawer of his bedside table and fishing something out before answering. "So you want me to bring you some?"

"Either that or I live here now."

The "something" was made up of flexible stands of black balls that he bent and twisted. "I guess you live there now. Or at least until I need the bathroom."

I laughed. She inhaled. "Is that Huck? Am I on speakerphone? Win!"

He tossed me the object. Clearly a phone clipped to one end, but what were the three strands for? "Tripod," he mouthed before answering her. "You called me from inside the house. How was I supposed to know it was a secret conversation about poop and not you being too lazy to walk across the hall?"

At this point it might be safer for him *not* to deliver the TP, because it was going to be *A Study in Murdered Siblings* if she ever got out of the bathroom. "And I guess I should've known Huck's here, because he always is. Maybe if he was here less, you'd have more time to change the roll after you finish it."

"Still on speakerphone," he said.

"I'm going to kill you," she growled, and I mentally high-fived myself for predicting this.

"Threats won't get you TP." But he was sitting up and swinging his legs off the bed.

"Fine. I'll use your towel."

That got him moving. And while he was opening the hall closet and having a through-the-door squabble with his sister, the doorbell rang. I wandered past them and opened it for Morris.

"Oh. Hey." He blinked and rocked back a step in surprise. "You're still—you're *here*?"

"Why wouldn't I be?" He gaped and hedged and looked so uncomfortable that I decided to save him. "Because of Win's iLive post about future ex?"

"Yeah. Sorry." He sucked on his upper lip and shoved his hands into the front pocket of his green hoodie. "I didn't know if you'd seen it and didn't want to start something if you hadn't. You guys are cool?" Morris looked so concerned that I *almost* forgave him for believing the page.

"Yeah, we're cool."

"Good. I was coming to check on how Win was doing between that and his eye. Guess I'm not needed."

He hesitated on the stoop, but I waved him inside. "I didn't punch him. Promise."

Morris frowned and pulled off his Phillies cap. "Yeah, I know. I was there when Cole did."

"I was..." I trailed off because nothing good came from pointing out a failed joke, plus I wanted Morris to like me. "Anyway, I'm not mad about the post. Win's funny like that. I mean, how has he wronged you over the years?"

He laughed, then paused when I didn't join in. "Oh, you were serious? He hasn't. Should he have? Is this the new 'squad goals' thing?"

I shrugged again. "It seems to be a pattern." It's not that I was testing Morris—except, fine, I was testing him. Annoyed he was another person who believed the page could be Win's. And maybe he knew I was peeved, because he was watching me as warily as I was watching him.

"Hey, Morris." Win and Wink came into the kitchen, still nudging each other. "What are you guys talking about?"

Morris blinked, his scrutiny melting into a grin as he held out a hand for Win to bump. "Huck was telling me you have a pattern of 'wronging' people—I'm trying to decide if I should be offended you don't care enough to offend me."

Win's eyebrows rose as his gaze shot to me. I flipped my palms up in a subtle shrug. That was certainly one interpretation of my words.

"Work on that, okay?" Morris's laugh sounded forced. "If you don't insult me soon, I'm going to be seriously hurt."

"Sure thing." Win pivoted for the cabinet where snacks were kept. "Popcorn, corn chips, or—" He broke off and narrowed his eyes at his sister; with one ringed in purple, the effect was lopsided. "What's wrong?"

I didn't believe in twin intuition, but I also had zero explanation for how Win knew anything was wrong. Two minutes ago she'd been issuing threats of fratricide—and, yeah, their bickering and joking was a bit pricklier today, but I attributed that to residue from last night. Win's jaw hardened and his legs widened to a protective, reactive stance. He tossed a bag of corn chips to Morris and faced her.

Only then did I see any evidence of distress as she squished her lips to one side and sank onto the couch. "Sorry I was a jerk earlier, Huck."

I nodded. "You okay?"

"It's stupid." She hugged a pillow, the same thing Win did when overwhelmed. "Just... Reese and I said we'd go to the freshman formal together. But Paxton asked her today and of course I told her to say yes, but now I'm the only one who's dateless."

The bag Morris had been opening tore in an explosion of chips. He chuckled self-consciously. "Well, now that I've got your attention: I'll take you."

Win laughed. "No, you won't, and get a broom." He

snatched up another throw pillow and threw it at Wink, but both the toss and his voice were gentle. "I'm not going. You can stay home with me."

"But you don't *want* to go." Wink's chin sunk into the chenille fringe as her lip quivered. "I do."

"Again, I can take her." Morris was ineffectively shoving the chips into a pile with his foot, breaking most of them.

"*Again*, you cannot." Win's voice was edging toward impatient, Wink's lip headed toward trembling. Morris had picked a *bad* day to come over, because he had no idea of the emotional showdown that had taken place last night or the fallout the twins were still sorting through—both picking at and protecting each other, everything still so raw.

Morris abandoned his mess, taking crunching footsteps closer. His face was briefly thunderous, then he laughed and clapped a hand on Win's back. "Wait! You're doing it. I told you to try and offend me and you went for it. Good one. You got me." He turned and headed to the closet, grabbing out the broom. "So, I'll take Wink. Consider it done."

"Um, I don't get a say?" asked Wink. "It's only *my* date. You can't just 'consider it done' when you didn't even ask me."

Morris's face fell, and Win's hardened into stone. He'd picked up another pillow and was squeezing it with white knuckles. No part of this was going to end well. I didn't know how Curtis was faring, but both Cavendish twins were emotional jack-in-the-boxes, ready to spring in the face of whoever turned their crank.

There were way too many volatile feelings trapped in this room—but it suddenly occurred to me that we didn't have to be.

"Time out!" I called, and all three faces swiveled toward me. "Win, you're not grounded, right?"

"Yeah," he said cautiously.

"So let's go somewhere."

He dropped the pillow and reached for his shoes. "Okay. Where do you want to go?"

22

Since Morris had to clean up the chips and Wink said we were going to be "disgustingly adorable" on the walk, it was agreed that they'd stay and sweep while we went ahead and tried to snag a table at Cool Beans. They'd join us when the kitchen floor would no longer make Mrs. Cavendish break into hives.

It bought us a five-minute head start. And I suspected Morris would spend most of it apologizing to Wink and trying to talk her into going with him to the formal. I also suspected her answer had nothing to do with Win's objection and that she wouldn't change her mind.

I gave a satisfied hum, knowing I'd get a chance to prove my hypothesis soon enough.

Win grinned and bumped his shoulder against mine. "I'm kinda digging how excited you are about getting coffee. It's cute."

I blushed and wondered if I should tell him coffee was only part of the appeal, and puzzling out Wink and Morris was secondary too. Mostly it was that we were outside his house—together—without risking punishment.

"Here's the thing." I stopped at the end of his block, gesturing vaguely to get his attention.

"Where?" He followed the motion of my hand and was studying the neighboring yards. He glanced back down the sidewalk at his house, then the other direction toward Main Street. "What thing?"

"No." I waved my hand like I was wiping away the words, and he tracked the motion with an increasingly furrowed brow. "There's no—it's not an actual physical thing. But I need to know something."

He laughed. "You always do."

"One question, I swear." I held up a finger and gave him my most winning, dimpled smile.

He groaned and rubbed the back of his neck. "Can we go back to looking for the nonexistent thing?"

"Just this one question, I promise." I grabbed his hand, and his surprised eyes swung to mine.

"Fine." He sighed as he squeezed my fingers. "Ask."

I waggled my eyebrows and paused dramatically. "Why'd you have to invite Wink and Morris?"

But in truth, it was fine when they joined us. Catching up before we'd even reached Cool Beans, Wink pretended to gag when she saw our clasped hands. "See? What did I tell you? Disgustingly adorable."

All three of them mocked me when I ordered a dark roast in the size they called "mega," and the barista paused before ringing it up. "You sure? We don't sell many of these outside of finals time."

I was sleep-deprived and I was sure.

We snagged the table by the electric fireplace, and Wink mixed sugar into the foam of her cappuccino and ate it with a stirrer. Morris offered to share his giant cookie. Win had his cranberry juice. Wink had brought cards. Apparently gin rummy was their game—and Bancroft was right about her being a card shark. Morris was scorekeeper, and Win was patient with explaining the rules, laughing at my beginner's luck when I won the first hand without having a clue what I was doing.

It felt like an afternoon from the future—like I was getting a sneak peek at life post-iLive. And I hoped that was true, but there was still so much unresolved. I laughed along with them when Morris almost spilled Wink's cup while knocking to end a round—and rolled my eyes when she won *again*. And protested my innocence when Win accused me of trying to look at his cards, but really I just wanted to sit closer to him. Through it all, though, my stomach ached—and not the acid burn of too much coffee. There was so much I was actively trying to compartmentalize, so many frayed pieces that I needed tied up in neat knots.

By the time it got dark, Wink's foam was long gone, Morris's cookie was crumbs, and Win had recycled his bottle. Those of us who were smart enough to order the mega still had coffee left.

"We should get going," Wink said, pulling out her phone. "It's pizza night. Mom and Dad want to do family dinner."

"Oh. Right." Win frowned. "Do I have time to walk Huck home?"

She shook her head. "Their ETA is five minutes—they're already going to beat us."

"It's okay," I told him. "I might stay awhile."

"Do not get a refill," he said with a finger point as we all stood and he started bussing our table.

I raised my half-full cup. "I'm still good."

"Wink." I pulled her aside while Morris was in the bathroom and Win was packing up the cards. "I had a thought about your formal. What about Lance? He can't already have a date to it because he doesn't go to your school, and he was saying the other day that he's the only single person at his lunch table."

Her mouth opened. "Do you think he'd go for it?"

"I don't see why not." It'd be platonic, because I knew he still was pining over someone, even if I didn't know who it was. "And you'd have great photos—he's hot."

"He's definitely that." Wink tapped her lip. "Do you have his number, or should I get it from Curtis?"

"I've got it from lacrosse. I'll send it to you. And give him a heads-up."

"Thanks," she said. "And thanks for *this*. I needed it. I'm sorry we were all such crab apples earlier."

"Understandable," I said, giving the word all the sincerity it deserved.

"Wink." Win tilted his head toward the door, where Morris was already waiting. "Stop monopolizing Huck. We've got to go."

I wanted a big goodbye. Or at least a private one since I wouldn't see him until Monday. But it ended up being a handslap with Morris, a hug from Wink, and an awkward "Have a good trip. And, hey, at least I've got my phone back" from Win.

I watched them exit, then pulled out my cell to text Lance about Wink's request. He responded immediately. She's thinking friends, right? If so, it's totally cool.

Part of me wanted to dig deeper, find out who Lance's secret crush was, but I let that go. For now, not forever. Because this felt good, having the solution to Wink's problem. I felt like *me*.

And maybe the reason I'd failed so much before was that I'd had no knowledge, I'd had no connections. I was finally starting to put down roots, to find my place in this town. My people.

I left Cool Beans but stopped in front of a store a few doors down. The sign looked like a mug shot. The window had stylized prison bars. **FRAME ME**. The name was so apt it hurt.

The bell over the door jangled when I entered, and a white-haired man looked up from a counter halfway down the narrow store. The front was racks of frames and albums. There were locked glass cases of fancy cameras behind the checkout, and the last third of the room was a photo studio. Backdrops and lights and bins of props. It was currently staged to look like a meadow. A pink parasol open beside a picnic basket.

"Can I help you?" The man pushed his glasses up his nose.

"I saw your sign in the window—Help Wanted?"

He brightened. "Ah! I'm Mr. Rivera. Do you know cameras?"

"Nope. Not at all," I said cheerfully. "I couldn't tell you the difference between aperture and exposure. I only know those are things because of my camera-savvy friend."

"Well, does your friend want a job?"

"He might. Because he talks really fondly about when he used to work here."

The man let out a breath. "Your friend—is he Winston Cavendish?"

I nodded.

"He was one of the best photographers I've ever worked with—not just teens—any age."

"Can I ask why you fired him?" This was a qualitatively different question than "Why'd you fire him?" The first allowed the answerer to feel like they were in control. It didn't demand information, so they were more likely to give it. If I'd posed the question directly, I'd probably be met with "Why are you asking?" or "It's none of your business."

"Winston used to be so dependable. For the first three months he worked here, he never took a single sick day. He was always on time or early. And then that changed."

"How?"

"He started emailing constantly, asking me to switch up the schedule. Then he wouldn't show up for the time he asked for. He was showing up for times he shouldn't. It was the darnedest thing. And what's the point in having an employee if you have no idea when they're coming?"

"Can I see these emails? Did you save any?"

"That's on odd request." Mr. Rivera studied me with eyes that were used to seeing things through lenses and viewfinders—practiced in screening out all sorts of busyness and capturing the heart of a shot. "You say you're Winston's friend? Why are you here?"

"Someone's been trying to make him look bad. They've sent other emails impersonating him. Win's told me how much he loved this job—and how confused he was when he was fired. I'm pretty sure the fake emailer was the one asking for the schedule changes."

Mr. Rivera gaped as he banged on the keyboard in angry hunt-and-peck typing. "Why? Why would anyone do that to our boy?"

Our boy. If I accomplished nothing else today, at least I could get Win's job back.

"I've got half a mind to reply to one of these emails and tell that cretin what I think—"

"Actually, could you?" A plan was forming as I skimmed the email he'd pulled up. A curt demand to switch shifts from Saturday to Thursday night.

"Give him a piece of my mind?" Mr. Rivera looked delighted by the idea.

"No. I'm thinking offer his job back. Say you'll call and let him know the details—but don't do it."

"I don't follow."

"We're looking to see if they respond. Or if anyone says anything to Win about the job. If they think you've called, they might let something slip or ask a leading question."

"You're making this all sound mighty mysterious." He tipped his head back in a look that was speculative. "I've always liked those double-oh-seven movies, but never thought I'd be in one."

"If you get a response, forward it to me." I grabbed one of the business cards on his counter and wrote my email on the back. He stuck the card in his shirt pocket and patted it. I slung my backpack on my shoulder and thanked him.

"Wait!" I was halfway to the door but turned to see Mr. Rivera following me. "How will Winston know he really *does* have his job back?"

I clamped down on my grin. "If no one spoils it before then, call him at the end of next week and offer it to him."

The bell rang again when I exited, and either my coffee had kicked in or the buzz in my veins was from a different source—the knowledge of yet another member of the Winston Cavendish fan club. Maybe if I recruited enough of us, he'd *have* to face the reality of how awesome he was.

23

My visit to Aspen Crest was short and focused. I'd submitted a list of students I wanted to talk to; the ones who'd returned their permission slips met me in a small room off the library during homeroom and first period. The list included the two Aspen Crest students who'd appeared on the iLive page, another four who'd gone to Mayfield, and two randoms. When asked how I made the list, I gave a vague, "They came highly recommended."

People often scrutinized criticism, but they rarely questioned flattery.

Of the eight students I'd requested, six returned their waivers. Most importantly, one of those six was Colleen Allen.

I interviewed her first, and she was quick to gush about Hero High. "I'm actually hoping to transfer. I had my interview two weeks ago. It went so well."

"Good." I tried to make the word sound sincere, but I was already crossing my fingers she wouldn't get in. Sorry, Sherlock—I wasn't unbiased here, and it was hard to smile and ask, "When you think of Hero High, what word comes to mind?"

"It's the best," she said. "And Aspen Crest is—"

"Sorry to interrupt." I wasn't sorry. "But I'm not making a hit piece on any other school. Can you focus on Hero High?"

"Oh. Sure." She drummed her fingers. "Hero High has a reputation for being an Ivy League feeder. I've been tracking its stats at placing graduating seniors in top-tier colleges, and they're—" She bit her lip as she tried to come up with a noncomparative way to phrase it. "I like what I see."

"Good to know," I told her, already going off-script because who cared about the stupid video? "I know someone else who's applying to transfer. Do you know the Cavendish twins?"

Her nose wrinkled and her upper lip curled. "We were at Mayfield together. Is Lincoln transferring?"

"She's already in. It's Winston who's applying. Too bad you guys didn't have interviews on the same day."

"Yeah, too bad." She almost managed to say it without sarcasm, but since she hadn't, I pounced.

"Not a fan?"

"Well, if Hero High wants a cyberbully, they should definitely admit Win. That's all I'll say." She crossed her arms. "It's just that—I don't know how he surrounds himself with so many nice people. Like, Lincoln is a sweetheart. And Mac and Morris and Reese—their whole group are good people. What do they see in him? Oh, is the camera still on?"

I made a show of turning it off and putting my phone down. "You want to go off-record?"

"Only to say this: I'm not worried. I highly doubt Winston Cavendish is getting in." She waved an airy hand before leaning in like we were best friends.

"Oh?" I arched an eyebrow, dimpled conspiratorially. "What do you know? Tell me."

"Well." She flipped her hair over her shoulder. "I caught him cheating last year, and that's got to be on his record."

Yeah, so she hated him...but she wasn't actively working against him. She was too busy being smugly superior.

I stood and held out a hand to shake, signaling that we were done. "I wish you luck." *Bad luck.*

"Thanks." She beamed. "I'll probably be seeing you on campus next year."

I prayed to the gods of petty grudges and fresh starts that we never crossed paths again. And then I double-checked for backlighting, adjusted Win's tripod, and sped through the rest of my interviews. Getting the sound bites I needed and getting out of there.

"Aspen Crest?" Mrs. York peered at me over the top of her glasses as she read my excuse note.

"Just for a project. No worries, I'm not transferring." I dimpled; she smiled.

"Pity," Mira said, then fake coughed. She was sitting by the office door with her backpack at her feet.

I turned to face her. "You're supposed to cough *while* saying the word." I demonstrated: "Cough*pity*cough."

Her cheeks turned pink, but she didn't lower her chin or look away. "I didn't want there to be any chance you misunderstood."

I laughed. If she didn't hate me, I really think we might be friends.

"Okay, that's enough." Mira and I swung toward the office

door. Clara stood there with a look of down-the-nose disapproval that rivaled any teacher's. "If I'm not mad, you're not allowed to be."

Mira stood. "You're too forgiving."

Clara gave a short laugh. "You absolutely know that's not true. I'm still holding a grudge toward that stylist who gave my hair a relaxer treatment in seventh grade. I love you for being all momma bear, but Huck does not deserve your holy wrath."

I was doing my best impersonation of the wallpaper as I tried to inch by them and out the office door. Mira cut side-eyes at me and grumbled an exaggerated, "Cough*sorry*cough."

I laughed and nodded, not wanting to endanger our fragile peace by trying to one-up her joke.

Clara caught up with me in the hall. "Don't take it personally. Mira doesn't like new people."

"It's March. I don't think it qualifies as 'stranger danger' when we're three-quarters of the way through the school year." I shrugged to make it clear I wasn't upset or blaming her. "And you really don't have to stick up for me."

"Oh, shut it." She shoved me gently. "Don't be ridiculous. Besides, I need to ask you something. I hear you're making a video."

The warmth in my chest turned sour and my pulse kicked up. "It's literally the opposite of what yours was."

She raised an eyebrow. "So it's about a teacher who only calls on girls?"

I flushed. "Okay, not literally."

"I got that." There were zero signs of panic on her face—I should've noticed that. She was joking; that was a good sign.

And her hair was curly again. These felt like baby steps back toward the Clara of *before*, and they made me hope I'd only dinged her, not caused any lasting damage.

"Are you doing okay?" I asked. "You don't have to answer, but I do care."

"It's getting better," she said. "Mostly because I've decided strangers don't get to change how I feel about myself."

"I will never stop being sorry about what I did."

"And I'm sure someday I'll take advantage of that." She twirled a curl and tucked it behind her ear. "But right now I just want to be in the video."

I stumbled over my own shock, then hurried to catch up with her. Clara walked *fast*. "You do?"

"To talk about Hero High? Of course. I could practically be the school mascot. I'm third-generation. I had Crimson Knight onesies. If I'd been a boy, I would've been named 'Reginald.' You need me in your video."

I grinned and held out a hand. "Sounds like I do."

She shook it. "I have your number. I'll call you to schedule."

Leave it to Clara to make it sound so formal. I had plans to interview Bancroft, Shi, Elijah, Rory, and Merri when I got back from New York. Maybe Clara and—dare I hope—Mira could come over and I'd get them too?

Then with Win's help, I'd edit it into something cohesive and be done. Just the thought of crossing *one* thing off my to-do list felt like relief. But that was a week away. In the meantime, I needed coffee.

Luckily, I'd left a cup from Cool Beans in my locker while signing in at the office. I fetched it, planning to chug it between the bells for second and third period.

And since I'm such an excellent friend, I swung by the humanities building to wait for Rory outside of English. "Hey, Campbear. How was class?"

"Fine."

I narrowed my gaze. "What are you getting away with?"

"What do you mean?" Her eyes darted up and to the left; they always did that when she was hiding something.

"It's got to do with English. And I know you're not that happy about poetry." I tapped my thumb against my lip. "What alternative assignment did you talk her into?"

She sighed in exasperation. "How do you always do that?"

It was simple. She'd charged out the door like she was ready to take on the world. And while Rory's being the first one out of class wasn't new, her doing it with a smile on her face was highly unusual. I took a sip of my coffee. We hadn't turned in an assignment recently, so there wasn't one she could've gotten back. Plus, Rory didn't grin for grades. This had to be art related. Art and English? I took another sip.

"Huck!" I didn't realize how fast I'd been walking until I noticed Rory jogging to keep up. I paused and drummed my thumb against my leg as she wove her way through the students.

"What are you drawing?"

"Fine. I'm doing a series where I create visual interpretations of poems we read." She stretched toward me, and I was trying to figure out why when she plucked the cup from my hand. "But, hello, Captain Caffeine. What number is this?"

I reached for the coffee, but she held it behind her back. "It's only..." My frown deepened as I tried to count. Cup one at three a.m. when I'd given up on sleep. Two at four thirty while studying my bulletin board, worried it was starting to resemble one of those red-string serial killer walls. At least my string was blue? Dad poured me a mug with breakfast. I'd smuggled a travel mug with another two cups to Aspen Creek. Then Mom had been drive-through amenable on the way here.

I rubbed my eyes. "More than one, less than ten."

Rory sniffed. "You know I love you like the brother I never wanted—but you need to cut back on the coffee. Do you even realize you're jittering?"

I hadn't. But I looked down at the hand Rory had placed on my arm—the muscles beneath her fingers were trembling. I dropped my arm, no longer trying to steal back the cup. If they hooked me to a seismograph right now, I'd register an eight point two. Not the Richter scale. I'd heard Eliza tell Curtis that scientists didn't use that anymore. I'd be an eight point two on the "moment magnitude scale"—and, son of a monkey, Rory was right. My thoughts were as jumpy as my feet—which felt like they could tap-dance but knew they didn't have the skills to pull that off. "Coffee is my cocaine."

"Excuse me?" She gaped. "You want to run that by me again? Only this time listen to the words you're saying."

"Sherlock injected drugs. I caffeinate."

"I'm pretty sure Sherlock Holmes is not the best role model." She tilted her head. "Or real."

Ms. Gregoire had been gliding past but paused. "Welcome back, Huck. I trust you had a productive morning?" She said "Good" in response to my nod and took the Cool Beans cup from Rory. "Did you want this back? Personally, I think Aurora's giving you good advice."

"I don't need it." The words felt like a lie, and I tried not to flinch as I watched the pink cup arc from my teacher's hand into the trash.

"Excellent. Also, I highly recommend you get yourselves off to class before the bell rings."

"C'mon." Rory tugged my arm since my eyes were still glued to the trash can. Once I started moving, she asked, "How'd it go at Aspen Crest? Did you learn a lot?"

Nothing at all about Winston or the case. Nothing but more dead ends. But it hadn't been a waste. I bumped my shoulder against hers. "I learned I'm so glad I'm *here*."

24

Do you have a second, Huck?" Ms. Gregoire popped from a dark alcove at the back of the Convocation Hall, blocking my exit.

I wanted to say no, to protest "train schedules" and "weekend." Freedom was just two steps away, but I was too busy trying to pretend my vertical leap was some sort of slick maneuver and that I was straightening my tie, not clutching my chest. I was fully committed to denying that the anemic mouse squeak of a scream had come from me, but I was hopeful—maybe delusional—that it had been covered by the student noise in the echo-y hall. Seriously, though, it was like she'd materialized from the shadows.

Or... like my body was still trying to process all the coffee I'd dumped into it lately. I nodded and followed as she stepped to the side, undamming the student traffic jam her jack-in-the-box appearance had caused. She sat in the last row, calmly waiting until the building was mostly empty. Mostly quiet.

"You keep making references to Sherlock and 'a case,'" she said. "And you've been erratic and exhausted in class lately. I'm not sure if this is related to the Clara video or an entirely different problem, but if there's something I can help with, please let me know."

Could she help? I wasn't sure. But she was on the admissions committee, and she may or may not be magic. It couldn't hurt. "Remember that day I was supposed to have a date?"

"Of course." Her forehead creased. "With Curtis's brother—and I met him when you were taking pictures."

"Winston." I didn't need to clarify, I just liked saying his name. And maybe other people would think it was "uncool" to talk to their teacher about their love life, but those people didn't have *this* teacher—and I'd take any help I could get.

I missed the first train as I filled her in. The Convocation Hall had emptied, and then even the lights went out.

"Hang on." She stood and waved her arms. The action should've looked unhinged, but somehow even when popping out of alcoves or flapping like a bird, Ms. Gregoire did so with a panache that just...worked. Maybe because she didn't take herself too seriously. I used to be like that too: Good with a quip or dimpled joke. A diffuser of situations, fixer of problems. Man, did I miss *that* version of Huck. The one who slept and didn't have to actively *not* think about stopping for coffee. The lights clicked back on and she sat. "Cost-saving eco-measure. Many a night I'm grading papers and the lights go out. Usually I take that as my signal to go home, but we're not going anywhere until we finish talking this through. Though, I can't say this is entirely new to me."

"What? How?" I squinted at her.

"I've seen the page—the whole admissions committee

has. There was a link to it in the email that withdrew his application. And while I had his application reinstated after talking to you both on campus, I didn't know this whole rigmarole about the fake page—or the fake email. I thought it was sent in a panicked moment. This changes things."

"But the page is set to private," I protested. I'd been holding on to that fact, hoping it kept him safe.

"The school profile was given full access," she answered. "And you can imagine how well that went over with the committee."

"So he's doomed?" I dropped my face into my hands.

"Not necessarily." She pressed her lips together, and I gave her space to think. But while she was doing so, my pocket buzzed with an iLive alert.

"There's a new post."

She didn't crowd me as I navigated to it. In fact, she was sending her own text message, one I caught from the corner of my eye. Going to be a bit late. Start dinner?

It was on the tip of my tongue to apologize for keeping her, but then the post finished loading.

There had been plenty of posts *about* Hero High, but they'd all been about the school, not the students. Not anymore.

In the posted picture Lance was wearing his Hero High uniform. And based on the muddy sidewalks, it looked pretty recent. He was turned to the camera but not facing it. Like he'd been talking to someone who'd been cropped out. The shot was poorly framed, poorly lit. Overexposed. Maybe underexposed? Regardless, anyone with even passing knowledge of photography could've shot better. Win would've made something frame-worthy.

`What's that word for when a guy hits on his best friend's little sister? Oh, right: SCUM.`

"It's not from Win." I wasn't sure if I was reminding her or myself, but I was also clicking on the photo making sure Lance hadn't been tagged. Would someone tell him? Should I? Or at least give Curtis a heads-up so he could? It was only an hour ago that Lance had stopped by my row in this building to tell me the Chester formal was a go. Who even *knew* about it?

Ms. Gregoire hit the button on my phone that made the screen turn off. "Let's go back to the post about you."

I lifted my phone. "Do you want me to pull it up?"

She shook her head. "Every post, by their very nature, risks exposure. Each one is predicated on the assumption that the subject *won't* doubt Win wrote it and won't confront him."

"Or, if they do—won't actually give him context." I was thinking of Cole and his fists or others' cold shoulders. Attitudes Win had found inexplicable before.

"Right." Ms. Gregoire tapped a finger against her lips. "So it's clear the person behind this doesn't know you."

I frowned. I'd followed her logic to this point but couldn't see the steps to this conclusion. "How so?"

"Your post was much riskier. You're not reactive—you wouldn't knee-jerk break up with Winston without explaining why."

"*I* wouldn't ever believe he wrote it." Maybe after our meeting on the Campbells' driveway, but not since our first conversation when he walked me home—no way.

"Exactly." Ms. Gregoire nodded. "Whoever wrote it doesn't know how perspicacious you are."

"Also," I half stood as pieces connected. "We're *not* dating. Not yet. But whoever wrote the post doesn't know that—and they implied we'd already kissed. We haven't." A fact that I'd whined about to Rory, and Curtis, and Miles—and I'm sure Win had been likewise complain-y to his circle. Which meant... it had to be someone who'd heard about Morris's Chester-lunchroom proclamation and made assumptions. "Thanks. This helps."

It was another filter to funnel suspects through. But first I needed suspects...

Ms. Gregoire mimed dusting off her hands. "Remember, all cases have a ticking clock and a motive. You've got a week. A week from right now is the last admissions meeting. When an applicant is polarizing, we put off the decision as long as possible—and Winston's on that final list of students to debate. I can convince everyone the page is fake, I can win sympathy about how it must feel to be so targeted. But I need something from you—from *him*, really."

"What?" It was a croak. Five days until we took the page down. Seven days until my video was due and the final admissions committee meeting. Eight days until acceptance and rejection letters got mailed. I'd picked a heck of a time to cut back on coffee.

"Does he actually *want* to go here? Because even disregarding the fake email and page, the impression he's given is that he... *doesn't*."

I tamped down the pressure that bloomed in my chest—the urge to shout *I want him here*—because all it did was emphasize that I didn't have *his* answer. I only had everyone else's.

Ms. Gregoire patted my shoulder as she stood. "And if he does, it would be great if we could see some evidence of that."

25

I boarded the 4:37 train—my head spinning with motives, ticking clocks, evidence, and caffeine craving—and stumbled out into Penn Station seventy minutes later with them all still crowding my thoughts.

Miles was waiting at the stairs that lead from the tracks into the pandemonium of people headed to subways and train lines, bathrooms and restaurants. A policewoman with a dog passed as he lifted the duffle bag off my shoulder and slung it onto his own. “Hey, Puck.”

“Hey, Half-G.”

Miles was still in a suit, tie loosened, briefcase in hand. He’d come straight from work. Since I was still in my uniform, we more or less matched.

We emerged from the building into the loud chaos of Seventh Avenue. The sidewalk was crowded with pamphlet-wielding tour-company hawkers, people walking briskly and having to step around others who’d stopped to read a text or pull up a ride-sharing app. A group of tourists in matching neon sweatshirts had accidentally absorbed a stroller-pushing mom—no, nanny—and she was trying to get out without running anyone over.

New York overwhelmed me. It was sensory bombardment. The smells: traffic and kebabs and a wisp of perfume from the woman who'd bumped into me while digging through her purse. The sounds: beeps and a thousand footsteps, the one-sided conversations of people wearing earbuds, the two-sided conversations in a half-dozen languages. It was too much to take in. I was blinking in the twilight, making sure I didn't walk into anyone stopping to take a selfie, and trying to listen to Miles tell me about his day.

I doubted even Sherlock would find New York to be good detecting ground. But then again, had nineteenth-century London been any easier, with its opium dens and hansom cabs?

Maybe the problem wasn't the setting but the detective.

"How's my little sister?" Miles asked. He'd met Rory when she'd dragged me to an exhibit at the Met in February. Miles had skipped the museum but taken us out to dinner after. And within five minutes declared, "Rory's in, you're out. I only have time for one sibling, and I've decided to adopt her."

I hadn't objected. Frankly, I loved him more for recognizing her awesomeness.

I dug around in my bag for the sketch of Luna she'd slipped me in Convocation. "This is for you. And I'm under strict orders to tell you hi and that she's hoping to be interning for Andrea Snipes in the city for the second half of July, so don't plan any trips then."

Miles pulled out his phone to add the dates to his calendar. "I assume you'll be crashing on my couch?"

"At least part of the time."

"Cool. You hungry? Ramen?"

I nodded, following him down two blocks, around a

corner, then inside a dim restaurant whose smell made my mouth water.

The waitress took our orders, filled our water glasses. She was two steps away and I was only twenty-three minutes into this weekend when Miles asked, "So what's new with you and this guy?"

And for the second time today, I told the whole story.

Our food arrived, but neither of us lifted a spoon—despite two visits from the waitress checking to make sure it was all right.

"—and the admissions committee meets next Friday for the final time before letters go out." I slumped back in my seat. My ramen was on the lukewarm side of edible. I still ate it without complaint, repressing the urge to order an espresso to go with it.

Miles slurped absently, his forehead creased the way it did when he was figuring out a problem. He was analytical too. And calculating—in the mathematical sense, which served him well on Wall Street. It also made him an excellent big brother, even though we'd spent the past five years living in different states. "What do his parents say?"

"They're so traumatized by what their lack of belief has put Win through. I'm half convinced I'll get home on Sunday to find out they've gone to the police about the page."

"I'm not so sure they shouldn't," said Miles, signaling for the check. "Whoever did this is seriously messed up. But I have one question." He frowned and dabbed at a spot of broth on his sleeve. He wasn't prioritizing his dry cleaning over me; this pause was him figuring out his wording. "What does Win want? Because at this point his parents and siblings believe him—which seemed to matter most to him. You could shut down the page, use that to clear his name, and call it a day. Maybe whoever is behind it would try something else, but they mostly got away with it because no one was taking his side. That's not true anymore."

I poked my noodles with a chopstick as I considered this. What did he want? Besides, well, *me*. And the fact that he'd been so clear about that when he wasn't about much else made my chest warm. I was chipping pieces of yolk out of the tea egg in my bowl, watching them turn the broth unappetizing colors.

Ms. Gregoire and the admissions committee had wondered this too—had read his attitude about Hero High as ambivalent. Was that right? If so, maybe the police and some cybercrimes unit *were* the way to go; it was only beating the admissions timetable that made my involvement make sense.

Miles had gotten the check, paid it, and put on his jacket while I pondered this. "I don't know if he's *let* himself want it," I said slowly. "I don't know if anyone's asked him."

Miles clapped a hand on my shoulder. "Then someone probably should. I nominate you."

I'd been hoping Miles would have some breakthrough suggestion about the case, but all his advice had been about Win.

Win and Me.

Man, it was obnoxious when he was wise. New York had given me distance, and Miles had offered perspective. I might not be able to solve this case. And if I couldn't, Win and I still remained. What were *we*?

Win had asked me way back on the day when I crashed his chores, "Is a puzzle still interesting if it can't be solved? What if I don't get into Hero High?"

My answers, then and now, were the same. But what had changed was that *then* I'd been too busy chasing clues to speak them.

Now I realized he needed to hear them. That they weren't as obvious outside my head.

My thoughts were crowded with things I didn't know and hadn't spoken. With observations sans analysis and analysis sans conclusions. And as I watched suburbia smear past the train windows on Sunday morning's ride home, I didn't know what to do with it all.

Ms. Gregoire didn't ask me to write response journals for *Sherlock*, but maybe I was used to it from the other books she'd assigned, or maybe it was just something I needed to get out. Because when I balanced my laptop on my knees and began to type, instead of completing the homework on Walt Whitman, I wrote about Holmes.

My family used to have this tradition where we guessed presents before we opened them. We'd try to fool each other with our wrappings—strange shapes, oversized boxes, padding material, slipping in a handful of dried beans to change the noise it made when shaken. Used to—and it's my fault the tradition ended. Because the unwritten rule no one tells you is: People don't want you to guess correctly. They want to feel clever, like they've fooled you or gotten away with something. They want the surprised reaction when the duct tape and bubble wrap and paper towel tubes have been cleared away. They get a sense of accomplishment from hearing, "I had no idea."

And I was too good at guessing.

The last time we played was my parents' fifteenth anniversary. Dad brought in a long, rectangular box. It was wrapped in newsprint and tied with ribbon—there were fifteen helium balloons attached. But in one corner you could see the packaging underneath—from a florist. Mom shook her head and chuckled. "Is it roses? You know they're my favorite."

My older brother said, "Good one, Dad."

I'd shaken my head, interrupted as Mom began untangling balloon strings and tape. "No, wait. He already took the roses out. I bet they're hidden somewhere—" I'd smelled fresh-cut leaves when I walked in the house and the box had come from Dad's trunk—where he wouldn't have left roses on an eighty-five degree day. "It's something else in there. I'm guessing diamond earrings—Mom's been hinting and Dad has a jewelry store receipt in his wallet." I'd seen it when he stopped for gas.

I'd been right. I'd spoiled the surprise. I'd ended the tradition.

Sherlock Holmes tells Watson of "the curses of a mind with a turn like mine"—how he can't shut it off, how he sees everything through the lens of his profession. I get that.

How do you try not to notice things? I can't. But I've trained myself not to share them. Not to give in to that urge to be right. Which is so hard—there's so many times a day I feel deficient. I crave chances to feel clever.

And what's the use of noticing things—noticing everything—if I can't sort clues that are relevant from those that aren't? If I just collect more and more facts to weigh on my mind but can't solve anything?

I was looking at sneakers online last week. I could filter by color, style, price, size—weed out the ones I didn't want and create a list that fit my specifications. I can't help thinking that if I could just figure out how to do that with the contents of my head—that I could make things finally make sense. That for once I wouldn't be the weirdo for making deductions; I'd be the hero.

26

I hadn't meant to throw a party. But as far as accidents go, this was a good one. I thought I'd have Bancroft and a few others over on Sunday night to do their Hero High interviews. But then Clara had showed up with a back seat full of friends, and her brother, Penn, had decided to stay instead of dropping her off. He'd called his girlfriend, and Lynnie came with her twin, Byron. I'd asked for Wren's number, and they'd agreed to stop in and lend their voice to an interview. Rory and Toby showed up. Lance dropped by with the rest of his lunch table. Pretty soon my basement was full of classmates.

And while I hadn't meant for it to be a party, the fact that I'd thrown one had scored me infinite points with my parents. I could practically see their stress levels dropping with each doorbell ring. They were taking this as proof I'd finally acclimated after the move.

And maybe they weren't wrong.

"Do you guys need more snacks? Pennsylvanians really like pretzels. I should go get some. What kind? Rye, extra salty, the big ones? Snaps?"

I interrupted Dad's encyclopedic knowledge of the pretzel aisle—*why?*—to ask, "Could I use your office for—"

"Sure!"

"—interviews. It's too noisy downstairs." It was a little alarming he'd agreed before I'd finished the request. One of these days I was going to sit my parents down and lecture them on the perils of their new popularity fixation. Yes, we'd moved—and I was *fine*. But right now I was going to answer the door, because Rory had called her brother-in-law, and Trent had gathered a few of his Hero High alum friends so I could cross those interviews off the list too.

It was late when people left. Bancroft had upgraded me from choreographed handshake to bro hug, and between what they'd all revealed on camera and the time we'd spent chatting during setup and afterward, I got to know the rest of them a little better too. Not that Rory had to worry; I wasn't going to snatch the BFF bracelet off her wrist and regift it—despite the fact that she'd spent a good portion of the night making faces at me through the glass door of Dad's office while I was trying to record interviews.

But my conversations with everyone hadn't been fake. I'd talked as much as I listened. I hadn't felt awkward or like an outsider. Maybe I wasn't anymore.

Elijah even suggested that he and Shiloh and Win and I go out sometime.

"I'd like that," I said sincerely. "Though if I ever wrangle him into a double date, I promised the first to Rory and Toby. You guys can have second." I left unsaid that Win and I should have *any* date before I agreed to plans with his ex.

"Fair enough." Elijah gave Shi the type of open, soft-eyed smile that made my stomach twist with longing for the guy who *wasn't* here tonight. I'd considered inviting Win, even though I'd already done his interview. But I wanted him here because *I* wanted him here. And if he'd come, I'd have resented or rushed through recording everyone else so I could be with him.

Shiloh patted my shoulder. "Thanks for having us. We're going to head out so I can walk him home before curfew." At Mom's insistence they took a cup of snacks for the road. Dad's "pretzel bar" with the fifteen different options I hadn't been able to stop him from running out to purchase had—shockingly—not been as popular as he'd anticipated. There were *many* weeks of salty-doughy-yeasty lunches in my future. I wasn't looking forward to pickle flavored.

Surprisingly it was Mira and Clara who closed it down. And not only closed it down, but stayed to help me pick up. Mira had firmly waved me off when I'd protested that she didn't need to get out the vacuum.

"Let her." Clara gave Mira a thumbs-up as she switched the Dyson on. "She's going to have nightmares about carpet crumbs unless she sees they're properly taken care of. Seriously, if you want her to like you, let the girl vacuum."

"By all means, go ahead." I stepped out of the way as Mira sashayed toward us, humming as the pretzel crumbs disappeared beneath her precise sweeps of the rug. "But I want it on the record that she's volunteering."

"Let the record reflect that," Clara teased.

"Speaking of things on-record." I put down the empty soda cups I'd been stacking. "There's an idea I've been wanting to talk to you about." Because I'd heard from Charles again. I'd heard from other reporters too. I refused to give out Clara's number, but if she was interested, I could pass along theirs.

By the time Mira turned off the vacuum with a self-satisfied flick, Clara and I had hashed out a plan.

"I don't want to seek this out." Her mouth was as flat as her straightened hair. "But if any opportunity presents itself, I'd think about it."

Opportunities continued to present themselves to my voicemail several times a week, so I had no doubt this could work. And more than *could*, it *should.* When it came down to it, Clara and I had similar fixer skills, but she'd proven tonight that she belonged on the other side of the camera. Her interview had the potential to be the one I built the rest of the video around. It was witty, it was charming—it had the kind of enthusiasm that made you want to believe and it was grounded in her deep knowledge of the school. If I used a written overlay during her section it would only be to highlight the facts she said; there was no need to add or correct anything.

Mom and Dad had already gone to bed by the time I walked Mira and Clara to where Penn and Lynnie were waiting in his car.

I was exhausted and caffeine deprived enough that I might actually sleep, but first I needed to send a text. I'd heard from Win a few times over the weekend, mostly teasing updates as he tried to salvage footage from the Chester interviews I'd recorded before his instructions. I'd sent the files after I'd had an important realization, courtesy of more unsolicited big brother advice: *I had to let Win know I needed him too.*

"When you get nervous you try and fix things—whether or not they need fixing," Miles had said. "That's fine if it's a crooked lampshade or your middle school's recycling program, but Win's a person. And you guys have been dealing with real problems. Make sure *he* doesn't feel like a problem. And let him take a crack at some of yours too."

Hey.

I could stop there and wait for Win's response, let him steer the conversation, but that felt cowardly. *I missed you. And I have more interviews. I think these are less hopeless. You sick of hearing about Hero High, or will you use your vid-master skills to help me edit them into something watchable?*

It was late. It was a school night. Despite all the reasons not to expect a response, the three dots appeared almost immediately. I gave a quick whoop that startled Luna from her perch on Mom's cookbook stand.

I don't know if I'd call you hopeless. I mean, my five-year-old cousin takes better selfies, but "hopeless" feels harsh.

I laughed; Luna hissed. The lights were off. The kitchen was supposed to be her domain until dawn. I lifted my phone to respond, but Win beat me to it.

Good thing you have me. Send the interviews. See you tomorrow.

27

Huck, have you read *The Sign of the Four*?" Ms. Gregoire had been infinitely patient with me today. I'd spent most of class on the wrong page, the wrong poem. Too lost in my head to participate in discussions. The bell had rung and she could've let me be my next teacher's problem, but that wasn't how she worked; she didn't only care during class hours.

So I set down my bag and tried to focus on her question. *The Sign of the Four*. Stolen jewels, prison camps, prisoner uprisings, boats. Lost treasure. It was the novel where Watson met his future bride, Mary, and within a few shared hours they'd gone from introductions to declarations of feelings. Somehow *him* being involved with her case hadn't prevented them from getting together. I scowled, but nodded.

"Do you remember the part where Sherlock says, 'A change of work is the best rest'?" She handed me a marked-up version of my ad hoc response journal. "You need a change of work. Or a night *off* work."

I folded the page and stuck it in my bag. I'd read her commentary later, once I was ready to face the overshare I'd vomited onto my keyboard. "I just took a weekend away. I went to New York."

"That's a start, but..." She gestured around us with a flourish. "Take a night off *here*. Do something fun."

Fun. Like figuring out how to ask Win if he wanted to go to Hero High?

"I'm running out of time." I rubbed my forehead. "The admissions committee—"

"I'm handling them. You handle taking a break. Sherlock's orders."

I might need to reread that story, because I didn't remember Sherlock ever voluntarily taking a night off. But I did recall—and resent—how quick and easy romance had been for Watson. Him declaring, "If treasure's not in the way, I can say I love you, Mary."

Once the case wasn't standing between Win and me, then I could say... well, not *that*. But something. "Change of work." I told her. "Got it."

Meet me at Cool Beans?

It was super convenient that Win wasn't grounded anymore.

Less convenient that he was already deep in editing mode when I arrived at the coffee shop. A half-empty bottle of cranberry juice was uncapped beside him, and he was splicing and playing with light levels, importing all the individual interviews into a larger movie file and tweaking their order and text overlays as he went.

Maybe I should've been more specific in my text, mentioned that we were taking the night off—Ms. Gregoire and Sherlock's orders. But how could I complain when he was doing work *for me*—work I had no desire to do for myself, but that I dutifully paid attention to? Watching his hands and noting the sequences of clicks and buttons each skill took. But mostly I was regretting my choice of location. Regretting all the coffee I was smelling but not drinking.

I blinked when Win snapped his fingers at me. His amused expression made it clear it wasn't the first time he'd tried to get my attention. Maybe I should've apologized or thanked him for his help, but no one interrupted Sherlock when he was musing. "Why can't you just follow me around and shower me with accolades?"

Win sat back. "Excuse me?"

"That came out wrong. Sorry. It's just..." I groaned and rubbed my temples. A cup of coffee would help in so many ways, but I'd already hit my quota. "Sherlock Holmes has Watson, who's his biggest fanboy and helper, and sometimes I want one too." A sounding board. A partner. I couldn't tell Win about my worries, because they were all about failing *him*.

"Hey." Win's voice was quiet, and I jumped at the soft touch on the back of my hand. "Another headache?"

I nodded.

"Are you okay?" His brow furrowed. "You've been getting them a lot lately."

"How did you—" I shook my head, then winced. "I haven't said anything."

"You're not the only one who can observe." His darkening expression looked especially ominous when paired with the lingering green and yellow bruises around his eye.

"It's nothing. Just stupid caffeine withdrawal. I'm down to one cup in the morning then two cups spread throughout the day."

Win whistled. "*Down* to three cups? Do I want to know where you started?"

"It could be worse," I snapped.

"Okay, true." Win rummaged in his backpack and handed me a pair of sunglasses. They had advertisements for an HVAC company on the purple plastic arms, and there was no way they were UV protecting. But for filtering the light coming through the café windows and fixing my sun sensitivity, they were perfect.

"Thanks," I said. "It'll get better. At least that's what everything I've read says. Just have to be patient."

"I don't know about you, but I'm so tired of being patient. I want to fast-forward to when you tell me, 'Elementary, my dear Watson,' because you've figured it all out. And it's over. And we get to get to the interesting part."

"That line's not actually in the books. At least not in any of the stories I've read. I think it comes from the movies."

"Yeah, that's not interesting either."

I didn't take it personally. I didn't write the books, and Sir Arthur Conan Doyle was too dead to care. Also, Win's posture made my chest tighten. There was so much tension balanced on his shoulders.

I reached over and shut the laptop. "You know what? Ms. Gregoire was right. We need a night off. No more talking about Hero High or Sherlock Holmes or iLive. We're going bowling."

"Bowling?"

"We need to throw something. Knock things down. And eat rubbery pretzels dipped in fake cheese."

Win was out of his seat almost as fast as that time I'd vaulted a couch to escape a kiss. He chugged the rest of his juice and three-pointered the empty bottle. "I could go for some fake cheese."

Normally he was a fortress. A poker player. That he was broadcasting his enthusiasm was a gift, and I wanted to offer him one too. "You're not the only one who's impatient," I told him as we gathered our coats and he shoved his laptop into its case. "I want to get to the part where I get flirty with a snarky, hot guy—" I paused, in case this needed clarifying. "That's *you*, by the way. The hot guy."

Win glanced up from zipping his bag. "I figured. And thanks. But if that's true, then... why?"

"Why pick detective over boyfriend?" I sucked in a breath, because so many people had offered different opinions. But Rory and Miles and Curtis were all wrong. It wasn't just Sherlock's theories on emotion, or that I was scared, or that I didn't know what to do with requited, or that I felt the need to "earn" good karma after Clara. "Because no one else was stepping up for the role. And you deserve someone who's on your side with no ulterior motives."

He opened the café door and gestured me out, but then caught my arm as I passed him and quirked those irresistible eyebrows. "*No* ulterior motives?"

"I mean, don't get me wrong, I want to kiss you—" We sidestepped to let a frazzled woman with a stroller through the door. Then, after catching her raised-eyebrows eavesdropper's face, we continued down the sidewalk past the outdoor tables, pausing when we reached the corner of the building. My face was a furnace, not from being overheard but from the honesty I was about to drop as Win leaned back against the brick wall and waited. "I want that so bad. But I also want you to have someone taking you seriously. Believing you."

Win was inscrutable, but that didn't mean he wasn't scrutinizing me. And every emotion I'd offered up felt printed in bold on my flushed cheeks. It became too much and I dropped my gaze, only to have it snag on his mouth. On the way his bottom lip was slightly chapped from how he always tugged and bit at it. How would that feel against mine?

I shifted left, ready to bolt down the sidewalk. I needed a walk in damp air, a bowling alley full of strangers and crashing pins to beat these thoughts from my head—but Win tightened his grip on my arm.

"Just so you know." His voice was low, raspy. His eyes darker than they'd been when I'd last met them. "Watson and Sherlock have nothing on me: I *am* your biggest fanboy."

I laughed. Apparently we *weren't* doing the thing where we actually stopped talking about Sherlock. "You just can't make it easy for me."

Win's hand was still bunching the sleeve of my blazer. "I don't make it easy for anyone."

"True." This was one of the first facts I'd deduced about Win. If you wanted to be in his life, you had to prove you wanted him in yours. And not just once. Daily. "And in case my obsession with clearing your name isn't clear enough—I'm your biggest fanboy too."

His expression flickered. It was there and gone. A tiny glance left. A loosening of his fingers on my arm. It was a drop of doubt poisoning our well. And the only way to counteract his fear that I'd run was to stand.

I planted my feet wider. His hand was on my arm, so I put one on his shoulder. Put the other on his neck, where he could probably feel the tremble in my fingers.

When I was five, during my very last swim lesson the

lifeguard had led me out to the edge of the diving board. I'd shaken as hard then as I did now. And while she'd been poised in the water beneath, clutching a long red float and promising to catch me, I'd dropped to my knees and crawled backward off the board.

This time I leapt. Crashing forward into the boy who was leaning in to catch me. Pressing my lips against his in a sigh that melted trembles into shivers of electricity.

This kiss was...

There were no words.

Just...

Lips.

And Win.

I thought he'd broken me, because it was the first time I could remember my mind being quiet. The only time I'd been fully in my body—fully fixated on sensations and...

His tongue had teased past my lips and twisted with mine.

And.

He groaned.

I drank down the sound and added my own to the chorus. I was off-balance. Even though I was firmly planted on the sidewalk, it felt like I was falling. It echoed my fears from the diving board—and I pulled back, straightening, gasping like a person who'd gone under and nearly drowned.

In actual drownings, the victim often endangers those trying to rescue them. They cling too tightly and thrash so wildly that they can drag them both under. I did the opposite. Practically shoved Win away—not that there was anywhere for him to go. His back was already against the wall.

Both our chests were heaving with ragged breaths. His eyes were wary, his voice soft. "You okay?"

"Wait." We were supposed to wait. I braced my hands against his shoulders, locking my elbows to keep distance between our mouths, but curling my fingers into the fabric of his shirt, like I dared anyone to try and make me let go. I didn't have time to get distracted. I didn't have room to make mistakes. I didn't have the strength to keep resisting him. "There's only four—"

"No." Win shook his head, then leaned a cheek against the back of my hand, bringing his own up to rest on top of mine. "You're not—we're not doing this. No. You make a lot of decisions, but I'm not letting you make this one. What difference is four days going to make? Are you going to change how you feel about me?"

Miles's advice had proved itself ridiculously accurate—not that I'd ever tell him. But I *would* tell Win. That was the whole point. That I needed to speak my truths, not just think them. My arms went slack, my feet scooching closer. "No, of course not."

"Then I'm not letting us hit pause. We're not doing that. I won't make it through another four days—not after . . ." His eyes focused on my mouth with a look that made me swallow and pray to the gods of lip balm and sibling wisdom.

"I have one question."

His laughter rumbled beneath my hands. "You always do."

"Do you want to go to Hero High?"

I didn't emphasize the pronoun or list off all the people whose opinions I didn't want. I didn't need to when we were standing so close our sneakers overlapped and our words ghosted across each other's cheeks.

I watched him process the question, felt his pulse flare beneath my palm. I waited for his expression to shutter or his posture to stiffen. Instead he met my eyes with a look that was pure, vulnerable, and raw—and nodded.

Our gaze held, and I was microseconds from leaning in to kiss him again—I figured we were owed a reward for our courage and honesty—when he blinked and pulled back.

"Come with me."

"Where are we going?" But I put my hand in his and followed without waiting for an answer.

Which was good, because clearly I wasn't getting one beyond "You'll see when we get there."

We turned toward his house, but that wasn't our destination. Instead he squeezed my hand and headed into one of the small parks that dotted our town. Having no real reason to visit playgrounds or dog parks, I hadn't been here before, but I felt my dimples emerging in anticipation of whatever memory Win was about to share.

Had he and Morris terrorized Wink on that pirate ship play structure? Had Curtis fallen from one of these trees? Had he won some photography award capturing the way the seasons revealed themselves in the branches of the maples and oaks?

We were communicating in presses of his fingers around mine, each pulse sending energy up my arm and sparking electricity in my blood. Because whyever we were here, it was just a precursor. After he shared his nostalgia, we'd be making our own memory. At least that's what I assumed from the way our eyes kept landing on each other's mouths and the shivers of anticipation that seemed to originate in my chest and resonate in his.

He led me past pickleball courts and across a jogging trail to a tree beside a tall chain fence. His free hand closed around the links, but I barely spared a glance for the concrete expanse on the other side. I wanted my explanation from him.

"This public pool is where I learned to swim." The lift of his eyebrows and hesitant lilt in his voice communicated its personal significance. "It was my first swim team too. I was here every summer morning when I was little. And when Mom went back to work full-time and needed us in all-day camp, the swim director invented some fake junior lifeguard position so I could stay on the team and then spend the afternoons here instead."

"They must really like and believe in you."

He shuffled his feet at the compliment but didn't deny it. Progress. "This summer I'll be old enough to actually lifeguard, once I pass the course." He was looking through the fence, but I doubted he was seeing the taut gray pool cover, the salt- and leaf-strewn concrete, the stack of picnic tables, or the lifeguard stands that had been lowered to their sides. I wanted to know what it looked like in his mind—when the water sparkled and there were ladders and slides and diving boards, crowds of people laughing and splashing, a line at the boarded-up snack bar, people headed in and out of the locker rooms, towels on the grass. *Him* in red trunks sitting on one of the stands, sunglasses on, a whistle around his neck.

New summer plan: invest heavily in sunblock, because I was about to become a poolside groupie.

"I'll teach you to swim here," he said. "We'll wait till the end of June so the water has a chance to warm up."

"Um, no." My lifeguard fantasy was rapidly fading into panicked images of myself sinking awkwardly in the middle of a group of three-year-olds more adept at floating like a starfish or whatever.

His laugh was a low rumble as he turned toward me. “Where’s the trust?”

The question made me pause, because the amount of trust he’d shown *me* was extraordinary. It made my chest tight as I thought over every secret and fear and flaw he’d laid bare, offered up, and endured. “Fine.”

He grinned as he stepped closer. “They’ll be lessons before the pool opens or after it closes. You, me. I won’t let you sink—just like you haven’t let me. I would’ve drowned these past couple of weeks if you hadn’t been holding me above water.”

They were words punctuated with brushes of his lips to my cheeks, my jaw, my ear. Until I could practically feel the future sunburn on my skin and taste chlorine on my lips as I nodded and lowered them to his.

28

I floated home with swollen lips and two dozen texts from Rory. Mostly made up of !!!s and emojis, all responding to the one message I'd sent her: I kissed him!

I was giving myself until eight p.m. to revel—to bask in Ms. Gregoire's brilliant, brilliant idea to take a break—but then I had to buckle down. Win's answer about Hero High had raised the stakes but hadn't given me any clarity.

Hopefully clarity would come at 7:59.

But first: family dinner. Pork chops, mashed potatoes, and green beans, served with a side of parental gloating about last night. "You finally put yourself out there and look at all those nice kids who've just been waiting to be your friends."

I nodded and uh-huh'ed and estimated I needed to sit there for fourteen minutes and clear approximately two-thirds of my plate in order to avoid raising their suspicions. Both tasks felt Herculean—it was hard to tone my smile down from megawatt to sure-I'm-listening. Impossible to actually listen.

Eventually Mom said, "Okay, Huck, we'll stop picking on you now," and prompted Dad to share something about his day.

"A student fell asleep in my afternoon class." Dad helped

himself to more beans. "Normally, I just let them get their REM on. It was a really good lecture—on aggregate demand—so I figured anyone who wasn't rapt must've truly needed the sleep."

Mom nodded as he paused to cut a bite of pork chop, and I grinned into my water glass. They were both dead earnest; they couldn't imagine a scenario where Dad's economic lectures would be anything but scintillating.

"But this boy—Colin—started snoring. At first I thought it was a radiator. Everyone sort of froze and—"

There was a knock on the door. A banging really. Even though the doorbell was right there, waiting to play "Hello!" from *The Book of Mormon* when pressed.

Mom and Dad looked at me. "Maybe one of your friends forgot something last night. Why don't you go see?"

I put my napkin over my plate. Regardless of who was at the door—and I was praying to the gods of interruptions and getaways that it was Rory—I was done eating.

"Curtis?" It was the reverse of our usual pattern: me on their doorstep. Except I usually managed to stand still while waiting, and he was pacing our front porch like Dad right before midnight when he hadn't met his step count goal.

"We need to talk."

I nodded and called over my shoulder, "It's Curtis—official Knight Light stuff."

"Does he want any dinner?" Mom asked.

"Or to come in and tell us about his brother?" added Dad.

"Another time, Mr. and Mrs. Baker," Curtis called before yanking me onto the porch and shutting the door.

Our porch wasn't small—it ran the length of the house—but the only place to sit was a white wooden swing. It could technically fit two, but this didn't feel like the setup for a cozy, swinging conversation—and with Curtis as fidgety as he currently was, he'd probably flip us over.

"Are you sure?" Curtis abruptly stopped pacing and pointed a finger at me. "Are you *really* sure that Win's not behind the page?"

If he hadn't looked so hurt, I would've hit him. But thank the gods of neural pathways and reaction times that instead of a fist, I formed a response. "I'm absolutely, fundamentally positive. Why? What happened?"

He groaned, cupping his face in both hands.

I grabbed a wrist and pulled it down so I could see his expression. "Tell me you didn't tell him you were doubting."

"No." Curtis pulled away to pace again. "At least I didn't screw that up. But there's a new post."

"Hang on." I grabbed my phone and pulled up the site. "Give me context."

"Win and I got in a fight at dinner. A real one, not just, you know, our usual passive-aggressive sniping." He sighed. "I thought we were past the whole 'anything I do is to make you look bad' mind-set, but my parents brought up how there's going to be this stupid thing at Convocation this Friday. It's a congrats-on-the-Avery slash good-luck-at-the-international-science-fair hoopla."

"And Win said something snarky?"

"No. My parents want the whole family to come—Win refused."

"Can you really blame him?" I asked. "You're being honored by the school the same week he expects it to reject him."

"Can you blame *me* for wanting him there?" He tugged his hair. "This is a big deal for me."

"Fine," I said. "You're both wrong. Finish the story."

Curtis shrugged. "Then we fought—though nothing we said to each other was as bad as that—"

He nodded at my phone and I looked down at the post: `Is there a word for when your peak is the high school science fair and the rest of your life will be a disappointment? Maybe in German? #MeinBrotherCheated #HeroHighCheaters`

I sucked in a breath. "Who was there during the fight?"

"My parents. Win. Wink. Reese."

"When did it go up?" I could see the timestamp, but I meant in relation to the rest.

"Reese left almost as soon as we got shouty, and Wink went to hide in her room. Win stormed off a few minutes later. I stayed at the table because we can't *both* sulk in a shared room. I still wasn't thinking it was that big a deal, so I was making jokes about needing hundreds of cupcakes to demo the project for all of Hero High." His words and feet had been racing, but both slowed to a crawl. "Then Lance called. He's been watching the page since the post on him. I saw it, and I came straight here."

I pressed my lips together, dreading the question I was going to ask, because I already knew the answer, knew what it meant I would have to do. "So Win doesn't even know?"

"If you're sure he didn't post it? Then no. Not unless Wink told him, and I seriously doubt it. She was whining on the phone to Reese when I left."

I sighed. Looked like my break was ending early. "Okay. Let's go."

29

"Go away, Wink. I don't want to talk about it." Win didn't look up from his math notebook when I knocked on his bedroom door. Not that he appeared to be doing homework. He was etching dark *X*s down the margin of his page. They were probably just angry doodles—but the visual, like he was marking problems wrong before even trying them, hit a little too close to home.

"I'm not Wink."

His chin shot up and his eyes lightened. "Oh, hey." His gazed dropped to my mouth, his own lips curling. "Miss me al—" But then he read something on my expression and narrowed his eyes. "No. I thought we agreed we weren't doing this four-day pause."

"That's not why I'm here." I stifled a groan of regret, because I didn't want to mix the guy who'd spent an hour kissing him with the guy who gave him bad news. But I was *both* those people, and separating them felt impossible.

"iLive?" His posture stiffened, but his voice was deliberately disinterested as he drummed the eraser end of his pencil on his notebook. "Who did I piss off this time?"

Yeah, I should've guessed he'd take the transition even worse than me. "Your brother."

His mouth gaped, but I shoved my phone at him before he could ask. It was only a two-line post, but it took him fifteen increasingly shallow breaths to look up. And when he did, there was a weariness in his eyes that made my chest hurt. "What now?"

"This post went up within fifteen minutes of your fight with Curtis. Whoever is doing this knew about that." I watched his face bunch then panic as he came to the first logical conclusion. "It's not Reese."

"Are you sure?"

Reese knew we knew the page was fake; if she'd been savvy enough to run it for months, there was no way she'd give herself away like this. Plus, her reaction when I told her about the page had exonerated her forever. I gave him the same answer I'd given Curtis when he asked about Win. "Positive."

He stared past me to his door, like he was looking through it to the hall and bedroom across. The color drained from his face. His inhale was a marathon, and the exhale sounded like he was pushing against the weight of the world. "I...I have to tell you something."

I put a hand on his dresser, because while other people might claim Spidey sense, my Sherlock sense was tingling, alerting me that I'd need to brace myself. I looked at the slump of his shoulders, the set of his jaw. I wished I was wrong about what he was going to say; I knew I wasn't. "I'm listening."

"I did the post about Curtis. The other ones too. And the

emails." He still wouldn't look at me, but I could see a sheen on his eyes, or maybe it was on mine, because the whole world had gone distorted. He turned away with a muffled "I'm so sorry."

"Stop." I pressed a hand to my chest for emphasis and to counteract the pain blooming there. "Just stop."

Old habits were hard to break. He may have promised to be my lifeguard today, but he had years of experience saving someone else. Even when she didn't need saving.

"Can you say something?" he begged. "You can't really be surprised. This is *me* we're talking about." His hands were tight fists, and I remembered the morning they'd been split, how he'd winced each time the cleaners got in his raw cuts. This stung more. "This is what I do: I screw up. You've got so much evidence of it—"

"You don't get to dictate my opinion of you." My voice was low—more like a growl—but it got louder as I continued. "You don't get a say in how I feel about you. Or to take away all the kind things I've observed you doing. And the fact that you're sitting there trying to think of a way to put yourself down breaks my heart."

"Huck—"

I shook my head, ignoring the wetness that was gathering in the corner of my eyes. "I'm not going to stand here and pretend you're not lying. I quit. I'm done."

It was the dishonesty that hurt the most. I would rather he *had* done it than have him tell me this lie. Like I wouldn't see through it. Like I hadn't been there to gauge his first shocked reaction to that page, or been beside him while he processed the ramifications. Like I didn't know his pattern of sacrificing himself for his sister. Like I hadn't spent the past two weeks reassuring him I believed his innocence and trying to prove it.

"Huck..." But he didn't follow my name with an explanation, an apology, or anything true. Except maybe that was the deepest truth: that like his voice, he was broken and all regrets.

It hurt to turn my back on him and face his door with its growth-chart markings. I didn't want to remember how tall Win was on his fifth birthday and how tall he was the day he kissed then gutted me. "I talked to Ms. Gregoire about your application." I hadn't had a chance to tell him this; we'd been too busy kissing. "She says the biggest obstacle you're facing with the admissions committee is that they don't believe you *want* to attend. That you spent your interviews acting like you don't. So the thing standing in your way is... you."

"What else is new?"

I ignored him. "It's you not sticking up for yourself. For what you want. You need to know that you deserve to go there." I looked over my shoulder and swallowed against a tightening throat. "You deserve me. You deserve anything you want. You just need to be willing to fight for *yourself*. Because I'm fighting for you. So many people are fighting for you. But we need you to step into the game too."

"Were." Win's eyebrows challenged me to correct his use of past tense. "You *were* fighting for me. But were you ever interested in me as more than a problem to solve?"

"Are you kidding me?" I raised my hand to lips that'd so recently been touching his.

"You didn't have to save me to date me." Win half rose, then froze—maybe realizing this was a conversation we should've had weeks ago. *The* conversation we should've had instead of me throwing up boundaries and roadblocks to us getting together. "I didn't like you *because* you were trying to solve this. I wouldn't have stopped liking you because you couldn't."

"I didn't like you because you were a puzzle. I like you because you're *you*." I couldn't use past tense. And maybe he wouldn't notice, and maybe it didn't matter, but my heart and my hand were still extended—with caveats. "When you're ready to tell me why you lied just now, you know where to find me."

Then, because I already *knew* his answer, and knew he'd hold it in and torture himself with the belief, I added a parting gift as I let myself out. "And by the way: Wink didn't do it."

30

What the heck, Huck? I vacuum your basement and you don't even tell me something this major?"

It was too early for me to handle Mira standing hands-on-hips and glowering. I was too under-caffeinated, and there were too many things wrong with her statement.

"You *asked* to vacuum." I turned to Clara. "It was on the record." Also, what major thing hadn't I told?

Clara winked at me, and Mira's stern expression cracked into a smile. "Of course I did—your parents have a *Dyson*. Seriously though: You and Win? It's a thing?"

I blinked. She was a very odd girl—I kinda liked it.

Clara added, "Bancroft told us—but I'm smacking myself for not figuring it out sooner. You guys are perfect."

I turned toward my locker, stealing a second to compose my face.

"Also, Win won't accept our friend requests on iLive and I'm annoyed," said Mira. "How am I supposed to tell him I approve?"

"Frankly, I'm surprised he has one." Clara twirled a curl as she mused. Her glittery sneakers matched her glittery nails, and these were both *good* things—signs of the old Clara coming back. But I was too emotionally drained to care. "He and Mac used to jokey-argue about it. Win always said, 'You either have a life or you iLive.' He's not wrong."

"You're not missing much," I told them, then realized there was no reason *not* to say more. Wink was supposed to be taking the page down, and *I'd* been the one who'd insisted on secrecy, back when I'd thought I could solve this. Back before Win had lied to my face to cover—again—for his twin. This time for something she didn't even do. "Actually, the page isn't his. I know it's his name and picture, but—"

I gave them the barest of stories, staring at a Model UN poster behind them so I didn't have to watch Clara brainstorming or Mira's fierce protectiveness expanding to include us.

"What can we do?" Clara asked. "Besides obviously making sure everyone hears this."

"I'm already on it." Mira waved her phone. "Wait here. I'll go get you pretzels."

"Pretzels?" I asked Clara after she'd stormed off.

"Aren't they your favorite?" She tilted her head. "We figured they must be since you had so many kinds at the party."

I laughed so hard my eyes welled—then I was balancing on a knife-edge, trying not to tip over to real tears.

Clara squeezed my arm. "Need a topic change?"

I nodded. And actually, I had one. "I got another call from Charles last night. I sent his phone number to your Hero High email, but there's no pressure for you to use it."

She raised a shoulder in a casual shrug before pivoting on the toe of one sparkly sneaker to greet Mira, who was rushing back with four mini-bags of pretzels that she'd scavenged from who knows where.

"Oh, no worries," Clara said. "I already did."

"How'd it go last night?"

I stared blankly at my English teacher. It probably wasn't that different from the blank expression I'd given her all class, or the one I'd worn while watching my clay spin aimlessly on the wheel in art. But there must have been some subtle giveaway because she grabbed a pen. "Oh dear. I'm going to need to write you a pass to your next class, aren't I?"

"No." I rubbed the base of my neck and reached into my backpack for the bag of chocolate-covered coffee beans Rory had given me as a weaning-down present. It took twenty beans to equal the amount of caffeine in one cup. This conversation would require at least five. "But only because I'm headed to Mayfield. My mom should be here in ten minutes to sign me out."

She put down her pen and sat back in her chair. "The night off didn't go well? Are you okay?"

"It had moments of promise..." Lucky me, I now knew what I was missing. "But it didn't end up being a good night." I traded beans for pretzels and used my foot to push my backpack away. "You know, sometimes Sherlock scares me."

She raised an eyebrow. "How so? The way a scary movie scares you? Or causes you personal fear?"

"I want to be as good at fixing things as him. But he's good because he's objective and unemotional." I stared down at salt on my thumb. "I don't know how to do that. To not care. I make people feel like projects *and* I have emotional blind spots." I lifted my chin. "I'm failing from *both* sides."

"Oh, Huck." Ms. Gregoire pressed a hand to her chest. "You're not failing at all. Don't stop caring—your big heart is one of the best parts about you. You want to fix the whole world—and maybe that doesn't happen at once, but you are making it a better place."

"But—" I thought of the times I'd asked questions that hurt Win because they felt like the right detective move. I thought about the answers I'd never found. "Sherlock's not—it's not a *love* story. Holmes cares for Watson more than any other human, but it isn't romance. And it's not a balanced relationship; he's always a bit patronizing when he tells Watson to make observations, then points out all the things he got wrong or missed. What must that feel like for Watson?"

And what must it feel like for Winston when we focused only on his mistakes, his past, his flaws?

Ms. Gregoire cleared her throat, waiting for me to meet her eyes. "Then it's a good thing you're not Sherlock."

"But you wanted me to read these stories?" And wasn't that what she did? Paired people via literary parallels?

"The lessons we learn from literature aren't prescriptive. There's not always a direct correlation; their endings aren't ours." The bell for third period rang, but she didn't blink or look away. "I appreciate that you admire aspects of Sherlock Holmes, but I also strongly discourage you from faking your own death or running around with a pistol."

I laughed. "Obviously."

Ms. Gregoire tapped her lip theatrically. "Hmm. So if *that* is obvious to you, why isn't this: you write your own ending. It's every bit as malleable as those of the people you make into projects."

"True, but..." But there was no but. If I expected to be able to change things for Rory or Clara or Win, why did I think I couldn't do the same for myself? I swallowed. "True."

She smiled at me. "And speaking of projects, you need to get to Mayfield to work on yours."

Ms. Gregoire was wrong about one thing. Did I *need* to go to Mayfield Middle Academy? Not really. But I already had the appointment, and a lack of interviews from Hero High's feeder school might look conspicuous.

But I didn't get anything usable. Every single student I interviewed had applied to Hero High. Which meant every one of them was a stress mess waiting to see if they'd get an acceptance or rejection letter mailed this weekend.

None of the frantic, sycophantic footage made me eager to sit down and edit. Especially since the last time I'd done so had been with Win.

When I got back to campus after a coffee-free drive-through lunch with Mom, Headmaster Williams stopped me as I was signing in. "Huck, let Mr. Welch know if you need any special setup for Friday's Convocation."

I blinked at him. "You want me to show my video at Convocation?"

"Well, make sure you show the final cut to Ms. Gregoire for approval first."

A slow grin spread across my face: Friday was when Curtis's family was supposed to come see him be honored. It was right before the admissions committee's last meeting. I didn't know how I'd put all these pieces together yet, but I'd come up with something.

31

Maybe there was something to Mom and Dad's Huck's-a-lonely-latchkey theory—because moping around my room Tuesday afternoon had been torture. Wednesday after school I tagged along with Toby and Rory. Tomorrow, maybe I'd go home with Bancroft, or ask Clara what clubs were meeting. Anything to fill the cavernous Cavendish hole in my days.

"Did you forget where you live? Or is Campbear too lazy to walk across the fifteen feet of grass between your driveways?" I asked when Toby pulled into hers.

He laughed. "Neither. I'm just dropping you guys off. I've got piano."

I got out of the car as he kissed her goodbye. In the past I would've been abstractly jealous, but now that I knew what it was like to kiss someone you cared about, I was glaring envious holes in the lawn.

Rory emerged from the car, bright-eyed and smiley, then dragged me to her kitchen and demanded, "Catch me up on all things Win and Sherlock and life in general."

She sketched lazily on a barstool as I sat at the Campbells' kitchen table and ate my way through most of their fruit bowl while explaining and complaining. "Between the school visits I've talked to a lot of the people who've been insulted on the page." I banged my head gently against the table. "Some of them don't like him—but none of them don't like him *that* much."

In "The Adventure of the Copper Beeches" Holmes tells Watson, "I have devised seven separate explanations, each of which would cover the facts as far as we know them." And I hated him for that line. Seven explanations. I had zero.

"Poor Huck." Rory reached down and patted my shoulder, probably leaving charcoal smudges on my blazer, then she resumed whatever she was shading. "If you don't think it's any of them, do you think... Could he have done it?"

I groaned against a poodle placemat. "No."

Her pencil stopped moving. "If it was me and Toby, I couldn't be open-minded. Are you sure you just don't want him to be innocent?"

I lifted my head and met her eyes, making sure she saw I was serious. "Yes. It's not him. Drop it, Campbear."

"If it's not someone who's on the page, then who's conspicuously not?" I turned to see Eliza standing in the kitchen doorway. She was holding the storage container I'd once moved to wipe down a cabinet. It was full of cupcakes. I knew their stress-baker. "Who else stands to benefit from Win being isolated or not getting into Hero High?"

While Rory picked out a cupcake for Toby from Curtis's baked goods, I mentally scanned the list of people insulted against the people in Win's life. Eliza was right—there was someone conspicuously absent. As Holmes had said, "Eliminate all other factors, and the one which remains must be the truth."

"Eliza, you're a genius!"

"I know." She frowned. "But that's the second least interesting thing about me. Did you figure it out?"

I stood and grabbed my bag. "I think—I think I did."

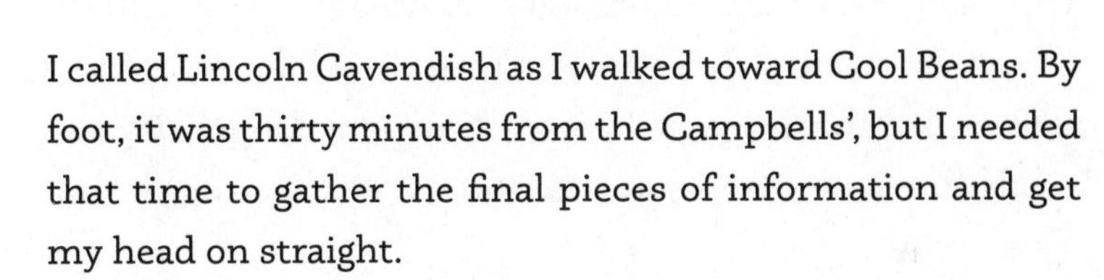

I called Lincoln Cavendish as I walked toward Cool Beans. By foot, it was thirty minutes from the Campbells', but I needed that time to gather the final pieces of information and get my head on straight.

"Hey, Huck." Wink's voice was hushed. "Curtis has gone through five pounds of flour, and Win appears to be doing a photo series of only broken things. Please tell me you're calling with good news."

"Close. I'm calling with questions. You know that kid Erick?"

"Yeah?" She sounded wary. "Is it him? I knew he was sneaky."

"Nope. But the kid he pantsed, the one who was commando—who was it?"

Win hadn't remembered, but Wink was an encyclopedia of social currency. I should've asked this sooner—not that I really needed her answer. Still, I sucked in a vindicated breath when she gave it.

"Another question: That fight Win and Curtis had about the science fair—did you talk to anyone about it?"

"Well, Reese was here, but after she left, I called—"

I could've completed that sentence for her too. And like a row of dominos, all the pieces were falling into place. It made sense why the only kind post on the page was about Wink.

Because Morris liked Wink. Because the page was Morris's.

I gritted my teeth, remembering how I'd glibly asked him, "How has Win wronged you?" and he'd had no answers. At the very least he could've cited the cheating thing and having to miss the class trip. Morris wore a Phillies cap; he was a fan. Hence the retaliation post about tattling Colleen.

And baseball! Bancroft told me that he, Elijah, and Morris were cut from the Mayfield team. The same team Erick had made. Erick who'd pantsed him. Erick of the dropped-ball revenge gif.

Shiloh had told me dating Win had "alienated friends" and that "middle school jealousy is real." Reese was Wink's BFF, and she'd asked Morris out, rendering him at least temporarily off-limits. Ergo the petty posts about both of them.

Frame Me had occupied Win's weekends, meaning Morris lost access to *both* Cavendish twins. The job had to go.

Lance became a target when he'd agreed to go to Wink's formal. It was a favor, not a date. Morris wouldn't care. Especially after Win had blocked him from taking her.

Hero High—that was obvious: an acceptance would take Wink and Win away from him.

Me? I'd monopolized Win's afternoons. But Ms. Gregoire was right: the person posting hadn't known me; he'd thought we'd break up. That I'd give his words that power. No chance.

No, it had been Win's words—Win's lie that had accomplished that.

But none of this was *proof*. It was all connections and coincidences. There was no smoking gun.

"Are you and Win fighting?"

I almost dropped the phone. I'd forgotten I was holding it and that Wink was still on the line.

"Yes." The truth was simple and strategic. "Actually, I could use some advice about him. Could you give me Morris's number?"

"Oh. I could—if you want, I—" I pretended not to hear her half offers, waiting her out until she rattled off his digits.

If Wink weren't so distracted by her brothers' bad moods, she definitely could've followed the pattern of my questions and drawn her own conclusions. But she didn't, and I further diluted the conversation by asking for Cole Martin's number too. There was no way I was letting him return from suspension still thinking Win had deserved that punch.

"If you haven't already, submit the takedown form to iLive," I told her. "Ask them to tell you the email address associated with the account."

I already knew how that would turn out—it would connect to the fake email used to retract Win's application and change his work schedule. One more clue that was also a dead end.

Except now I knew the culprit. I just needed to figure out how to get him to admit it.

I glanced up from my phone when the chair across the café table from mine scraped backward. "Morris. Hi. Thanks for meeting me."

"I wasn't surprised you called." He set down one of Cool Beans oversized in-house mugs. They were coated with chalkboard paint, orders and names scrawled on the side.

His read "green tea," which was as disgusting as him, and "Mortis"—Latin for "of death," which felt so fitting.

He nodded at my cup. "No mega today?"

I kept my face neutral but internally seethed that he'd brought up the last time we'd been here, sat at this same table while he'd played cards, played at being friends with the people he was betraying.

"Nope." I set down my cup. "Hunk" was written over "decaf pour-over," and I turned it to face away so I wouldn't be bombarded with the memory of when Win first walked me home. My drink was half finished, so it wobbled but didn't spill when Morris banged the table as he sat. He winced as tea splashed into his lap. "Let me guess: Win screwed up."

I shifted in my chair—not because I was uncomfortable or surprised by his words, but because I was supposed to be. "Yeah. How did you know?"

"Listen. I love the guy, but it's what he does. He'll do it again if you let him. It's good you're recognizing this and cutting your losses now."

Wow, that was a leap. And not at all subtle. I couldn't have disagreed more. So, of course I nodded emphatically.

"And what *I* do is pick up the pieces." He spread his hands and gave me a smarmy grin, along with a hint of his motive. Once I was eliminated, Win would *need* him. "People always call me when he screws up."

"What do you mean?"

"Well, *you* did." He frowned at my "confusion," annoyed I was asking questions instead of complaining about Win. "And Wink has me practically on speed dial."

"Wink has you on speed dial?" If you repeated the end of a person's statement back at them, changing the inflection to make it a question, they elaborated. It was simple and effective.

And infuriating.

Morris's ears turned red. "She's sensitive. And every time Win messes up or gets yelled at, she needs someone to vent to. She can't complain to him, because she's worried about making it worse."

I set down my cup with a clink. "So then you get to step in and play hero?" In my head it was sarcastic, but I'd kept my tone neutral.

"I don't know that I would've phrased it like that." Morris chuckled nervously, flattered by the words but not sure if they were complimentary. "But, basically. Yeah."

"Breaking things off with Win . . ." I bit the inside of my cheek until I could breathe steadily and speak calmly. If my façade was cracking, hopefully he attributed it to my being heartbroken—not that I thought he was the human equivalent of phlegm. "It's probably for the best." I took a slow sip of coffee to get Morris's full attention. "I mean, soon he won't have time for me anyway."

"Why?" His puzzled expression cleared. "Oh, right. Because of the job. I'm shocked the old guy rehired him. It won't last."

I pinched my leg to keep the *gotcha* off my face.

Win hadn't been offered the job yet. The only people who knew about it were me, Mr. Rivera, and the owner of that email.

Gotcha.

32

In Sherlock's stories, once he had solved the case, the villains, the victims, or a bystander all said some version of "I will soon make everything clear to you" and produced a convenient explanation or confession, often with details about their motives and methods.

I wasn't going to get anything like that from Morris. He wasn't going to admit anything he'd done or tell me the *why*. And while Sherlock said deduction needed to be devoid of emotion, crime was wholly motivated by it. If I stayed across from this monster who said things like "I love the guy" while working to destroy Win's life, I'd make the leap to the wrong side of the paradigm. Lash out with fists and accusations that weren't mine to inflict.

And once I realized that, there was no reason to stay at Cool Beans.

I didn't bother with bussing my mug, or goodbye, or acknowledging his surprised "Huck? Where are you going?"

I just stood and walked out the door.

But having an answer didn't give me a direction. It didn't get me a confession.

I had all new questions, though: Did I tell Win, or Wink, or Curtis? Did I tell anyone?

I pondered this while I edited the video. It wasn't perfect, but it was magnitudes better than the shaky, under-the-desk horror that had gone viral. And all credit for that improvement went to the guy I kept picking up my phone to call before putting it back down.

Finally I walked downstairs and handed it to Mom. "Can you hold on to this for me?"

It was what she'd made me do in middle school: surrender my phone until my homework was done. And now, because I'd done it voluntarily, I got a hug and a squeaky, too-proud comment about "my Pucky being so grown-up and mature."

Yeah—she was preventing me from texting Morris is a liar, liar, pants on fire. So grown-up and mature.

Despite my wishful thinking, there weren't any texts from Win waiting when I retrieved my phone the next morning. There *was* an email from Ms. Gregoire though, agreeing to meet me before school to approve the video.

She nodded and *uh-hmm*'d as it played. Then shrugged. "This looks perfectly acceptable."

That was lukewarm praise by Gregoirian standards, but I let it go. I had something else to ask before first period. "If I figured out who was behind the iLive page and that knowledge will hurt Win, do I still tell him? Or do I confront the person myself? Report it? I could go to the police. The page is down now."

"Who was it?" she asked. "Also, well done."

"A friend."

She sucked a breath through her teeth. "Yikes. So you weren't exaggerating that the truth would hurt." She was quiet for a moment. "I think Winston has had a lot of choices taken away from him lately. The things that have been done in his name have made him feel disenfranchised. This is his friend, his hurt. It should be his choice about if or how to confront them and what the consequences should be."

"But isn't that worse? If I could figure out how to take care of it, then he won't have to." I couldn't control what Morris might say to Win. Couldn't stop him from spewing venom that would only add to the emotional baggage Win insisted on carrying.

Ms. Gregoire gave me a look soft with pity. "Sherlock only solves the cases; he doesn't serve as judge or jury."

The door opened and seniors were filing in, so I spoke faster. "So, I tell the twins . . . then what do I do?"

"Well, you have a video to finish. Go get your big win."

But it *was* finished. And did she mean that in the victory sense, or was she talking about the person? Capital-*W* Win, or the lowercase antonym of lose? Because I'd lost Win. But could I win him back with the video?

"Did you mean—" The bell rang, cutting off my words.

"Absolutely!" She nodded and handed me my laptop. "You've got this. Convocation tomorrow is going to be unforgettable."

I spent hours that night staring at the video. Something was missing, but I couldn't identify what. I had alumni and hopefuls. Outsiders and those currently enrolled. I had

Win's gorgeous photographs and even his gorgeous—albeit bruised—face among the interviews. But Ms. Gregoire was right: it was currently "acceptable," and she'd set the bar at "unforgettable."

I kept my cell phone next to me while I waited for inspiration. Not because it was any less of a distraction tonight, but because I was hoping Win would respond to the text I'd sent: Hey. We need to talk.

The texts I *was* getting were all from Rory.

We need to talk?

Seriously, you sent him "We need to talk"?

AKA, the worst words in the history of communication.

Did you want to make him LESS likely to respond? Because, good job.

I laughed and groaned and scowled at the bottom of my coffee mug. I'd been so good about sticking to my three-cup limit, but tonight might need to be an exception. I pushed the mug out of sight and replied to Rory: As always, your unwavering support is noted and appreciated.

I looked at the bruised face frozen on my computer screen. I'd promised him "unwavering support" too.

I put down my phone and picked up my pen.

33

"Huck!"

I'd spent hours listening to that voice in the past couple of weeks. Hearing it sound jovial and sarcastic, vulnerable and reserved. And in our last encounter, angry and anguished. So even above all the student voices in the Convocation Hall, I could pick out Win's.

"You decided to come." I didn't know what to do with my hands. I wanted to reach for him, but for what purpose? And how would he react? My fingers drummed against my pants until I shoved them into my pockets. "I'm glad. You'll get to see my video too."

"Are you nervous?" His hair was wet, like he'd just gotten out of the shower—like the evidence this really had been a last-minute decision was still dripping onto his collar. And the realization that he'd almost missed it made my stomach cramp.

"A little. Did you get my text?" I still needed to tell him about Morris.

"Yeah, but I only have a minute. My parents and Wink are grabbing seats. I just—" He pulled a tie from his pocket and held it out to me.

I looked from it to the one I was already wearing. "What's this for?"

"Me?" He shrugged and toed the carpet. "I stink at tying them. I figure you do them every day... Or I can ask my dad."

"No!" I took the tie and a step closer. "I've got you. Got *this*."

He was right: I did do this every day, and the muscle memory should've made it easy. I stepped behind him, standing close enough to smell the chlorine on his skin and feel his breath on the backs of my hands as I reached out with unsteady fingers to flip up his collar. I looped it around his neck. But how many times did I adjust the length of my own tie before I began crossing and twisting? Because I couldn't seem to stop sliding it back and forth. The back of my fingers skimming against the white fabric of his shirt as I did, and the lungs beneath hitching in ways that matched my own shredded breath.

"Is that too tight?" I asked as I pivoted around to face him and slide the knot up. I placed my left hand on his shoulder to hold us both still.

"No, it feels good." Win's voice was husky, his eyes dark. I wanted to ask if I was still past-tense, but I was lying by omission at the same time I was being trusted to tie knots around his neck. Asking for anything from him before I'd come clean about Morris felt like the worst kind of violation.

The knuckles of my right hand brushed the bare skin above Win's collar as I made final adjustments to the knot. His throat moved against my fingers as he swallowed. "By the way, you weren't wrong."

I froze, both hands still touching him. "About what?"

"Everything. You weren't wrong that Wink didn't do it. You weren't wrong when you said I was covering for her." He reached up and covered my right hand with his. "And you weren't wrong about me—that I needed to step up. I needed to stop playing the martyr and start driving my own life. And more than that, I needed to decide if I wanted to be here"—he gestured around us, to the nearly full Convocation Hall—"both for Curtis today, and next year as a student. You weren't wrong, Huck."

"I was right about one other thing too." I shrugged like it was nothing, even though his words meant everything. But the other options were bawling or mauling him, and I didn't have time for either.

He laughed and rolled his eyes. "Oh? What's that?"

"That you were worth *all* of that effort." But I couldn't prove it now. My parents were standing and waving us over. Dad had his phone out, and I'd bet a week's worth of coffee he'd taken a picture of me fixing Win's tie and planned to print and display it next to the one of Miles putting on his prom date's corsage.

"C'mon." Grabbing his hand felt presumptuous, so I looped my fingers around his wrist. "Meet my parents. It looks like they've already met yours." His family was one row up, turned around and chatting over the seats.

"Do we have to?"

"Sure do. And I should warn you: Mom's a hugger."

He paled as we approached, sticking out his hand for a shake—like that would stop her. "Hi, Mr. and Mrs. Baker. I'm Winston."

"It's so nice to finally meet the boy who has my baby Pucky all aflutter." Mom was five feet nothing but clearly deadly, because I about died of mortification as Win choked on his laughter in her stranglehold hug.

"Marlene, we talked about this." Dad shook his head, and for a second I thought he was going to tell her to notch back the humiliation. Instead he added, "Huck may be our baby, but he doesn't want you calling him—or his boyfriend—a 'boy.'" He held out his arms. "It's nice to meet you, young man."

"Yeah, um, Dad's also a hugger," I added when Win glowered at me over his shoulder. "Probably should've mentioned that too."

It might've gotten worse. There really were no limits to the degrees of embarrassment my parents could inflict, but thankfully Headmaster Williams tapped the microphone and began the usual announcements.

Then Dr. Badawi, Curtis's biology teacher, was taking the podium to talk about his winning project from the Avery Science Fair and sing his praises. I tuned out and stared at the back of the wet head one row up.

Did he think that label came from me? That I was casually combining "boy" and "friend" when I talked about him? Not that I did. Talk about him with my parents, that is. At least, not much.

"Huck," Dad whispered.

"I don't!"

"Don't what?" he asked. "Never mind that now. Your teacher—"

I followed his finger to where Ms. Gregoire was beckoning me from the edge of the row. "Are you ready?" she asked.

I patted my blazer pocket, then nodded. The video file was saved in my school Dropbox. All I had to do was double-click on it. Whether that was all I *did* do remained undecided.

"Good. Headmaster Williams wants a quick word." She led the way to a tiny anteroom and he looked up from his phone.

"I wanted to confirm that you're all set. I don't want any antics."

"Define 'antics,'" I said with a smile, the kind that disarmed people, before I added, "*Kidding*"—even though this time, I wasn't.

Headmaster Williams didn't seem disarmed. "Might I remind you, you're on your third strike, Mr. Baker."

"I've seen and approved the video." Ms. Gregoire stepped forward with a bright smile. "Huck has been nothing but motivated and cooperative."

Headmaster Williams nodded. "I'm glad to hear it. I look forward to seeing your hard work." He ducked out to join in the applause for Curtis, and I took a deep breath.

"I need to tell you something." I'd waited until the last cowardly second to come clean. Not as cowardly as afterward. Not so late she couldn't stop me. I held on to those truths. "I made some changes to the video. It's not the version you've seen."

She smoothed the front of her skirt. "I know."

"You do?" I glanced over my shoulder at the stage. Curtis was at the podium, and hopefully he'd be his usual charming and chatty self, because I had questions. "How?"

"Just because I'm telling you to be *less* like Sherlock doesn't mean I don't have a little sleuth in me as well. The day I don't know my students well enough by March to tell when they're lying to me is the day I should quit teaching."

"Do you think it's a mistake?"

"I don't know." I didn't like her answer, but I appreciated

its honesty. Well, ten percent of me did. The other ninety was worried about sweating through my shirt. "Like those last students whose admission status will be decided at today's meeting, *your* ending isn't written yet. But I'm not going to talk you out of it."

"I'm nervous," I told her.

She squeezed my shoulder. "And I'm here. Well, out there, rather. Because it's time to go on."

34

The Convocation Hall looked bigger from the podium than it did from the seats. I cleared my throat awkwardly by the mic. "Hi, I'm Huck Baker."

"Wahoo! Go Huck!"

The audience laughed, and I wasn't sure if that was Merri or my mom, so to be safe, both were dead to me now.

"I, uh, made a video a month ago that accidentally went viral, so here's one I made on purpose. Thanks."

My hand wobbled on the laptop remote, but there was a guy in the second row giving me a look of raised-eyebrow challenge paired with a small nod of encouragement. And if nothing else, I wanted him to hear what I had to say.

I pressed Play.

I slid the remote into my blazer pocket. It nestled beside note cards I had memorized. I could still pretend they didn't exist—exit stage left and let the file play uninterrupted. There were two minutes and thirty-eight seconds until I had to make that decision.

Headmaster Williams joined me by the podium. He'd been clapping politely with the audience, but he reached out and put a hand on my shoulder. "Stay here and watch it with me. You should be proud of your hard work."

I gave him a nervous smile and pivoted so I could see the video screen in my periphery—but more importantly, see Win's reaction to it.

The opening shot looked like it could be straight from any admissions brochure. It was the view of campus coming down the avenue and into the lane where the stone buildings became visible. It was one of Win's pictures, and my voice from a prerecorded narrative track joined it.

"This is Hero High. Founded in 1889 by the famous tile maker Reginald R. Hero as a coeducational school that supports the academic, artistic, and athletic endeavors of all students. Hero High is a special place. If you ask the parents, they might rave about achievements or college acceptances, but if you ask the students—"

I felt the tension drain from Headmaster Williams's grip. He patted me on the back and then clasped his hands in front of his stomach as my narration continued. "Well, I'll let them speak for themselves..."

A question flashed on the screen: `Describe Hero High in one word.` I'd only included the responses of current students, and I'd made quick jump cuts between the videos of their answers.

Merri: "Magic"

Fielding: "Tradition"

Lance: "Teammates"

Rory: "Inspiration"

Eliza: "Family"

Bancroft: "Friends"

Curtis: "Intellectually-stimulating"

There were giggles at his disclaimer: "It's one word. I'm using a hyphen."

I'd split the screen to show Shiloh and Sera both say, "Acceptance."

Then subdivided again for Mira, Elijah, Hannah, Wren, and Dantes's "Community."

The video zoomed in on a single face for the last answer: Clara's.

"Home," she said. "It feels like home."

The narration picked back up with more of Win's glory shots of campus: The sunset off the greenhouse, the light through the Convocation Hall's stained glass windows. A close-up of a book left on a bench, a row of lockers, student posters, the famous sidewalk tiles. "It's easy to see why people want to come to Hero High."

In the past two weeks I'd conducted dozens of interviews, had a hundred answers to my three questions. I let myself glance at Win, let myself drink in his attentive gaze, knowing he was probably making mental notes on how I'd done with the filming and editing. I caught his surprise, then his smirk as he realized that the first interview I'd included was of a boy sitting on a bed, starring at the camera through a black eye with his heart on his face and in his words.

"It feels like Hero High is a safe space. I've seen what it does for my brother—for other people I care about. It's a place where you become a better version of yourself. Where you're heard and supported and given a chance to grow from your mistakes."

I turned from the screen as other answers played, text overlays affirming or correcting the words of current and former and hopeful students as well as people who had no affiliation with the school. I saved Clara for last again, zooming in on her smile as a choral version of the school song played in the background.

"I've wanted to be a Hero High Crimson Knight for as long as I can remember. It's possible I was the youngest person to submit an application—I was seven. They said they'd hold on to it for me. I have my acceptance letter, which came six years later, framed."

The audience laughed, and I searched for Clara, finding her in the third row. Her head was high, her shoulders back. Mira's leg pressed firmly against hers. I'd gotten her permission to use one of the gifs, and she met my eyes as it flashed on the screen, then she held up her phone and typed something with glitter-painted nails. I felt mine buzz in my pocket and knew what she'd sent: a date, a time, a TV station. I grinned.

The audience had stirred in surprised discomfort at the sight of her gif, but they leaned in when her interview came back on the screen. "But Hero High is more than an idea that can be hung on the wall. It's a community that challenges and changes you. And being accepted into this school doesn't mean accepting the status quo. They let me in because they valued my voice, and I'm so lucky to be surrounded by people who remind me to use it—even when it's hard. Even when it's easier to stay quiet."

I could've edited out the pause after this, but I left the three seconds where she looked down and regrouped. The potent silence in the Convocation Hall told me it'd been the right choice.

"When the video went viral, Headmaster Williams came to check on me. He sat at my kitchen table and told me, 'Our school doesn't graduate students—it produces *heroes*. These next couple of weeks are going to be hard for you, Clara, but know you're already one of mine.' I hope he knows the feeling is mutual."

The tall, bald man beside me tried to be subtle as he sniffled.

My video cut from Clara to Ms. Gregoire, smiling across the expanse of her desk. "Anything can happen in these classrooms. My job isn't to fill my students' heads with facts; it's to provide questions and guidance and get out of the way. Then it's my privilege to watch them become the people they're meant to be."

The school song began to swell, and if I'd let it play a second longer, people would've rocked forward to clap—instead I hit Pause and stepped up to the mic. This was where I'd diverged from the version Ms. Gregoire had seen, and standing off to the side of the stage, she lifted her coffee cup in salute.

"I watched this video a dozen times last night and couldn't figure out what was missing. I was proud of the voices and opinions I'd collected—but the thing that was missing was mine."

I scanned the audience, taking courage from my parents' faces and Win's curious smirk.

"When I started these interviews, I recorded everyone else's answers but didn't have any of my own. I was 'the new kid,' and I blamed that for why I stayed on the periphery, why my only real friends were the other new kid"—I nodded to Rory—"and my Knight Light mentor. I liked school, had some great and not-so-great teachers"—the audience gave an uneasy chuckle—"but I didn't have the big feelings Hero High seemed to inspire in everyone else. I didn't understand why people were so proud to wear the sweatshirts with their names on the back, or the reason for their school spirit. It was just a school—and paying hefty tuition didn't make it any more special."

There was an uncomfortable stirring in the rows as people exchanged looks, an obvious footstep closer from the man hovering behind me. I caught Ms. Gregoire gesturing for him to wait. And I took a deep breath.

"That apathy? That disconnect? That was on me. I was so busy looking back at my old life that I wasn't investing here. But I've spent the past few weeks talking to everyone about this school—meeting new people, hearing their ideas, letting them in. Somewhere along the way I started to get indignant if someone said something negative about Hero High. I had to remind myself not to interrupt and correct false assumptions. I had to stop myself from chiming in with my own praise."

I took a deep breath. This wasn't just a jump, it was a high dive. And this was my last chance to back off the board. Instead I let momentum and honesty carry me over the edge. "Somewhere along the line, I became smitten. Not just with the school. But it's because of Hero High—because of Knight Lights—that I met the guy I fell for."

"Um, it's not me!" Curtis called out, interrupting an audible "aww" from Merri and Mira and many others I couldn't see or name. "Just clarifying." The wave of laughter rolled past me; I was too busy swimming in the shocked joy in Win's eyes.

Ms. Gregoire cleared her throat, and I raised my chin to address the room again. So many faces—many still strangers, but hopefully they wouldn't be for much longer. I had more words on my note cards, but they'd fled from my memory, replaced by ones so emotional that Sherlock would cringe—and to be fair, I probably would later too. But the admissions committee was meeting right after this, and what good was my voice if I didn't use it?

"Curtis is right, it's not him. The person I fell for is applying to this school. And it was in wanting it for *him* that I realized the depths of my own Hero High pride. I want him to have these teachers, these traditions, his own Knight Light. I want him to walk these halls and across the mosaics. He'd have so much to contribute here. I want him to be a part of the Hero High community that was waiting to welcome me, just as soon as I was ready to let them."

The words were out, but I was still in free fall. I pried out my dimples and hid my shaking hands behind the podium. "That was the long answer to my questions—but here's the short version. Describe Hero High in one word: *Possibility*."

35

I stumbled off the stage after pressing Play, the school song chasing me out the side door. Was it supposed to feel like this after declaring feelings for someone? Like my rib cage had shrunken and my heart and lungs were being crushed? Had I made a huge mistake? Was I going to get kicked out?

"Huck!" Win's voice came from the main door, and I turned to see him marching toward me, one hand gripping the back of his neck, the other loosening his tie.

I'd used up all my words on the podium, so I leaned against the side of the building and let him speak first. He rubbed his bottom lip while studying our shoes. "I didn't need you to do that for me."

"But—" It killed me a little that we were still having this conversation.

"No, listen. I didn't *need* you to do that for me, because I already did it for myself." He raised his eyes from the sidewalk and met mine. "My hair is wet."

"I—I noticed that," I said slowly, not quite sure where he was taking this conversation but willing to follow.

"Because about an hour ago, I did a swim demo for Coach Yang. And before that, I had another meeting with Headmaster Williams."

My hand tightened into a fist in my pocket, like I was clutching all my hope. "Why?"

"There were some things I needed to clear up about my application. I wanted to make sure that if he'd seen the iLive page, he knew it wasn't mine. And explain I hadn't sent the email pulling my application—that I would never have because I really, really want to come here."

I fought back my dimples. "So when you said I didn't 'need' to do that—you meant it. I *really* didn't need to."

He nodded. "Pretty much. I had it covered. I don't know what will happen, but—I tried."

"So, I just humiliated myself for no reason?"

"Well . . ." He raised an eyebrow in challenge. "Not *no* reason. You—you fell for me?"

I pointed over my shoulder. "Were you not paying attention? Because I'm pretty sure there are a couple hundred witnesses in there who heard me."

"I see," Win said slowly, pulling his bottom lip between his thumb and finger in that way he knew drove me to distraction. "So you're staking a claim in case I do come here next year?"

"I'm staking a claim regardless."

"Maybe you should just say it again," he teased. "Just to clear up any confusion. There are a lot of people you met making that video. How do I know you weren't talking about any of them?"

I rolled my eyes and squeezed the podium remote that was still in my pocket. I considered restarting my video. Would that buy us more time? It had to be almost dismissal. "Because none of them are half as frustratingly impossible as you."

He crossed his hands over his chest. "I'm not a case anymore. Not a puzzle or a project."

"No, you're not any of those things," I agreed. "But you're the guy I fell for. And you could be my boyfriend. I'd like you to be." I took another step forward, and his nostrils flared. His hands were white-knuckled as they gripped his opposite arms. And of all the times for him to be inscrutable, for me to see all the signs and not be able to read them. I froze, a half step away. "I can't tell if you're angry or into this. And while I want to kiss you right now, I'm not okay crossing those signals. Give me something here."

I'd meant an answer, but I guessed Win's response was acceptable too. He grabbed the collar of my blazer in both hands and pulled my mouth down to his.

He drank my kisses like questions—like this was one more game and I was figuring him out. And maybe I was. Maybe I always would be. The contradictions and challenges, the sweet and the sarcastic. The texture of his hair, his skin, his mouth. The taste of his tongue when he let me in. The sound of his voice when he pulled back. "So much for your observational genius. Shouldn't you already know? I've fallen for you too."

If I'd ever wondered what I'd sound like with the rasp of bronchitis, I had my answer when I laughed hoarsely against his neck and said, "You scramble all my radars—because you're too important to make a mistake."

"Then maybe you should just ask. We've got this question game down to an art."

I swallowed. "Win, will you be my boyfriend?"

"Sure. Now your turn to answer: Huck, will you be mine?"

I nodded, and his hand came up to touch my face. It was when he traced my dimples that I knew I was smiling.

"Is this what you texted me about yesterday? The video? Or asking me out? Because, I gotta say, I'd prefer you never use the words 'We need to talk' again."

Rory would feel so vindicated, and part of me wanted to go the easy route. Laugh and tell him about her upcoming *I told you so*.

Instead, I shook my head. "We need to talk because I solved the case."

36

Like blazer-wearing salmon, we swam against the stream of students exiting the Convocation Hall to find Wink. I wanted to tell this story only once, so she needed to be there for it. Objective achieved, I led them to the small room where I'd met Headmaster Williams earlier.

They both stared at me, but it was Win who asked. "So who made the iLive page?"

"Morris." Win drank coffee only when it was saturated with milk and sugar, but bad news: he drank that black. Undiluted, unsweetened.

Wink asked, "Morris Henderson?"

"Morris? You're sure?" Win was already seated but reached forward to brace himself on the chair in front of him.

In *A Study in Scarlet* Holmes says, "It was easier to know it than to explain why I know it," and he was so dang right it hurt. I knew Morris had done it, but he hadn't confessed. All I could do was lay out my evidence—and let them choose what to do with the information.

But perhaps I shouldn't have started by sharing that quote.

"Um, what?" Wink looked at her brother.

The corners of his mouth flickered, but his eyes stayed

flat, his snark was feeble. “If you skip the Sherlock now, I promise to fanboy later.”

I lifted my eyebrows. “I’m holding you to that.” But it was the last moment of levity as I moved on to a breakdown of the motivations behind the iLive posts I’d decoded. Wink stared at me. Win studied the window. Pinched the bridge of his nose. Shook his head.

I finished by revealing why Mr. Rivera had fired him and Morris’s advance knowledge of Win’s forthcoming job offer. “Congrats on that, by the way.”

“Um, thanks, I guess.” He shook his head the way Luna did when she’d misjudged a leap and fallen short of her goal. Like he was trying to recover from a disorienting blow and get his bearings. “But... *why*?”

“Because he didn’t want you to leave him behind at Chester High. And...” I wasn’t sure if I should pause and let them process or get it all out while they were still stunned. But this part felt harder to reveal. I pointed to the girl leaning against his shoulder and chewing her lip. “Because of Wink.”

“Me?” She might have pulled away if her brother hadn’t put his arm around her shoulder.

“According to Morris—and I’m not sure we should believe anything he said—you vent to him if there’s drama. And he was using that page to stir up a lot of drama.”

“I did this?” She was twirling a strand of hair—not flirtatiously, but in an anxious way that made me concerned she was going to knot her fingers in it.

“No.” If they processed nothing else I said, they needed to hear this. “*He* did. Not either of you.”

Win put his hand on top of hers, tugging her fingers free. “It’s not your fault. I can’t—he’s...”

He looked out the window and trailed off, like he couldn't come up with an insult bad enough, or maybe he twinspoke it right into Wink's brain, because she was nodding. "I just liked... He always listened. And everyone was so busy yelling at you or praising Curtis, and Reese gets all 'Suck it up, buttercup.' He always told me I was right."

Win looked at their hands instead of her face. "It's not like I don't ever complain about you. Remember the two things Mom said people say to her about us?" He counted them off on his fingers: "'I always wanted twins,' and 'Better you than me.'" He peeked at her to gauge her reaction. "That's kinda how I feel most days: I will always want you as my twin, but some days I don't want to *be* a twin."

"That makes perfect sense." Wink stared down at her hands. "So what do we do?"

Win's jaw hardened. "I'll handle it. Morris and I already had plans tonight. Why don't you head straight to Reese's or something? You don't have to be there. It's gonna be ugly."

They both shut their eyes for a second as it sank in. If the mood wasn't so serious, I would've cracked a joke about them doing a "creepy twin thing" as they took simultaneous deep breaths.

When Wink opened her eyes, there was a sharp resolve in them. "Thanks for saying I don't have to be there—but I think I should be."

Their gazes swung to me, but I looked away. To quote Ms. Gregoire, "Sherlock doesn't serve as judge or jury." It wasn't my place to suggest how they handle this. "I'm really sorry." I pointed toward the hall. "I should check if my parents grabbed my stuff."

It was true but also an excuse to give them privacy. I

didn't know Morris like they did. I didn't share the good memories they had to balance against these brutal revelations. I couldn't understand what they were feeling or how it was compounded by the unique love-guilt bond of twinship.

"I'll come with you." Win squeezed his sister's shoulder as he stood. "Tell Mom and Dad I'll be home soon."

As we stepped into the hall, he said, "Can we not—let's not talk about that right now. I need..." He scrubbed his hand across his face. "Just a break."

Instead of answering, I reached for his hand. Or maybe that *was* my answer, because he gave me a weary smile as he squeezed my fingers.

When Miles and I were little, we used to do this thing whenever Dad insisted we hold hands in parking lots or crowds or pictures. Basically we squashed the heck out of each other's fingers until one of us—me—squealed.

Holding Win's hand felt nothing like that. Sure, I was as aware of it as I'd been all those times Miles tried to cut off my circulation, but instead of the pain of my bones being ground together, my hand was comprised of electricity, of sparks of sensation that were somehow hardwired to my smile. And when I peeked sideways at him, he was smiling too.

Instead of heading outside where students would still be lingering, the faculty preparing to meet to discuss a list with his name on it, I headed to the alcove in the back. The one Ms. Gregoire had emerged from when she'd given me a heart attack last week.

If my first kiss had been a revelation, and my second a declaration, this one was pure captivation. It was a good thing I didn't know how amazing kissing—kissing *Win*—was weeks ago, because I never would've stopped doing it long enough to ask him questions. Or maybe it was this amazing *because* I'd spent so much time getting to know him, letting him get to know me. Either way, I had a new favorite pastime.

"Man, I hope I get in," Win mumbled against my jaw. "If so, let's make this—"

I pressed a finger to his lips, pulling him deeper into the alcove as footsteps approached.

Headmaster Williams sounded weary. "Remember when Convocation was a nice, orderly way to end the day?"

"I don't know." Ms. Gregoire seemed to pause right outside the alcove as she added, "It's so much more invigorating this year! I think the school needed and needs some new voices."

If Headmaster Williams replied beyond a disgruntled "Hmph," it happened when they were out of earshot.

"Invigorating, huh?" Win touched my cheek. "That's one word for it."

I nipped at his fingertips. We needed to wait a few minutes for the coast to clear before sneaking out of the building. I knew just how to spend them.

37

Hey, can we sit here a second?" Win was pointing to my front porch swing, and I was already halfway down the steps. We'd just escaped the gauntlet of my parents taking pictures and were headed—finally—to our first date. But I backtracked and sat beside him.

"What's up?"

"I was kinda hoping we could do the whole Morris update here—and then leave it here," he said, staring down at his clasped hands.

It was Sunday night. The rest of Win's weekend had been engulfed by "the whole Morris thing." His family was still undecided about what to do—whether they wanted to press legal charges or ask Chester High to impose consequences.

The news of the fake page and who was behind it had spread quickly—courtesy of Clara and Mira and Reese and Bancroft. Win told me he was half tempted to let social justice run its course.

"But I think I want the decision to be Wink's." He tipped his head back against the swing's chains. "It was 'for Wink' that Morris said he'd done it. He assumed if I didn't get into Hero High, Wink would stay at Chester. And that if I screwed up enough, she'd eventually fall for the guy who kept stepping up to comfort her."

He gave a flimsy smile. "She was a rock star though. She put together this slideshow of screenshots of *every* post. And then made him account for every single one when she played it in front of our parents and his."

"Whoa. When she decides to step up, she goes all in. I like her style," I said.

"Yeah. She was super stoic. Better than me." Win lowered his head, and his expression made my chest ache. We were already thigh-to-thigh on the swing's bench, but I put an arm around his back, tracing the striped pattern of his shirt.

"I don't think there is a 'better' here. You feel how you feel. React in whatever way's authentic. His was a massive betrayal; no one's judging if you're stoic." I leaned in to press a kiss on his shoulder, wishing I could carry some of the weight.

Win nodded distractedly. "The worst part is, Morris kept insisting he was still my friend. Saying things like, 'It's not really a big deal,' and 'We both know you won't be happy at snob school,' and 'I wouldn't have done it if I'd known you'd be so mad.'" He sighed and rubbed his forehead. "And I kept having these moments where I wanted to believe him."

I didn't have advice, but I had empathy, and ears, and a hand. Which I held out to him when he stood and reached for me. And which he didn't let go of. Not on the walk to Pizza My Heart, not when he held the door for me. Not even to serve or eat his pizza. That felt like a pretty good solution: listen and hold on. And I was committed to it for as long as he'd let me.

"Question," he asked as we walked from pizza to bowling.

"You would've ordered garlic knots if you were here with your family?"

"Oh, absolutely," I said. "You?"

"Yup. Definitely. Still sorta regret not getting them."

He was laughing right up to the moment my mouth met his. I kissed him till his hands migrated to my hair and hips, then pulled back to whisper, "Still thinking about garlic knots?"

I ducked from his arms and ran down the sidewalk, his footsteps and laughter chasing me until I let him catch up. He poked me. "Fine, we'll both order them next time and cancel each other's breath out. Deal?"

"Sure. My question. Least favorite nickname?" There'd been so much talk of "the twins" lately: "the twins" as victims of Morris, "the twins'" decisions about how to proceed, "the twins'" uncertain schooling future as they waited for a decision letter. But really it was Win's friend, Win's letter, Win's uncertainty. Did it bother him to be lumped into a set?

The corners of his mouth dropped as his eyebrows shot up. "Last week I would've told you 'Win.'"

It took a minute for my expectations to catch up with reality. "What?"

"It felt like a punch line—'cause all I did was lose." He gave me a self-conscious smile and met the hand I was extending halfway. "But I think that's changing. I've had some pretty decent victories lately—regardless of what happens with Hero High." He squeezed my fingers. "So I guess my answer is 'Blubs'—it's what my grandma calls me. You?"

He looked up expectantly, like he hadn't just blown my mind or made me fall even deeper. I wanted to be here for all his victories. I wanted them to be infinite. "Um, yeah. I—uh. Your brother's stuck on 'Huckleberry,' but I'll live."

Win groaned and lifted our joined hands to cover his face. When he lowered them, he was shaking his head. "He told me that was your real name, and I believed him."

"For how long?" I asked.

"Until two seconds ago. I was this many years old when I found out it wasn't true."

I'm not sure which of us laughed first, but it was the kind that was contagious and uncontrollable. That stole our breath and made our shoulders shake. Tears leaked out of my eyes when Win fanned his, muttering, "Okay, okay"—then he snorted, which had us doubled over again.

Eventually we bowled—I needed my hand back for that. Though Win probably didn't. Even if I'd been hanging off his other arm like a giant anchor, he still would've wiped the lanes with me. He was worried about stacking spares and strikes, while I was wondering if we could get a lane with bumpers.

I tried everything: switching hands, counting my steps, changing ball size, even bowling two-handed between my legs. None of it made a difference in my score. All of it made him laugh. And there hadn't been nearly enough of that sound in my life. Tonight felt like a good start.

"Gelato?" I asked after we'd finished a game, which had been one more victory for him to add to his balance sheet.

"Tomorrow," he said.

And for just a second my smile slipped, because once upon a month ago I'd told Mrs. York that I'd be bringing Win ice cream the day Hero High letters arrived—that I'd pair it with a bow or tissues. That day was tomorrow.

"It's a date," I told him, folding up that fear and hiding it far from our clasped hands and good-night kiss.

38

First period had barely started on Monday when the art studio phone rang. Mrs. Mundhenk's eyes darted my way a few seconds into the conversation, so I began to clean up even before she crossed the room.

"Huck," she whispered, like she could somehow stop every eavesdropper from listening. "Headmaster Williams would like to see you."

Campus was quiet. Except for a tardy senior, no one else was out, and I was tempted to take a forbidden shortcut across the lawn to get to the office faster. I resisted. If this meeting was in reaction to my third-strike "antics," then this might be my last chance to enjoy the campus as an enrolled student. So I paused to admire the stone buildings, the stained glass windows, the reproductions of Reginald R. Hero's famous tiles that sat at the corner of each walkway. I passed globes and quill pens, theater masks and maps. Followed the path of tiles with judicial hammers—the one that lead to the administration building.

Mrs. York ushered me into the room with the too-large portraits. "He'll be in shortly."

The paintings made me feel even smaller without my

parents to act as buffers. Should I call and ask them to come? Could he expel me without a guardian?

"Mr. Baker." Headmaster Williams beckoned me from his office. "Please, join me."

The two other times I'd sat in this room, it had been on the punishment side of his desk. This time he led me to a pair of wingback chairs in a corner lined with bookshelves.

I sat. He did too. For fifteen long seconds I had so much sympathy for Fielding and Sera Williams, because their father was way too comfortable with silence. I *knew* the wait-it-out technique; I used it myself, yet it was killing me not to fidget or dimple or make small talk.

It took all my remaining self-control not to fist-pump when he spoke first. "Your video was quite good. With your permission, we'd like to share it on the school's social media accounts."

"Of course."

"But your speech at the end..." He stood and crossed the room. "Over the years, the admissions committee has gotten all sorts of attempts at bribes or threats. But I think your speech was the first time anyone used a romantic declaration to try and sway their hand."

"Do I get bonus points for being creative?" I asked, and either he ignored me or he didn't hear me over the *snick-snick-snick* of the blinds he was raising.

"It gets dim in here, all the dark wood." I blinked at the sunlight, not quite sure what was happening.

"Headmaster Williams, sir." I cleared my throat. "Am I being expelled? Is that why I'm here?"

"No." He reached into the lower drawer of his desk and

drew out a tissue-wrapped package, placing it on top of the blotter. "I placed a rush order for this on Friday."

I craned my neck but couldn't see what it was and didn't know if I was allowed to leave my seat.

"We had decided to decline the younger Mr. Cavendish's application." I sucked in a breath and opened my mouth, but he raised a hand to still me. "That was the early recommendation of the admissions committee. Then the email about withdrawing his application was sent and it seemed like the matter was settled.

"But Winston had quite the advocate on the committee." Headmaster Williams quirked an eyebrow at me. "Ms. Gregoire was singularly impressed with him—surprisingly so for a person she'd only met in passing. And Coach Yang was sent a video from summer swim meets and a follow-up email from the coach at Chester High who says Win has the discipline to train on his own. Mr. Welch got a phone call from the owner of a local photography studio who vouched for Winston as both an employee and an artist."

I grinned, full dimple. Full, authentic dimple—because while I could take credit for talking Win up to Ms. Gregoire, I'd had nothing to do with the rest. Win had meant it when he said he was here to play. He was here to *win*.

"And your video . . . speech . . . whatever you want to call it." Headmaster Williams chuckled. "While unorthodox, you made your point. As did he when we met on Friday. He's communicated his desire to attend, and Winston clearly inspires strong devotion from those around him."

I winced. Not *everyone* was inspired or devoted to him.

While I was in *this* office, Win was across town in Principal Nunes's with Morris and his parents. Wink and

Mr. and Mrs. Cavendish would be there too—hopefully their support outweighed the awful. Hopefully they found some sort of justice and peace. And I had to give their parents some credit; it wasn't just Wink who'd stepped up. Mr. and Mrs. Cavendish had been working hard to right past oversights since learning about the page. And since the Morris reveal? Well, it was a good thing I was already inner sanctum, because they'd gone full overprotective helicopter parents, and I wouldn't be surprised if they guilt-bought him a pony—or at least the new camera filter he'd been eyeing.

Headmaster Williams cleared his throat and I blinked, trying to figure out if he'd been talking while I'd zoned out or if he'd been doing dramatic silence again. "Maybe we need a little bit of unorthodoxy around here."

Since he'd picked up the same conversational thread, I was going to assume dramatic silence.

Except, wait. I stood. "Do you mean—"

He pushed the tissue paper away from the bundle, revealing a gray sweatshirt with *Cavendish* across the back. "Would you like to be the one to deliver this? Winston's acceptance letter should be waiting when he gets home today."

I hugged the sweatshirt to my chest. "No."

"No?" Headmaster Williams was too surprised to notice I was trying to hand it back, so I folded it and placed it on the desk.

"There's been enough drama around his admission. If I deliver the sweatshirt—I don't want him to think he owes me. I want there to be no question he earned this on his own."

If anyone had told me my meeting with the headmaster would end with his shaking my hand and calling me a "Good man," I would've laughed and told them to switch to decaf.

But it did.

And I walked out of the administration building whistling and counting down the minutes until I could show up on the Cavendishes' doorstep and ask Win to model it for me.

First, however, I had English class, where I pulled a black hardcover from my bag and returned it to Ms. Gregoire. "Thanks for this—for everything—but I'm done with Sherlock for a while. I'm ready for my life to be a little *less* of an adventure."

"Oh, Huck." She laughed as she took the book. "Your story is only getting started."

39

I'd never imagined I'd open the Milverton video file again; had thought I'd be taking a break from *all* editing software. But I'd spent the week making a gif. It wasn't as complicated as I'd thought. Or maybe Win was just a good teacher. He was definitely a good distraction, which is why it had taken a whole week. To be fair, several nights had been monopolized by Hero High acceptance celebrations—his family taking him out to dinner Monday, my parents having him over Tuesday.

Wednesday I made him model his new sweatshirt and we went out for gelato on our own.

The gif was the same as so many others; it featured Clara raising her hand on loop. The difference was the caption. Ours read: `WHEN YOU DON'T LET THE PATRIARCHY GET YOU DOWN.`

I'd shown it to her, of course. Gotten her approval and permission when we met her for coffee on Thursday. I'd ordered half-caf, then sat back and let her and Win talk about how it felt to lose control of their image and reputation, and the steps they were taking to regain a sense of empowerment. My role was to listen and learn. I knew Clara didn't blame me for the video. I also knew that didn't make me innocent.

That night I'd *carefully* clicked to send the new gif to two dozen of our friends. The plan had been for everyone to post it after first period Friday morning in the hopes of the new version going viral and changing the narrative.

It was the second post on Win's new iLive page. The first explained that this was his only page and that he'd recently learned there'd been another one using his identity to insult and hurt. The post included a picture of iLive's takedown notice and an apology for what had been done in his name.

It didn't identify Morris, which was far more gracious than he deserved. The Cavendishes and the Hendersons were in discussions. There were lawyers and school administrators involved, and while Morris was currently suspended pending a decision, the final outcome wasn't clear yet. Wink had quickly shut down any Henderson excuse that included "He just likes you and didn't know how to show it."

And Win and I rehearsed his response to their lawyer's request for leniency: "I'm offended you're so concerned about the impact being held accountable could have on Morris's future, when he demonstrated no concern about how his actions impacted *mine*."

If he wanted to, Win could do what Clara had done that morning—appear on a talk show and tell his story—but that wasn't his style. Clara might not have considered it *her* style either, but from the exclamation-point-heavy texts my parents had sent, I knew she'd nailed it.

The interview had aired first period. I knew some teachers had offered to turn it on, but everyone gathered in the Campbells' basement after school had promised to wait and watch it together.

We'd trooped down the stairs with snacks and phones.

Sera and Fielding were in full uniforms, but the rest of the Crimson Knights were taking advantage of spirit day freedoms.

The sight of Curtis wearing Eliza's red sweatshirt like a crop top still made us snicker—and him preen.

Since Chester High was ten minutes farther away, the Cavendish twins were last to arrive. Win bust out laughing when he looked from his brother to me. "How many times today did people ask if you were dating him?" he asked me.

"Not that many. Turns out Curtis did a pretty good job of establishing that fact at Convocation." I smoothed down the front of the sweatshirt. "But I still had plenty of chances to tell people that *this* 'Cavendish' sweatshirt belonged to you, my boyfriend and future Hero High student. You're not getting it back by the way."

He grinned. "That's fine. I'll keep yours."

Eliza wrinkled her nose. She'd avoided "all displays of romantic entanglement" by wearing her Hero High cross-country sweatshirt. But when she thought he wouldn't notice, she looked at her crop-topped boyfriend with such soft devotion. Right now she whirled on him with her hands on her hips. "Curtis, should I be concerned that someone has replaced your brother with a nonsarcastic imposter who's willing to talk about his emotions?"

"I'm teaching him everything I know, Firebug." Curtis punched my arm and said, "You're welcome," at the same time that Eliza told Win, "Please tell me you're not listening."

Win winked at her before being engulfed by Bancroft, Elijah, and Shi. "I hear you're coming to Hero High!" He nodded and ran through the handshake routine three times faster than I could do it once.

"Are we ready to do this thing?" Merri's voice came from the other side of the two enormous buckets of popcorn she was carrying down the stairs. Hannah was behind her with a tray of drinks. "Because if you make me wait any longer I'm going to break my vow and peek."

Merri reached the bottom of the stairs and thrust one of the bowls at Lynnie. "Have you heard from Penn? Is Clara happy with how it turned out?"

Lynnie nodded. "They're out to dinner with their dad, but he said she did great."

"Of course she did." Mira—who'd showed up with a giant bag of pretzels—sounded indignant that anyone would question Clara. Man, that loyal, vacuum-loving lioness was growing on me. "Now, who has the remote?"

Fielding held it up, and unsurprisingly, no one challenged his right to it. Even more than his father, Fielding had a quiet authority that made you *want* to listen to him. So when he said, "Grab a seat, I'll queue it up," everyone scrambled to sit.

He, Merri, Rory, and Toby were crammed on the couch. Lynnie and Lance sat on the love seat. Her twin, Byron, lay on the floor by her feet. Of everyone, he was the quickest to "*shhhhh*," the most focused on the TV. It was a fact I filed away for the future.

Wink was sitting on a faded beanbag chair with Mira and Elinor and Gemma. It was easy to see how she'd meld back into their group next year. Curtis had pulled the coffee table to the side, and he and Eliza were perched on top. The rest of us grabbed spots on the floor.

Fielding pressed Play, and Byron told him to turn it up before the theme music had even finished.

The muscles in my back stayed locked for the first

two-thirds of Clara's interview. It wasn't until the male host, Preston, told her, "I've got to say, you're an articulate and impressive young person," that I relaxed against the shoulder Win had pressed into mine.

Clara smiled and turned to the camera. "It's because of the environment where I spend my days. Reginald R. Hero High has taught me my voice matters—that everyone's does."

I did a fist pump. Clara was born to be heard.

"So explain that video then." Abigail, the female host, leaned forward with a sympathetic expression. "Why hadn't you spoken up when you were so clearly frustrated by not being called on?"

Clara started to reach for a curl but stopped herself and folded her hands on the table. "It was the opposite of what I'd always been taught, which is why it threw me. I got caught up in thinking that if the teacher gave me a chance, I'd be able to prove myself. But that was never going to happen. I'm done wasting my energy on people who don't value me. Whether that's a teacher or someone making mean memes with my picture, I'm over it. I know you've talked to Huck, so he's already told you he went about it in the wrong way, but he was also *right*. Something needed to be done. I wasn't using my voice, but I should've been. I'm not going to let anyone silence me again."

"Wow," said Preston. "What advice do you have for other young girls?"

"Surround yourself with people who value and challenge you." She glanced down at her nails. I couldn't see them, but I was pretty sure they were back to her usual color-coordinated glitter. "Don't dim your sparkle, or waste it on people who don't value you."

"What's the strangest thing that's come out of this?" asked Abigail.

Clara laughed. "I was offered a deodorant commercial."

"Will you do it?"

Clara turned her head and gave her armpit a fake sniff. It was a gesture that *only* Clara could make charming, and everyone in the basement joined the hosts in laughter as she said, "We'll see."

The show cut to commercial break, and I looked around the room. The interview was over, but eyes were on screens: the TV, phones. A few people were talking in animated voices about how well she'd done and what else she could endorse.

Everyone was engrossed.

I pinched the back of Win's hand and he elbowed me. Clearly we needed to work on our signals. I pinched him again and this time he looked over. I tilted my head at the stairs.

His eyes brightened. He rubbed his bottom lip like he was trying not to smile—but did he forget that every time he did that, I wanted to touch his mouth too? I'd remind him upstairs.

He flipped his hand over and I fitted mine inside.

If anyone asked, I was showing him where the bathroom was or getting a snack.

Lance and Lynnie had shifted closer on the couch, like they needed to make room for a third person, even though no one had taken them up on it. "I'm meeting with Ms. Gregoire about it tomorrow," Lynnie was saying. "And I already have a feeling she's going to assign me a book instead of giving advice."

I paused, jerking Win to a confused halt. Lynnie's face

was turned toward Lance as she spoke. I couldn't read her expression, but his told a full story. Whatever book Ms. Gregoire assigned Lynnie, I wished them all luck. Lance, Lynnie, and Penn—I wasn't sure where they'd end up—but hopefully their journey was easier than ours.

Win squeezed my hand impatiently.

"If you're going to make out, try the back porch, not the front yard," Merri called as our feet hit the bottom stair. "My parents are sitting in the kitchen, and those windows give an A-plus view of the front stoop."

"Short Stack, where was that helpful advice when your best friend and I needed it?" Curtis threw a pillow at her, but Fielding caught it.

"I think the side yard is better," said Rory.

"And pretend you're getting something from the car if anyone asks," said Toby.

"You're not actually fooling anyone when you two do that," said Eliza, but she was quickly drowned out by everyone else chiming in.

And while I liked them all, valued their voices and sparkles and stories, was glad to have found my place in this group and would rival Mira in defense of any member of it, right now I valued Win's most.

So while they bantered and bickered and tossed popcorn and pillows, I let him lead me up the stairs. He could choose whatever exit strategy he wanted, but wherever he went, I was ready to follow.

Being Win, he chose to blaze his own trail—one that was more direct and honest. He paused in the kitchen doorway. "Thanks for having us."

Mr. Campbell stood and shook our hands, switching the

one he extended so we didn't have to let go of each other. "You guys leaving already?"

Win nodded. "We're going for a walk. Huck might implode if I don't get him some caffeine, and I might combust if I have to wait much longer to kiss him."

I guessed raising a daughter like Merri meant being prepared for any possible combination of words, because the Campbells barely blinked before telling me, "I like this guy, Huck. Bring him around again soon, okay?"

"I like him too," I said. Then we headed out into an afternoon bright with sunshine and possibilities. Shiny with the promise of coffee and kisses. I still might not know how many planets were in our solar system—but I knew the guy holding my hand was my favorite across all universes.

ACKNOWLEDGMENTS

I first began daydreaming about a school where classic stories crept off their pages and a maybe-magical teacher guided her students toward their perfect book back in 2012.

Many years and four books later, I love these characters and this school like they're real. It's bittersweet to be stepping off the campus of Hero High and away from the lives of the Campbell girls and their friends. I'm the worst at goodbyes, so I'm struggling to close this final (for now!) chapter and express how much joy this series has brought to me or how grateful I am for those who've helped me along this journey.

Abrams, you've been a dream home for this project. Endless gratitude to Andrew Smith, Jessica Gotz, Brooke Shearouse, Marie Oishi, Brenda Angelilli, Jade Rector, Melanie Chang, Jenny Choi, Kim Lauber, Trish McNamara O'Neill, Nicole Schaefer, and Megan Evans. Anne Heltzel, you challenge me in the best ways and ask the perfect questions. Huge thanks to Michael Clark, whose mind rivals Sherlock's in its attention to detail.

To Barry, who never gave up on this project, and Kate Testerman, who felt like an old friend from the moment we first met—thank you.

And to those who've walked beside me, you know who you are and I love you. Sherlock and Watson, Anne and Diana, Meg and Jo, Lizzy and Jane all have nothing on my Scott, Courtney, Emily, Miranda, Jessica, Annie, Lauren, Amy, Amanda, Jennifer, Stacey, Nancy, Tip, Shannon, Rae Ann, Carly, Claire, Kristin, and Kate.

To every reader who's followed on this Bookish adventure: *thank you*. Those eight letters hold the whole of my heart. I hope you find your own Ms. Gregoire. I hope you find your book. I hope you feel seen, heard, and believed—and know *your* story matters.

Finally, my family: I couldn't do this without you. St. Matt, you're the reason I write love stories. Schmidtlets, you remind me every day of the power of BIG imaginations. Let's promise to never grow up and never stop make-believing.